WHERE EVIL LURKS

Other Boson Books by Robert Rodman

The Evil That Men Do

WHERE EVIL LURKS

A Dagny Taggart Jamison Mystery

Robert D. Rodman

BOSON BOOKS
Raleigh

Published by Boson Books
An imprint of C&M Online Media Inc.

ISBN (paper): 978-0-917990-80-9
ISBN (ebook): 978-0-917990-79-3

For information contact:
C & M Online Media, Inc.
3905 Meadow Field Lane,
Raleigh, NC 27606-4470
e-mail: cm@cmonline.com
http://www.bosonbooks.com

Contents

BOOK ONE: HARRY

BOOK TWO: TOM

BOOK THREE: DICK

BOOK FOUR: ASHLEY

BOOK ONE

HARRY

CHAPTER 1

"Who knows what evil lurks in the hearts of men?" began an old radio show. Who, indeed? In the 1940s, The Shadow knew. In the 1990s, in the thirty-first year of my life, I found out that evil may lurk in the hearts of women, too.

It was the last autumn of the twentieth century, in the city of Raleigh, on a crisp morning of Carolina blue skies punctuated by marshmallow clouds. The previous night I'd quietly celebrated the fifth anniversary of the remission of the breast cancer that had nearly taken my life. Statistics favored me now, not the disease. It was ironic, then, that that same day of closure would see the start of events that would be every bit as deadly and emotionally distressing as that terrible disease.

I was sipping coffee and working on the daily crossword puzzle. I had a six-letter word for *threatening snake* that went c--l--. I reviewed my snakes: krait, cobra, asp, mamba, adder, viper, rattler, hisser—but none fit. I racked my brains for the right word but it wouldn't come. Idly, I gazed out the front window. That was the first time I saw her. She had parked her ice-blue Lotus facing the wrong way at the curb in front of my house. A lithe body unfolded itself from the low-slung vehicle. With a glance at my house number, she came with a resolute step up the walkway. An old pickup truck chugged by, the driver rubbernecking at the blonde in the suede skirt.

Ah, got it! Hastily I penned in *coiler* and put the newspaper aside. The snap of the car door when it shut had alerted Hank and Midas, my two greyhounds, whose ears had pricked up at the sound. The footsteps of the approaching visitor set them to barking.

I hustled my two would-be guardians into another room and went to the front door. I opened the door at the same moment that the visitor was poised to knock on it. She lost her balance for a second.

"Oh, sorry," I apologized. "I saw you coming up the walk."

She was unruffled, however. Looking at a slip of paper she asked, "Are you Dagny Taggart Jamison, the private investigator?"

"Yes, I am." I opened the door fully and stepped back. "Won't you come in, please?"

She was an inch taller, a shade blonder, and two letters more curvaceous than me. Her clothes were immaculately tailored, and were a perfect match for the Lotus. Even her scent, I thought, had an element of the lotus blossom in it. Her only jewelry was a man's wristwatch and two diamond studs. Golden hair flowed down to her shoulders and the blue of her eyes matched the blue of the sky. There was a hint of harshness, though, in an otherwise cover-girl face.

"What can I do for you?" I asked when she'd entered the house and we were standing facing each other in my living room. A soiled tank top I had carelessly thrown over a chair for later removal to the wash caused me a moment's embarrassment, but she seemed not to notice or care.

"My name is Ashley Bloodworth. I believe you're the private investigator who unearthed the pharmaceutical scandal in California. A couple of people were murdered by hanging that was made to look like suicide, if my facts are correct."

"Yes, it was me, and your facts are correct, but I had some luck and a lot of help with the case."

"I found your Web site," she said, "so I know from your bio that you're licensed in California as well as here. If my memory serves, it said you'd been in the service and afterwards got your degree at UCLA. Let's see, what else?" She paused to smooth a perfect eyebrow with a finely manicured nail.

I cocked my head, curious to know what information on my home page was arresting enough to be remembered.

"Ah, yes, you had some law school education and I think it said your brother trained you to be a private investigator."

"You have a good memory."

"I also asked my legal firm to check you out—I hope you don't mind. They said you have a reputation for being objective and discreet. That's really why I've come to see you this morning."

"Thanks for the compliment," I said, blushing slightly, "but I just try to do a good job." I held out my hand. "I'm pleased to meet you, Ms. Bloodworth."

We shook hands. Her hand was cool and slight, but her grip was firm.

"Why don't you come this way," I said. "My office is back here."

I led her through my outsized living room, past the old Bösendorfer grand piano, around the large dog beds to my sunroom-cum-office in the rear of the house. The greyhounds whined behind the door that kept them shut out.

"Coffee? It's already made."

"Thank you. Black, no sugar."

I motioned her to the chair reserved for clients. When I purchased my home, it had a glass-louvered porch jutting out to the southeast. I converted this, along with some interior space, into an office. The chair in which I seat clients faces the bright exterior, while I always face the dimmer interior. This seating arrangement puts their features in high relief, the better for me to observe them.

After setting down cups of coffee for each of us, I took my seat and waited a few moments for her to settle comfortably. Then, leaning forward a little in my chair, I invited her to tell me what her visit was about.

"Ms. Jamison, please don't be insulted if I ask you for an assurance of complete confidentiality. I've no reason to doubt you, but I do need to satisfy myself on this point. What I have to tell you is extremely personal."

"I understand. Let me just say that I treat my clients with the utmost discretion. You can depend on that—you have my word on it. I wouldn't stay in business long if I didn't honor that code."

Ashley Bloodworth straightened in her chair and tugged at the hem of her skirt. She cleared her throat, then said somewhat hesitantly, "It's taken me a long time to arrive at this point, a length of time that may surprise you. I might have done this sooner, and I might have gone to a deluxe agency—no slight intended—but I want this to be a one-man—or I should say, a one-woman—operation. I don't believe I could tell a man my story."

"All I can do is to repeat my assurance, but I need to add that what you tell me isn't privileged, as it would be if I were a lawyer. I can be forced to testify in a court of law under oath, so if that's a problem…"

"No, it's not that at all. It's just, well, feminine matters."

"Then I think we're on safe ground, Ms. Bloodworth."

"Ashley, please, and may I call you Dagny? I'd like to dispense with some of the formality. I should guess we're no more than a year or two apart—'of an age,' as Jane Austen might put it."

"Okay, that's fine with me, uh, Ashley. I won't betray your personal matters as long as there's no question of perjury."

"There won't be. I have no crimes to confess, though crimes there certainly have been. I know I must put my trust in someone and I believe I can trust you."

She looked directly into my face, her lips pressed together, her head nodding slightly forward and back.

"Perhaps I might begin with some background?"

"That'd be fine," I said. "Go right ahead."

"I was born into an old, southern, moneyed family. For me this meant private schools, the best church, a debut, fine clothes and jewelry, expensive cars, social connections, and of course no drinking and no sex." She spoke detachedly, as if about a different person. "I conformed. I got good grades, and I was accepted right out of high school at Meriwether, just a few miles from here. The Bloodworth daughters were obliged to attend the most prestigious women's college in the old Confederacy, whether through achievement or family influence."

She paused to sip her coffee and asked, "Do you mind if I smoke?"

I didn't, and I went and fetched an ashtray, which I placed next to her cup and saucer. She lit a slim, green, gold-filtered cigarette with a gold-colored lighter shaped like a harp. A whiff of smoke made me wistful and reminded me how much I once enjoyed the habit.

Ashley took another sip and continued, "Imagine college life in the late '80s. You were probably a student then, too. You know things were wild. My parents warned me to abstain from alcohol and sex. That I should leave drugs alone went without saying."

Memories of my own school days danced in my head as Ashley spoke. I saw my fellow students doing lines off the chem lab tables, using short pipettes to snort the powdery cocaine. I smelled the sweet smell of marijuana smoke drifting over the laurel bushes behind the science building, those same laurel bushes behind which girls occasionally abandoned their panties in their haste to dress after sex. My demeanor must have changed because Ashley paused for a moment as if expecting me to speak, but when I said nothing she went on.

"A wildness came over me, as it did with so many of us when we left home for the first time. We drank. We experimented with sex, and soon after with drugs. This is important. Or maybe I shouldn't be telling you this?"

I shrugged. "Don't worry. Even if the actual statute of limitations hasn't expired, the practical limitation has. If they went back and arrested everyone who did drugs, half the Congress would be in jail."

She took a deep drag. I had a nearly uncontrollable urge to bum a cigarette off her, which I fought off by crossing my arms over my chest, reminding myself of my recent malignancy.

"Cocaine was as plentiful at Meriwether as sugar at the dining tables," she said. "Snow is white and money is green, and ever the twain shall meet. And Meriwether kids are sooo rich, and cocaine is—was— sooo sweet. Within months I was a cokehead, in with the in-crowd of cokeheads. When spring recess came in March, they asked me to pick up a delivery on my way back to school."

She paused for another sip and crossed her legs, allowing a black pump to dangle from her foot. "I drove a Lamborghini then—a high school graduation gift. The trafficker wanted to hide the cocaine in the door panels but I wasn't about to let anyone tear up my car's interior. Why the hell should I have? I had the good sense not to speed in the Lamborghini because the damn thing was a cop magnet. I didn't expect to be stopped or searched, so I put the half-pound of coke in the glove compartment. I didn't even bother to lock it up."

She took a final drag of her cigarette and stubbed it out. "I get bored on the main highway," she continued. "I know the secondary roads that lead to Raleigh and I'm cruising down one with pine forest on both sides when the Lamborghini dies. It just ups and quits, dead, kaput. I coast onto the shoulder and try the cell phone but I don't have power. I can't even lower a damn window. I hang an old T-shirt on the hood ornament and begin to walk."

She pursed her lips as she decided how—or whether—to go on. She withdrew a blue cigarette from a case that had a matte gold finish. She shut the case with a snap, put the cigarette between her lips, lit it, and took a deep, cancerous pull. I wondered if the blue paper added to the health risk. She turned aside to exhale a stream of smoke, which she followed with her eyes as it dissipated through the open louvers.

"What happened then?" I asked.

Ashley shifted her gaze back to me. "A break occurs in my memory," she said, speaking in a lower tone now. "On the other side of it, I find myself waking up in a hospital bed, tubes and bags everywhere. I don't know if I'm dreaming or truly awake. I hear a beeping sound that I recognize from a TV hospital program. It's my heartbeat."

I was shocked by this unexpected turn of events. "How dreadful! What, did you fall and injure your head?"

"I'll come to that," said Ashley, uncrossing her legs and slipping her foot back into the shoe. "A nurse was there. She was asking me questions—difficult ones, like my name, my age, what kind of car I drove, how many fingers was she holding up, and who was the goddamn president. When she was satisfied with my answers, she beckoned towards the door and up show my parents, if you'll pardon my down-home grammar. They're thanking the Lord and praising Jesus. I'd been unconscious for thirty-six hours and there was a possibility of brain damage. Their vigil had taken its toll. They were too tired to disguise their disapproval of what they thought I'd done."

"God, you must have been so upset and confused," I said. I was feeling agitated but didn't have the benefit of lighting up, so instead I took a large swig of coffee, and immediately regretted it as it burned its way down my esophagus. I gulped in a deep, cooling breath of air and asked, "What did they think you'd done? I mean, how did you even get to the hospital in the first place?"

She ran her fingers through her hair, then shook it back into place; she brushed a rebellious wisp off her face. "A state trooper found me in my car, unconscious," she said. "Cocaine powder was on my face, in my hair, in the upholstery of the car. I was gravely overdosed and near death. His quick action, and that of the EMS medics, saved my life, though not my memory."

That struck a chord in me. When I was in the army, I trained to be a corpsman and part of what I learned was how to deal with ODs. But mostly corpsmen learn to treat battlefield trauma—and those were peaceful times. There wasn't much trauma around, except for victims of auto wrecks and barroom brawls, and the civilian medics usually got to them first. Eventually I asked for Military Police training—anything to ward off the boredom of peacetime army life—and it meshed with the medical training.

Ashley's voice broke my reverie. "You look a million miles away, Dagny."

"Oh, I'm listening," I assured her. "It's just that I was thinking back to overdoses I've treated. I was a medic in the army once. You could've come out of this a lot worse, you know. Did you remember anything about the cocaine?"

"That was about the last thing I did remember, and I was scared that I'd be busted. Not even my father's influence and money would get me out of it. A bit of cocaine on the lips is one thing; a half-pound in your car was entirely another. But all they charged me with was possession of six-tenths of a gram and driving under the influence. I got off with a fine and three years' probation."

"You were lucky," I said. "Don't tell me they didn't find your stash."

"There was no stash to find. You'll see."

Ashley was going to tell the story her way, and she wasn't going to be hurried.

CHAPTER 2

The dogs had their own tale to tell. They were tired of being locked up while hearing us talk. Their whines, which had at first been a quiet entreaty, became loud, demanding yelps.

Ashley said, "Feel free to let your dogs out, poor little things."

"Uh, well, they only sound little. They're greyhounds—little throats, big dogs."

"That's fine. I need a break anyway." She stood up and stretched her arms toward the ceiling, yawning unabashedly at the same time. Her blouse came adrift, exposing a narrow swath of bare midriff. I knew guys who'd pay money for that sight. She tucked everything back in and said, "I'd be happy to meet your hounds."

I let Hank and Midas out, and they fell over each other to see who would be first to check out the guest. Ashley met them standing. She was a good sport and deftly parried the inquisitive muzzles before they could leave nose prints on the fine, shiny leather of her skirt. She gave each dog a rub behind the ears and a pat on their substantial rumps. Satisfied, they retreated to their large soft beds by the piano to watch the proceedings.

"They're nice dogs. Did you rescue them?"

"I did, actually. They used to race and I got them when their careers ended. They were pals in the kennel where they lived, so they were put up for adoption as a pair. But anyway, I'm mystified about this half-pound of disappearing cocaine. Do you want to tell me about it?"

"I don't mean to be mysterious or secretive. I'm just trying to relate events not as they happened in time, but as I came to realize them. So, let's see. After I left the hospital I rested at home. The first couple of days I was dazed most of the time. I dreamt awful dreams, violent and terrifying, and when I was awake, I'd find myself wringing my hands or grinding my teeth. I hurt inside, too, and bled some. By the end of the week I realized that I'd been sexually assaulted, but of the event itself I could remember nothing."

"You mean they didn't figure that out while you were in the hospital?" I asked incredulously.

"I believe I was so close to death that they focused on cleansing out the cocaine and counteracting its effect. They found me alone in my car, dressed, unmarked by violence, but stoned literally almost to death. Rape wasn't uppermost in their minds and so they missed the signs. But when I finally began to regain my senses, it was certainly uppermost in my mind."

"Did you report it to the cops, or tell your parents?"

"I couldn't. I mean, I didn't know what had happened and I was terrified. Terrified of the law. Terrified of my parents. Even terrified of myself—terrified of being insane. I just hunkered down and waited."

"Were you able to go back to school? I mean, how long did you stay at home?"

"I went back after a week, a changed person. I decided to take my education seriously, to make up the work I'd missed. I truly desired to redefine myself. There was the not-so-small matter of the missing cocaine. I said that I'd been robbed and forcibly overdosed. It was a prophetic lie, as it turns out. This helped break me out of the group I went with, and by the semester's end I felt I could achieve my goals."

"And this is your freshman year, right?"

"Yes, spring semester, and I was enjoying my new self a lot, except for one downer: I missed my April period. I attributed it to the trauma of the assault. When I missed in May, I blamed the stress of final examinations. When I missed in June, well, you can imagine and..."

My expression must have revealed my second occasion of incredulity on this subject because Ashley paused mid-sentence and restarted.

"Oh, I know. You've been raped and you're missing periods. Deep down, you know you must be pregnant. All I can say is that the rape at the time was surreal, and I so very badly didn't want to be pregnant—so very badly—that I practiced a naïve self-deception. But that's what I did. What can I say?"

"Yes, of course you're right. I don't mean to be judgmental. What happened next?"

"My GYN confirmed it. I was fifteen weeks pregnant, but I hadn't slept with anybody in six months. I may have been a druggie, but I wasn't a slut. My parents were dead set against abortion, and I was too far along to be comfortable with the risks."

"So you have the child now?"

"Children. I gave birth to twins, a boy and a girl."

My eyebrows rose reflexively. Ashley caught my surprise but carried on despite it.

"My parents live in the old Bloodworth mansion, called Hatfield Hall. We have live-in servants and various extended family in the house.

I left Benton and Jeanne-Renée in their care and continued my education. I had little time for babies."

"And you didn't know who the father was," I said.

She smiled wanly and removed another designer cigarette from the gold case and lit it with a snap of the harp-shaped lighter.

I gestured toward the pot of hot coffee but she placed her hand over her half-filled cup.

"I graduated from Meriwether in three years with a double major in business and dramatic arts—I'd done some acting—and went on to earn my Ph.D. in economics at the University of Chicago. My research was on how to maximize short-term investments by the use of computer models of my own invention. I worked under the late Professor Victoria Krofmin, who won the von Hayek Prize in economics in 1989."

I'm clueless about economics and economists and it must have showed.

"Oh, few people have heard of her outside academia," Ashley explained. "She was an extraordinary woman, though, Dr. Krofmin. She'd been a successful psychiatrist before switching fields—she was truly remarkable."

Ashley lost her train of thought, perhaps thinking of her old professor. The room darkened at that moment as one of the puffy cumulus clouds floated past the sun. The shadow on Ashley's face tempered her features and drew them back from the brink of harshness. I adjusted the floor lamp to gain a tad more light.

"One day, unexpectedly, Dr. Krofmin said, 'Ashley, something is deeply troubling you. Eventually it will surface to your detriment. Have you ever considered psychoanalysis?' This was a serious thing for one's professor to tell one, especially when that professor is Victoria Krofmin, M.D., Ph.D."

"Couldn't she just help you herself, since she was a psychiatrist?"

"Not really. She didn't offer, and I didn't feel it appropriate to ask. But when I showed interest she referred me to a psychiatrist who did hypnotic therapy. I turned out to be a susceptible patient. We soon worked our way to that day in March. Hypnosis is effective for certain kinds of amnesia. You not only recover what you might ordinarily remember, but you also recall hundreds of small details and images that are usually lost to the memory. This is at once frightening and, I was assured, therapeutic. It took multiple sessions to bring it all back."

Though it was cool in my office, small beads of sweat had formed on Ashley's brow. The fingers of her right hand were worrying a loose strand of rattan on the arm of the wicker chair. Her face, more disciplined than her hands, was impassive, though the indefinable trace of harshness had returned.

Speaking in a near monotone, she went on. "I'm walking away from my broken down car. A minivan looms up the road. It sees me and begins to slow down. Something about it is ominous, but what can I do? I keep walking, trying to pretend I live in the neighborhood, as if the car and I are not connected. The van stops beside me and a man jumps out of the passenger side, and another man jumps out of a rear door, and I'm between them. They throw a blanket over me. In less time than it takes to draw a breath to scream, I'm in the van, blindfolded."

"Jesus, so you're recalling this under hypnosis?"

"That's right. Until the hypnosis, Dagny, I didn't remember any of it. You'll see why I can't tell a man. The moment they dragged me into the van I knew what would happen. I could hear the sounds of a third man, the driver, removing his clothes. It was pointless to struggle and I didn't want to get beaten up. But I wasn't going to be compliant either, or so I thought."

Ashley was struggling to keep her composure. She tucked her hair behind her ears and smoothed her leather skirt. She pulled out a silk hankie and patted her forehead dry. The dogs, always sensitive to human moods, shifted uneasily in their beds.

"They removed my T-shirt and bra and pinned my arms behind me. Something touched my nipple. Pain exploded through my body. It was a cattle prod. Then the other nipple. I was so afraid they wouldn't stop. That they'd torture me to death. I pleaded with them to stop. Someone growled in my ear the single word—Cooperate.

A single tear formed in the corner of one eye and tracked down her cheek. She quickly wiped it away with the backs of her fingers. I needed to be a good listener, so I swallowed my horror. It left a metallic taste in my mouth.

"I cooperated. I'd have thrown my own children into a fire. When they asked me to do things I didn't think I could do, the cattle prod came out. When the three were finished with me, they tied my hands and threw me in a corner. One of them had searched my car and found the cocaine."

I was shaking my head involuntarily, appalled by the images that Ashley's words evoked. I reached forward and touched her hand. We made eye contact and my heart went out to her. I leaned back to listen. I didn't want to break into her story.

"After an hour of getting high, they raped me again. Afterwards, they forced me to snort cocaine until I couldn't anymore. The last thing I remember before I lost consciousness is them stuffing cocaine in my vagina and rectum. I know they tried to kill me that way. They dressed me and left me in my car. They spread cocaine around to make it look like I overdosed."

She stopped and sipped at the tepid coffee. With her forefingers she wiped the tears from under each eye. She didn't wear makeup, so there weren't the dark smears that make us women look so pitiful when we cry. She lit another cigarette, this one red, sucked deeply and exhaled a great stream of smoke through her nose.

I fought to hold down the wave of nausea that surged in my stomach. My neighbor had just fired up his noisy old lawnmower, and whenever he came close to my house, the louvers rattled under the blast of sound. I walked over to close the ones nearest the mowing, which gave me a few seconds to regain my composure.

"Why have you come to me, why not the police? This is far too serious a crime for a private investigator."

"Two reasons: discretion and motivation. The police lack both. If I guess right, you were named after a fictional character of great mind and courage. You demonstrated both qualities in your previous work—yes, yes, I know a lot about that case through my business network. You deserve credit."

Ashley had changed within seconds from the victim of a hideous crime to a woman with her emotions in check, icily detached and goal-oriented.

"But what do you want me to do?" I asked.

"Simple," she replied coolly. "You mentioned the father. It was 'fathers' actually. I want you to find them."

CHAPTER 3

I don't make a secret of where my name comes from. My parents were enamored of the writer-philosopher Ayn Rand. I was named after Dagny Taggart, the heroine of *Atlas Shrugged,* Ms. Rand's greatest novel.

I'd read most of Rand's books by the time I was sixteen. I understood that her fictional characters represented ideals. I never try to be Dagny Taggart, but I do try, albeit mostly in vain, to be as resilient as she is.

On several occasions my parents offered to help me change my name if I wanted to. Perhaps they had been overly zealous, they said. Maybe they had been, but I was okay with it. Lots of kids go through a stage of hating their given name and adopt a new one. When she was sixteen, my cousin Linda insisted on being called Cece, and for years signed her cards and letters that way. Then one day she was Linda again. I always liked the uniqueness of *Dagny,* and never suffered ambiguity as the Jennifers had to do.

It didn't surprise me that Ashley knew the source of my name. She was well read enough to refer to Jane Austen, and as an economist she must have read *Atlas Shrugged,* which is in part about economics and capitalism. The work also glorifies the spirit of the individual. It would appeal to the steely, independent Ashley.

"You have more faith in my ability than I deserve," I said. "Being named after a character doesn't make you as great or as smart as that character. I really think it's a matter for law enforcement. It's not my kind of work."

"I don't want law enforcement, nor do I think it possible at this stage—I think it's too late for that. Besides, if I went to the police the attention that would be focused on me and my family is too horrible to contemplate."

"So what's the point of finding them?"

"I want to know who fathered my children and I want it verified by a DNA test. This wasn't technically feasible until recently. I need some degree of closure."

"If I'm doing the math right, it's been nine and a half years since you were assaulted. That makes for a cold trail."

"I haven't told you everything, Dagny. As I said, one recalls a lot of detail under hypnosis. I'm not sure what to do with this information. Sometimes I'm not sure it's reliable, though Dr. Brodsky—he was my analyst—claims that it is."

"You underwent analysis three or four years ago, again if I'm counting right. Had you made previous attempts to find the father, I mean, fathers?"

"No. At first I was in school. After graduation, I set two goals for myself. One was to modernize the family businesses, which hadn't adjusted well to the new global economy. My family had supported me for my entire life, and this was my way to pay them back. And at the same time—though it seems contradictory—I wanted independence from them. I wanted my own money, and I wanted plenty of it. By applying the results of my research, I was able to form a successful investment corporation. But all that took time—lots of time and lots of work—and even when I thought about my, uh, situation…"

Ashley stopped in mid sentence, an unsure look on her face. I prompted her, "Yes, your situation, what did you think?" She leaned toward the ashtray and stubbed out the remainder of the red cigarette.

"I was always uncertain as to what to do. Even after my financial successes, I wavered. Should I involve the police? Should I engage a law firm? Should I employ a big-name investigative agency? Should I forget it and get on with my life? I flitted from one choice to another like a moth in the streetlights, always on the brink of a mental meltdown."

"And I gather that you've made a choice, seeing that you're here. What made you decide after all these years?"

"As I said, I need closure—I don't want this horror to consume me. And I need privacy, discretion and a competent person who will work hard on my case. I believe that you fit the bill."

Money aside, the case aroused my interest. I felt an impulse to act, to do something about this all-too-common crime of sexual violence against women. Additionally, I always welcome a small respite from the drudgework that takes up most of a P.I.'s time, such as delivering summonses or staking out errant spouses. I tire of countless hours spent in municipal buildings chipping my nail polish sifting through endless ranks of file folders.

Ashley watched me closely for a few seconds, and at the precise moment that she sensed I was at my most receptive said, "I'd like your help very much. At least will you listen to an offer? Can I tell you what it's worth to me?"

It was easy to give in. "Okay, shoot."

"First, I require total and complete anonymity. Nobody, without exception, is to know that I'm your client."

"Agreed."

"Second, I'll pay you $500 per day, including weekends, no overtime. You keep track of the days that you work. Payment will continue until I'm satisfied, or you give up."

That pleased me, but I tried to keep my expression neutral. My regular rate was $50 an hour, and I billed an average of 25 hours per week. This was more than double my usual earnings.

"Third, I want you to give the job utmost priority. You mustn't let other work interfere with or delay progress on my case."

That also suited me. There's a guy who takes over my practice when I need to be away for an extended period. I knew I could rely on him to take up my other cases.

"Fourth, your expense account. Naturally, I'll reimburse your out-of-pocket expenses. But I want you to take a broader view of expenses. It may be necessary for you to pay for information, or for access to information. Let me avoid the word 'bribe.' Your judgment is discretionary up to $10,000. Beyond that we'd need to confer."

I opened my mouth to protest but she waved me aside.

"You don't need to do anything that you find unsavory. It's entirely up to you. I'm only telling you what lines are available on your expense reports."

"Is there a fifth point?" I asked.

"Yes, but I'm not finished with four."

"All right, sorry to interrupt."

"While you work for me, you're to be generous with yourself, consistent with getting the job done. When you travel, I want you to go first class. Stay in good hotels and eat in good restaurants. I won't question those expenses. My motives are purely selfish. If you're well fed and well rested, you'll be in peak form. If you happen to be at your best eating fast food, sleeping in fleabag motels and flying cattle-class, well and good, but don't do so out of financial considerations. Do you understand?"

"It's easy to understand," I replied, "but I'm afraid my credit cards would give out in a hurry."

"I thought of that," said Ashley. She pulled her wallet from her bag, and a light-green plastic strip from the wallet. She handed it to me. It was a corporate credit card of the Bloodworth Investors Corporation. It had my name on it.

"I know, I know," she said. "It was presumptuous of me. What does it matter? I had this made in a day. If you don't take the case, I simply go snip-snip. Your limit is $50,000, by the way. The card is paid off monthly."

"Is that it for 'four'?" I asked, feeling a little giddy.

"Yes," said Ashley. "Fifth and last, you'll receive a $2,000 bonus for each DNA sample, one per rapist. You'll have to convince me that you have the right person."

"If I take your case," I said deliberately, "you'll have to revisit the crime in detail. You'll have to answer my questions, regardless of the pain. Are you prepared to do this?"

"Do you think I haven't reviewed those hours in excruciating detail? Dr. Brodsky recorded every hypnotic session, and I've listened to each of them many times. The good doctor mined my mind. I remember what the men said before, while, and after assaulting me. Hypnosis wouldn't bring back memories of faces, though I must've seen the two who snatched me, however briefly. But I could see straight down under the blindfold. I saw the tip of the cattle prod, and parts of their bodies. I have memories from all five senses, Dagny. I will not shirk. My role is to remember. Yours is to forge out of these recollections a path that leads to these men."

"Look," I told her, "it's Friday, and I've got some small jobs to wrap up. I have a colleague P.I. named Barry Hernandez, who can sometimes fill in for me. I need to check with him and I want to give careful thought to the entire matter. Can I let you know Monday?"

Ashley grimaced. "It must seem silly to you that I've waited years, and now I find it difficult to wait days. I'm ordinarily a patient person. My business requires patience and a keen sense of timing. In business, I never let my emotions interfere. This is different. It's pure emotion, distilled to the highest proof, and I'm antsy and impatient—I've waited so long. What about by tomorrow?"

"Give me your phone number. If I can sort everything out and come to a decision, I'll call you. If it's 'Yes,' I'll need a contract."

"No contract. This instead," she said, reaching into her handbag again. She placed two packets of bills on the table next to the credit card. "They're each $5,000. That's a substantial advance on wages. I'll keep to my side of the bargain because at worst, I lose a trifling sum of money. You'll keep to your side because your word is, as they say, your bond." Her steely blue eyes met and held mine. "Do I judge you right, Dagny?"

"Please keep the money and the credit card for now." I told her. "I'll call you when I've made a decision."

She put the money and the card back in her bag expressionlessly, never taking her eyes off mine. We each sensed the interview was over, and stood up. I escorted her outside, where we shook hands but said no more.

Ashley stepped off the veranda into the early October sunshine. She hitched her bag back over her shoulder and walked to the curb with a firm stride. Sunbeams danced in her golden hair as it swung gently from side to side in counterpoint to her swaying hips.

The Lotus had attracted some local attention. The immaculate, liquid-blue fiberglass body radiated with a soft light of its own. Several of my neighbors were admiring it. They kept their hands in their pockets the way you do in a fancy china shop. A teenager had gone so far as to crawl half under the car for a view of the engine. When he saw Ashley approach—he must have had an eyeful of her legs—he hastened to extricate himself, knocking his head with a loud crack on the undercarriage. His buddies tittered like a flock of sparrows.

Ashley didn't mind any of it. She put on her best southern charm and accent—not an "r" to be heard—as she wished them a good morning. She smoothed down her leather skirt and glided sinuously into the driver's seat. With an inscrutable smile, she drove slowly away, depriving the guys of an acceleration display.

She was cool. Too cool, I thought, or maybe too rich, or too something. But a client is a client, and a challenge is a challenge. It would test my mettle to find any one of those men, let alone all three.

I went back inside and received nose touches from Hank and Midas as thanks for returning so promptly. We all three returned to the living room, where the greyhounds nestled back in their huge pillows and I sprawled on the sofa to think.

I was too fidgety to relax, for I was agitated by Ashley's sordid account, and annoyed by the relentless surge and ebb of the mower's clangor. Soon, I was pacing up and down, much to the consternation of the dogs. They raised their heads to follow my movements.

The mowing stopped at last. I sat down at the old Bösendorfer and began to play a Schubert sonata I was learning. Classical piano playing is a hobby of mine, though not one at which I excel. It does, however, oblige a girl to keep her nails well clipped. More important, it diverts the conscious mind into other channels, leaving room for the subconscious to work. The sonata sings and dances through a variety of keys and moods.

My mind underwent similar modulations regarding Ashley's offer. The sonata ends in the optimistic key of A Major. I decided to take the case.

CHAPTER 4

I picked up the portable phone by the piano and dialed Barry Hernandez, pressing the buttons with my left thumb while my right hand doodled over the notes to the James Bond theme. He said he'd be happy to take over for me, and that he was fixing to get married and needed the extra bucks. I drove to his office with all the necessary paperwork. Inside of two hours I'd explained each case to him. I made a few phone calls from his office to tell clients of the switch. Everyone was agreeable.

I left Barry's office without calling Ashley. I didn't want a record of her number to show up on his phone bill. I had my cell phone but I didn't use it, either, because of security concerns. It had recently been discovered that the governor's own cell phone conversations had been plucked out of the air and played to members of the opposing party. I had little reason to think my calls were any more secure.

I called Ashley when I got home, but all I got was her machine. I left a terse "call me" message and returned to the Schubert. I slow-practiced several tricky passages, and when I tired of that, I moved to my desk and logged on to read e-mail. I was halfway through a reply to my brother John in California when the phone rang.

It was Ashley. I told her of my decision to take her case. She sounded pleased and we arranged for her to return to my place the next day. She'd bring notes from the hypnosis sessions so I could see if they contained any leads that might get me started.

Ashley was prompt on Saturday morning. The Lotus attracted a larger audience than on the previous day. So did Ashley. The expensive Italian blouse and leather skirt had given way to an ordinary T-shirt and a worn pair of jeans that fit snugly in the right places. A pair of boots and a matching leather bag, both of Italian design I guessed, turned the jeans and T-shirt into high fashion. Her earlobes were naked this time and she lacked even the lightest touch of eyeliner. If I dressed like that, with my short hair, I'd get taken for a gay woman.

I made the hounds back away from the door and had Ashley take her former seat while I fetched the coffee and a clean ashtray. She'd already taken out the gold cigarette case and had withdrawn a yellow-papered cigarette when I returned with two steaming cups. She lit up with a snap of the lighter and took a deep drag.

"Now then, how shall we proceed?" asked Ashley, smoke pouring from both nostrils as she spoke.

"Tell me everything you can about these men. I'll interrupt with questions when I need to. Also, I'd like to record the conversation, unless you object."

"I'd prefer that you didn't," she said. "If you wouldn't mind, just take notes. We can go as slowly as necessary. I have my own notes which you may consult afterwards. I don't like being recorded."

"That's fine," I said. "Tell me what happened. Don't leave anything out, no matter how unimportant you may think it is. Let me decide that. Okay?"

"Okay. There were three men. All of them had intercourse with me at least twice. I can give you some overall physical features. In fact, I think of them in my mind that way."

She took a sip of the hot coffee and a pull off the cigarette. She pressed her lips together before continuing.

"The first I call 'Strong.' He was a fair-sized man, but not fat. I caught glimpses of his skin. He had a medium complexion and a rich suntan. He also had dark blond hair, with a slightly reddish or brownish tint. But all I saw was body hair. I suppose the hair on his head might be a different color, probably blonder. He was a few inches taller than I am, so I'd estimate around six feet, 210 lbs. Strong had some other quirks. Should I tell you about them, or describe the others physically?"

"Anyway you like."

"All right, I'll tell you about the one I call 'Fatboy.' He wasn't as big-boned or as large as Strong but he weighed the same. He was a terrible slob. He drooled on me. I could feel his fat jiggle when he was, you know…He was the hairiest one, too. Hairy shoulders. Hairy back. A blubbery, slavering ape. He was lighter in complexion than Strong— almost white skin under the light brown hair. I don't think he had any tan. Oh, and he was missing a toe. Second toe, but I'm unsure of which foot. One time he did me standing up and I could see straight down to his bare feet."

"What about height?"

"Mmm, I'd say an inch or two less than Strong. Maybe high fives."

"And the missing toe. You're sure of that?"

"Quite sure."

"Was it recently missing? I mean, was it red or freshly scarred?"

"No, I think it was an old injury. I didn't see a scar, and the first and third toes were misaligned to fill the gap. If you can find someone you think is him, the foot is a giveaway."

I made her pause as I typed everything she said on my laptop. Midas was having a nightmare, or maybe a pleasurable dream—how could one know?—and he was making little yipping noises and his lanky legs were twitching epileptically.

"And what about the third one?" I asked.

"'Little' is my name for him, though 'Cruel' might work, except they were all cruel. He was the driver. It was the two big guys that grabbed me in the road. Little was a small, dark, wiry man. He smoked. The others didn't, or hadn't recently. He was a couple of inches shorter than I am, so around five seven or eight. He was left-handed, by the way. He used the cattle prod with his left hand."

"Were there any other distinguishing marks on any of them? Any scars, tattoos, facial hair such as a moustache? No other missing body parts?"

"No. All I noticed in that vein was the toe on Fatboy. I tried not to touch any of them except when they forced me to, so I didn't have any opportunity to feel a scar, and I only saw other things by chance."

"Can you remember anything about the van?

"It was dark blue. I must have noticed the hood ornament. I actually drew it under hypnosis. Then it was easy to figure out it was a Dodge. Unlikely it would still be on the road. It didn't smell new when I was in it."

"Hmm, any other details?"

Ashley referred to her notes. "I saw an unusual belt buckle, one of those large brassy ones. It showed a man in a robe astride a winged horse, you know, like the Pegasus. I also saw a crucifix and chain on a pile of clothes that I'm pretty sure belonged to Fatboy. It was silver-colored, heavy and ostentatious. It must've been three inches long. And, let me see, I also have notes about glimpses of clothing that I saw. Do you think any of that is important?"

"Probably not, unless there was something extraordinary. There weren't any ladies' clothes or the like, were there?" I asked.

"No, nothing like that, but there *was* something quirky about Strong. He wasn't able to, uh, perform unless he was looking at something—pictures, I think."

"What kind of pictures? Did you see one?"

"No. I assume dirty pictures of some kind—you know, pornography. And there's something else. I caught glimpses of cameras, video cameras, light fixtures, a lot of wiring, a tripod, all lying around in various parts of the van."

"Did they photograph you?"

"No. I'd have known that." She turned a page. "That's all the visual memories. I separated them from the memories of what I heard. Are you caught up?"

I tapped away for a few more seconds. "Yeah, go ahead."

"They didn't talk much. I don't think they intended to kill me at first. They made an effort not to reveal themselves. Let me just tell you what little I remember hearing. When Little finished with the cattle prod, Fatboy said, 'You got bloody ice in those veins of yours.' He sniggered, as if he'd made a funny joke. Little told him to shut up."

Ashley was reading ahead, a pained look on her face. I wondered if she could ever revisit the notes without inflaming her emotions. She stubbed out her cigarette and immediately lit another—yellow, like its predecessor.

"There were mutterings having to do with whose turn it was to do what to me. At one point, Strong called one of them 'Frenchy.' I think he was referring to Little. He also called Fatboy 'Jaydee' or 'Jaytee.' Those were the only names they used, except for one last thing."

"What was that?" I asked.

"It was after they poisoned me with cocaine. A final act of cruelty from Little. He put his face up to mine and said, 'You've been fucked by every Tom, Dick, and Harry.' The others laughed. Then I lost consciousness."

"God, what bastards! Any chance you could guess their ages?"

"Young, I think—early twenties. It's hard to tell."

"Anything about their voices? I mean, did any of them speak with an accent or have some speech peculiarity?"

"Hmm, come to think of it, I'll bet Fatboy is a good old southern fat boy, the way he said 'veins' with two syllables, and 'ice' more like 'ahce.' Strong might've been an easterner—New York, New Jersey, Brooklyn. I can't tell them apart. And Little—I'd guess he's not from the South, though many southerners manage to lose their accent. I did when I went to Chicago."

"Were you able to see anything else in the van besides the photographic equipment?"

"I stumbled over a duffel bag one time, and I thought I saw a backpack."

"Can you guess the age of the vehicle? Did it seem new?"

"The carpeting was in decent shape. God knows I spent some time with my face in it. I didn't feel any badly worn places or glimpse terrible stains. It didn't smell new, but it wasn't falling apart either."

I waited a moment before asking, "Can you think of anything else?"

She pursed her lips. "No. Nothing more in particular about any of them that'd help you track them down. Will you take the advance and the credit card now? Do we have a deal? Everything I said yesterday still goes." She placed the two packages of one-hundred-dollar bills and the credit card on the table.

"Okay, we have a deal." We stood and shook hands. "I'll do what I can," I told her. "You'll have to leave me phone numbers where I can call you, or where I can reach someone who knows where you are. I may have questions that need immediate answers. I may find a situation in which you, as my employer, will have to make a decision."

"I'll do all that. I live in a wing of Hatfield Hall in Kinston. I have an office and a secretary there. If you can't reach me on my mobile, my secretary will know how to find me. She's also my cousin and lives in the house, so she's there a lot during non-working hours. She's not privy to this matter. If you call, just leave your name. I'll get back to you as soon as I can."

We shook hands again at the door. She gently ruffled the ears of Hank and Midas, who had followed us, by way of saying goodbye.

People were out in numbers and there were more eyes on Ashley and the Lotus than ever. I thought that if I was a woman worried about secrecy and discretion, I'd bag the Lotus and the flashy leather accessories and get myself a McJapanese car and shop at the Gap. At the same time, if I'd suffered like Ashley, I'd want those men to answer to the law regardless of the attention it drew. Ashley Bloodworth was a bundle of contradictions.

I went back into the office and reviewed my notes. I organized the facts into related groups and looked for both consistencies and inconsistencies. My brother John, who trained me to be a P.I., recommended this technique.

John had written a book—*How to be a Private Eye* by John Galt Jamison—which, of course, I had read. He advocates the use of computers, on the one hand, and in a seemingly opposite vein, also suggests pacing, walking, or jogging while pondering the facts of a case, as a way to come up with fresh ideas.

When I'd finished typing, I opted to jog and think about everything Ashley had told me. I have a gym locker at nearby State College, by virtue of being a night student. I take conversational Turkish to stay fluent in a language that I learned growing up in Turkey, where my father was in the Service. As well, every other Saturday morning I take a mid-level martial arts class—also an attempt to retain skills once acquired, which tend to deteriorate if not practiced.

I drove over to the college, changed into my running clothes, and walked and stretched my way to one of the grassy playing fields. I put my legs on autopilot and let my mind work on the riddle that Ashley had laid out for me. Three riddles, in fact. Find three men who committed an atrocious crime nearly a decade ago, and do it based on the few clues that a tormented, blindfolded victim of horrific violence was able to recall under hypnosis.

I ran for a long time, mulling over the facts until each etched itself into my brain. I soaked long under the shower, too engaged in thought to be self-conscious about how others in the shower room looked away from me. The scars from my cancer surgery, while no longer red and angry, were distasteful-looking, or perhaps plain scary, to other women.

I turned off the water and stood dripping, naked, thinking, as I reached for my towel. As my thoughts gelled, the vehicle emerged as the best line of pursuit. I had to assume it was registered in North Carolina in the year of the crime. Then I needed the name of every owner of a dark-blue Dodge van manufactured in the mid to late 1980s. That would be a tremendous challenge, and it was sheer luck that I found a way to attack the problem that same night.

CHAPTER 5

That night it happened that my friend Cynthia was having a bash on her small farm in the country west of Chapel Hill. Cynthia works as a lab tech for a pathologist at Memorial Hospital. My boyfriend is a pathologist, so Cynthia and I had one thing in common: we knew all the pathologist jokes, which were so pathetic that it was somehow hilariously funny to retell them. (*How many pathologists does it take to change a light bulb? None, they just stain anything they need to see.*) Yuck!

Cynthia's shindigs are legendary. She had grown up locally and knew a passel of folks who liked to party. On this occasion, people started arriving around two in the afternoon just when the sun's warmth was at its peak and the mixed smells of the country—horses, hay, manure and diesel fuel—were at their most aromatic.

Everyone brought food and drink and soon the smell of barbecuing meat and the sound of tops popping added to the zesty atmosphere. Many brought along something to smoke, not all of it tobacco. Cynthia contributed a tractor and wagon for rides for the kids, the barn and its hayloft for amorous retreats, and music.

The day began its descent into twilight, the light draining almost imperceptibly from the sky. It remained warm enough to wear shorts and go barefoot, and that was the attire, or lack of same, of most people. I grabbed a fresh beer and decided to walk about the old farm before darkness set in. Away on the far side, beyond a huge yellowing oak tree, was a pond where some kids in straw hats were fishing. The tree frogs had just begun their nightly trilling, slow-paced and dolorous now that summer was a fading memory.

Scattered about the property are thickets of pine and poplar trees with the occasional dogwood. Wild shrubs and vines grow among the trees. These natural areas are enough to support a community of small critters, and that's where the trouble began.

An unwritten rule at these parties is that pot smoking takes place out of sight behind the trees. This is both for the comfort level of parents with children, and of any cops, judges or city attorneys who happen to be at the party. I rounded a copse behind which revelers were passing joints.

Suddenly a man screamed in panic, "Oh shit! It bit me, it bit me."
Another man cried, "Fuckin' A, it's a fuckin' copperhead."

I ran toward a fat, barefoot man hopping on one leg, his belly
undulating under a thin shirt. "Where'd it bite you? Quick!" I called.

"Right there," he pointed at the dangling foot, "on my fourth toe are
you a nurse?" A pair of tiny pinpricks marked the spot.

I knew what to do, but I was scared to do it. I balked for a moment,
full of doubt. Then I heard in my mind's ear the voice of Colonel Tom
Hart, the M.D. who had trained my class. I didn't hear any words, just
his voice, and it gave me confidence. I didn't think my lawyer would like
this.

"I'm not a nurse; I'm an ex-army medic." (I do love that look a man
gives a woman when she's unorthodox.) "Put your foot down flat," I
commanded. I took out my Swiss Army Knife and deployed the razor-
sharp small blade. There was no time for the niceties of sterilization. I
pressed the thumb of my left hand down hard on the transverse vein
located an inch behind the joint of the toe.

"Try not to move," I said. "This will sting." I quickly made a half-
inch incision to open the vein at a point just in front of my thumb.

The man yelped. One woman screamed at the sight of the
considerable amount of blood now flowing over his foot, while another
buried her face in her companion's shoulder. I was praying that my
patient wouldn't faint on top of me. He stood stoically, his eyes focused
on the thin red flush in the western sky.

While the blood and at least a portion of the venom were draining, I
asked for a T-shirt.

"I suppose you should use mine," said a voice. "I'm his wife. It's
just...I'm not wearing a bra."

"Use this," offered one of the men. He handed me a T-shirt from
which I cut a large strip. I was tying the makeshift bandage around the
foot, knotting it over the wound for pressure, when I saw that the other
foot was missing a toe. This jolted me. This was far too strange a
coincidence. I needed to know more about this man.

A number of people had been drawn to our little group. There was a
buzz of explanations going on around me, but one thing was clear: the
man needed to be taken to the ER at Memorial Hospital. "I'll drive," I
said. "I've only had a beer and a half."

"Shouldn't we call an ambulance?" asked the man's wife. Others
nodded in agreement, and one woman got out her cell phone, evidently
intending to dial 911.

"We'll get him there quicker ourselves. Cynthia's place is hard to find," I said, "and we don't want to wait for an ambulance that's got lost."

The wife and I began walking toward my car. Two of his friends assisted the injured man while the rest trailed along behind, chattering to one another. A light plane motored low overhead on final approach to the one-runway airport that served the town of Chapel Hill.

Cynthia had sensed something was wrong and ran out to meet us. I quickly explained what had happened.

"Oh crap, I'm so sorry," she said to the injured man. "This is my fault. I should've warned people not to walk around there without shoes. Damn it all!"

With the ordinarily serene Cynthia swearing, the entire party knew something was up. The sight of the blood-soaked bandage intensified the drama. People stopped what they were doing and came over to see if they could help. The more timid among them lent moral support by looking on sympathetically. We left Cynthia to deal with the crowd and continued on to my car.

I'd brought the hounds and had left them in the wagon. "I hope you're not bothered by dogs," I said. I ordered the startled greyhounds into the way back. The husband, panting from exertion, fell heavily into the passenger seat, pulling the bloody foot in behind him. One of the men helped the wife into the back seat. I got in and started the engine.

"That's Midas and Hank behind you," I said to the wife.

"I saw them earlier. They're beautiful," she said, trying to pet simultaneously the two heads that were now more or less in her face. I ordered the dogs to lie down so I could see while backing up.

All were silent as we jerked and jolted on the uneven country road. Occasionally a dog would stand up, only to be knocked off his feet by the careering wagon. Greyhounds have high centers of gravity and low centers of common sense. When we reached the pavement and the ride became smooth, we became more inclined to converse.

"I'm Philip Martin and this is my wife Beth," the man said, still a little out of breath. "I don't know who you are, miss, but I suppose you saved my life."

"I'm Dagny Jamison. I don't think I saved your life exactly. From the little I know, copperhead bites aren't usually fatal, but they can make a person sick. I think you were lucky. The snake couldn't get much venom into a toe."

We soon left the dimly lit rural roads and came into the town. I wove through the evening traffic with a lack of courtesy that I ordinarily detest, mentally composing a story for the fuzz, just in case. Time was essential, if not critical.

I had little trouble finding the emergency room of Memorial Hospital. I knew my way to every ER in the Raleigh metro area. This, too, was part of my training as a P.I. by my brother John. Indeed, John's book, *How to be a Private Eye,* is specific on that point:

> People who are licensed to carry handguns, and may have occasion to use them, must know where the ERs are located, either for someone they shoot, or for themselves.

Beth and I helped Philip out of the car and into one of the wheelchairs lined up outside the ER entrance. Inside, few people were waiting, it being early evening. Soon enough the knife- and gun-wounded would trickle in, the inevitable victims of too much alcohol mixed with too much testosterone on a warm Saturday night.

Philip's foot was beginning to swell and his breathing was shallow. Already the bitten toe was twice its normal size. I went to report a man with a copperhead bite to the check-in person. She was a hard-faced, middle-aged, white woman. Her rumpled uniform suggested that she was at the end of her shift.

"Oh, cripes, another one. S'that time of year. Damn snakes get aggressive when they're trying to fatten up for the cold weather. Back on Daddy's farm, always someone gettin' bit afore winter. Y'all bring him on back. We'll treat him with anti-venom and have a doc look at it. You his wife?"

"No—*she's* over there with him." I indicated the couple.

"Well, I guess she can authorize us to treat him. Best to bring him back now and get started. The missus can do most of the paperwork."

A man in green scrubs emerged to wheel Philip into an examining room. Beth barely had time for a quick kiss. "I'll be right outside here, lovey," she said.

We took two seats made of molded plastic with thin foam upholstery. The walls of the ER were light green, their monotony broken by several austerely framed prints of restful scenery. Every few seconds, it seemed, the staticky public address system paged Dr. So-and-So with a request to call station such-and-such.

Beth was an attractive woman with intelligent brown eyes and medium-length straight brown hair. Hers was the kind of figure that let her go braless under a T-shirt without appearing brazen. She sped through the mass of forms the nurse had given her. When she had finished, she put the clipboard aside and began to fidget with her rings.

Several more unfortunates had drifted in while Beth was writing. One had his left thumb dislocated so badly it pointed toward his wristwatch. Beth noticed it and muttered "Ouch" under her breath. Another, a chunky woman in a sports uniform with the name "Carrboro Giants" emblazoned in green across the chest, was lying on the floor with her left leg raised on a chair, the ankle swollen to twice normal size and turning blue.

"You don't need to stay with us," Beth said. "I'm sure we can get a cab back to Cynthia's when Philip has been treated. It's beginning to look like a long wait."

"I really don't mind. I'd like to know the outcome. I guess I've got a vested interest in your husband."

"How did you know what to do?" she asked.

"I had some medical training when I was in the army. We learned a lot of blood vessel anatomy. Bleeding to death is the greatest danger from getting shot or hit by shrapnel. We also learned how to treat venomous snakebites. Jungle warfare, you know."

"I'm so thankful you happened along. We owe you a tremendous debt. What do you do when you're not treating snakebites?"

"I'm a private investigator. I work in Raleigh out of my own home. What about you?"

"I work for the state. I'm the associate director of MVIS—motor vehicles information systems—in the Department of Motor Vehicles. I do computers, in short."

"So you work downtown?"

"Yup."

"Do you live in Raleigh?"

"In Cary, actually. Philip works in the Park for Green Cap, that software company that just went public. He's a computer scientist. That's how we met. We both majored in computer science at State."

"How long have you been married?"

"It'll be four years next month. How did you get to be a private investigator? I always thought that was a man's domain." She lowered her voice an octave on the last two words. "I guess that's sexist of me, isn't it?" she added.

"When people hear 'private investigator' they often think of fictional characters. The job is rarely as dramatic as it is in books or on TV. No Maltese Falcons in our daily rounds. Mostly it's grunt work, and a lot of that takes place in front of a computer screen, as a matter of fact."

A nurse called out. "Mrs. Martin, please."

Beth got up and walked to the check-in window. She handed in the clipboard and exchanged some words with the nurse. She called to me that she'd be right back, then opened the door to the hospital innards and disappeared behind it.

While she was away, I searched my memory for details of Ashley's story. Fatboy was missing a toe. Which toe? Which foot? Had she been specific? I did some deep breathing relaxation to help bring my mind around to Ashley's recollections of Fatboy. It was a second toe but I was nearly certain she didn't mention, or didn't remember, on which foot. Philip was missing a second toe from his right foot. And he'd be about the right age and body build, too.

"I'm sorry to make you wait," said Beth when she returned. "This is a busy place. He's going to be okay, but they want to keep him overnight just in case. They won't let me stay, so do you think you could drive me to our car?"

"Of course. I'm glad it's not too serious."

We left the ER just as a man with his head bound up in a bloody rag was coming in. His wife or girlfriend trailed behind, chewing him out in PG-17 language for brawling. The wail of an ambulance siren grew louder, its pitch rising as it drew nearer, and then descending through the octaves to silence as the vehicle came through the entranceway and stopped. We reached the car a moment later.

"I don't know how I can repay you for your kindness," Beth said to me.

"Why don't you let me drive you home," I asked. "I don't mind and it's barely out of my way. Please. I'd like to ask you something. You'd be doing me a favor. Tomorrow, whenever Philip's ready, we can go back to Cynthia's and collect your car."

Beth thought a moment. "Okay. I'm really tired. I know I shouldn't drive. I'm sure my sister will give me a lift back, so I won't have to put you out any more. But I'd love to know what I can do for you."

Traffic was sparse and we quickly made our way to the Interstate, which would speed us both home. I engaged the cruise control and stretched my legs.

In the passenger seat Beth was nodding off. Her face was drawn and she was struggling to keep her eyes open. She had already yawned several times, and now I was starting to yawn myself. I might have let her sleep but I needed to talk to her.

"Philip has bad luck with feet," I remarked. "I couldn't help noticing the missing toe on his other foot. I'm curious as to how he lost it, though it's none of my business."

"It's a funny story—I mean, not funny ha-ha, you know. He says when he was nine he was sitting on the curb one day and a steamroller ran over it. Can you believe that?"

"I guess it could happen, but it does seem odd."

"Well, that's his story, and his parents don't deny it. But anyway, you said you wanted to ask a favor of me."

An 18-wheeled rig passed us doing at least 80. The Volvo shuddered but held the road. I strengthened my grip on the steering wheel and said to Beth, "I think you can help me with a case that I have, because you must know a lot about getting motor vehicle information."

"That's for sure," she said.

"I have a client who wants to know who owned a certain vehicle in March 1990."

"That's easy enough. All you need is the plate."

"Mmm, that's a snag. We don't have a plate number. All we know is that it was a dark-blue Dodge van manufactured, we think, between 1985 and 1989."

"Do you know if it's still on the road?"

"I don't. Even if it is, I don't know whether it's still registered in North Carolina, assuming it *was* back then. It's a toughie."

She turned toward me, tucking a leg under her and brushing back some wisps of hair. "It may not be as tough as it is expensive."

"What do you mean?"

"The department keeps all of its records on magnetic tape dating back to 1970. It raises money by selling the tapes to businesses and election campaigns. I'm afraid the price is $25,000."

"Wow! That's a chunk of change, but would the tapes have the data I need?

"Oh yes. They contain the year and month of all registrations. Each record has the make, model, description, and year of manufacture of the vehicle, as well as details about the owner." She yawned deeply, deepening the lines in her face.

"I suppose the van I'm looking for would've been registered between March 1989 and March 1990."

"I can tell you that about five million vehicles were registered in North Carolina at the time. That's ninety-eight or ninety-nine percent of all vehicles on the road, but we never have one hundred percent."

"Suppose I have these tapes. Then what?"

"Then, unless you happen to have a mainframe in your living room and you happen to be a programmer and you happen to know the right database language, you still have a ways to go."

Actually, there was nothing in Beth's list of unlesses that couldn't be bought. Ashley had made a big show of "money is no object." It might be as well to see how far she'd go with that.

"If I wanted to buy the tapes, what would I do?"

"You'd put an application in at the main office downtown. It takes about a week to copy the tapes. You'd need a cashier's check for the exact amount. Are you really serious?"

"Very serious."

"What would you do with the tapes?"

"Find someone to write a program to print out every record of a dark-blue Dodge van from those years. I shouldn't think that'd be too difficult."

"It wouldn't be difficult, but you'd have about ten gigabytes of data to search for that information. That would eat up some computer time. And you might end up with a load of records. That's a fairly common vehicle in this state."

We took the Cary off-ramp. Traffic signals were in their late-night blinking mode and for the most part ours was the only vehicle on the streets. A few cars were parked at a 24/7 McDonald's restaurant that I happened to know was a refuge for pot smokers with the munchies who had depleted their food supply at home.

"How many of these vans would you guess were registered?" I asked.

"I don't know. Thousands for the whole state, I suppose. If you could eliminate parts of the state, that would cut down on the numbers."

"I guess I'll have to think about that possibility." I was feeling a little daunted by the sheer weight of numbers.

Beth guided me through the residential areas of Raleigh's chief bedroom community until we reached her home. "Thanks a million, Dagny. If you want the tapes, I'll get the job expedited. Just call me." She handed me a slip of paper with her phone number on it.

"I will. I'll call anyway to see how Philip is doing." I dug a business card out of my wallet and gave it to her.

I watched her walk into the house and waited for a light to come on. When she was safely inside, I drove away, wondering not so much about locating the van as whether beyond all odds I'd stumbled upon Fatboy.

CHAPTER 6

I was wound up when I got home in the wee hours of Sunday morning. The house was stuffy and I threw open some windows to let in the mild night air. While the house aired out, I walked the greyhounds around the block. When we got back I clicked on the TV to check college football scores. When I was a student at UCLA I hung out with some of the older guys on the football team, as I was a "non-traditionally aged" student at 25. I learned a lot about football and I've been a fan of the sport ever since.

The ribbon of scores at the bottom of the screen began to repeat itself. I got up and washed my face, removing what little makeup I wear. I gave my teeth a quick once over and tuned the TV to the American Movie Classics channel. They were about to show *The 4 Horsemen of the Apocalypse* and the host was pointing out that they were Famine, Pestilence, Destruction, and Death. The opening credits with the four chargers bearing ghostly riders in the sky were impressive, but the plot dragged, so I clicked off. I was half asleep, and before I could move off the sofa the other half of me fell asleep, and there I spent the night.

Just before waking I dreamed, but the dreams were more like nightmares, literally. I was in the football stadium of nearby Marquis University. They were playing Notre Dame, who had the so-called Four Horsemen from bygone years in their backfield. I was trying to name them but I was confused. I kept coming up with Famine, Pestilence, Destruction, and Death: wrong horsemen. They made me leave the stadium because I didn't know the players' names.

On the road outside, a man in a flowing robe, riding a blue Pegasus, pursued me from the air. I tried to run but my jeans were too tight. They soon caught up to me, but when the horse landed it became a large dog, a German shepherd. The man had disappeared. I knew that the best way to handle a dog is to act like the Alpha. I tamed it and it became my friend. We were walking back to the stadium to see who'd won the game, when I woke up.

It was late morning and I was stiff from sleeping on cushions. The morning light hurt my eyes and my mind was still half in the dream. I pulled myself upright, blinking to adjust to the brightness. Churchgoers were already walking home from services. Children were yelling and racing about. Several were tossing a mini-football around. A woman called out to her kids not to dirty their Sunday clothes, while her husband, now in his shirtsleeves, practiced his golf swing with an air-club.

I settled back, my fingers locked behind my head, to think about the dream before the memory of it faded. The tendrils that connected my dream to reality were easy to trace. It was football season; I'd seen flying horses on TV; and the blue Pegasus is the logo of Marquis University, whose football team is dubbed "The Flying Horses" by the sportswriters. The key insight, though, was the man on the blue Pegasus. He fit the image I had formed from Ashley's description of the belt buckle of one of her rapists. That raised the possibility that one of the men had been a Marquis student or alumnus.

I got up and walked into the kitchen with the hounds on my heels. I took a drink directly from the faucet and splashed my face. The cold water brought me fully awake. My face, reflected in the chrome, was indented with the pattern of the sofa cushions, and that, together with the state of my hair, would have competed well in a beauty contest for orangutans. My breath was at least as bad as the dogs', but they didn't seem to mind. I dried, gave them both a good-morning rub, and let them out back.

In the house behind mine lived five young men and women who ran a small internet company from the premises. One of the women was washing her car with a power brush. She saw me open the door to let out the dogs and waved. I didn't exactly feel like being seen—I'd intended to hop into the shower—but I didn't want to be rude either, and when I saw who it was I got an idea that made me forget how I looked.

I waved back and walked over to the low picket fence that separated our properties, while licking my fingers and applying them to unruly strands of hair. The woman switched off the power brush and came to meet me. Lily is a woman of Philippine extraction. She had grown up in California, had attended Stanford, and had received her computer experience working in Silicon Valley. She was smart, definitely one of the brains behind the company's success in a highly competitive industry.

"How's it going, Lily?"

"S' going great. I'm so glad fall is here. I never get used to the humidity. It's a great pleasure to wash a car on a morning like this."

"Say, how about coming over when you're finished for a cup of coffee. I'd like to ask your advice about something. Would you, please? I'd appreciate it."

Lily agreed. I went back inside, grabbed a one-minute shower, and made a small breakfast of fruit, cereal and skim milk while the coffee was dripping. I took my breakfast standing at the counter, and when I'd finished eating, I refilled my coffee cup and carried it to my office. The room was awash with the warm noonday sun and the leafy scents of autumn wafted in through the half-open louvers. Lily's power washer hummed in the background. I sat down at my desk and punched in Ashley's landline number at home.

A child's voice answered, "Hello."

"Hello. May I please speak with Ashley Bloodworth?"

The receiver was put down with a clunk and the same voice cried, "Mother, there's a telephone call."

I could hear Ashley admonishing the child in the background. "Benton, please don't answer my telephone. You have your own telephone."

The child said contritely, "Sorry, Mother."

Ashley came on the line. "This is Ashley Bloodworth."

"Ashley, this is Dagny. Can you talk now?"

"Yes, of course. I'm surprised to hear from you so soon. I hope it's a sign of progress."

It's a sign that you and some money may soon be parted, I thought. I hadn't cared for the way she'd been so curt with her son, but that was none of my business. This was a professional call.

"It may be progress, it may be wheel-spinning, I really don't know which. You have a decision to make."

I told her about the DMV tape and the possibility of a $25,000 boondoggle if the van wasn't registered in North Carolina. I also pointed out the drawback of too much data. What would I do with a thousand names of Dodge van owners? She wasn't worried about the money.

"Buy the tapes. If you take your credit card to any branch of Southeastern Bank and Trust, they'll cut you a cashier's check. You can pay for the consultant and the computer time in the same way. Cross the too-much-data bridge when you come to it. Oh, and save the tapes. I may be able to resell them."

"There's one other thing, Ashley. That belt buckle you described to me—it may be a Marquis University logo. One or more of those men might've been students, or former students, at Marquis. Does that ring any kind of a bell with you?"

"I'll think about it, but I'd like you to follow up anyway. My family earned much of their earlier fortune in tobacco. A goodly portion of the

Marquis endowment came from tobacco money. Let me give you a name and number to call if you need assistance from officials at Marquis."

There was a momentary pause while she looked up the number. The name was familiar.

"Did you say Theodora Jenkins? Isn't she the…"

"President," Ashley finished. "When you call the number, identify yourself by name. Either Dr. Jenkins or her administrative assistant will direct you to the right person. Is there anything else?"

"That should do it."

"Thank you, Dagny. Please keep me apprised."

I disconnected at the same time that Lily switched off the power washer. Shortly afterwards a quiet rap on the glass louvers announced her visit. I walked around to the side door and let her in. Sweat had beaded on her brow and she was flushed from the morning's exercise.

"Coffee's ready, but if you'd prefer something cold to drink…?"

"Actually, Dagny, I wouldn't mind a beer. I've worked up a bit of a sweat. I hope I'm not too disgusting."

"Don't be silly," I told her. "Bottle or glass?"

"A bottle is fine. Thank you."

I brought her a long-necked Black and Tan and refilled my coffee cup. The hounds, who knew Lily, were dozing unconcernedly in their nests under the piano. One or another of them had "passed gas" some minutes before Lily's arrival. Traces of the odor remained, and I was hoping not to be blamed. This is a bane of dog ownership.

"I need to ask your advice about something that's come up. I may be acquiring magnetic tapes from the Department of Motor Vehicles that contain vehicle registration data. I'm wondering if you know a company that would search the tapes for certain information."

"Mag tapes from the DMV, huh? First thing is to get it all on CD-ROMs. You could process the data on a laptop if you had to."

"I hadn't thought of that. Who'd be able to do that for me?"

"There are a couple of places in Raleigh. I can look them up for you. Do you know how much data's on the tapes?"

"Ten gigabytes, I'm told."

She whistled. "You might want to transfer it to a hard drive, so it's all on one piece of medium, you know. Otherwise, you'll have a shitload of CD-ROMs. Do you know the database?"

"No. I assume the tape comes with that information."

"Oh yes, it'd have to. May I make a suggestion?"

"I was hoping you would. I'm kind of clueless."

"See if you can hire one of the DMV programmers as a consultant. They'd probably welcome the chance to earn some extra bucks. Be sure that you get someone who's worked with the database. Buy some computer time somewhere and you ought to be able to do your searching."

"That's a great idea, Lily. I'm glad I thought to ask you. But if I can't get anyone, you can give me some guidance, right?"

"I'd be happy to. Just let me know."

That evening I called Beth Martin. Philip answered.

"Hello, Philip? This is Dagny Jamison. I'm glad you're home. How's the foot?"

"Dagny, good of you to call. The foot's sore as hell. I'm using a cane to get around but they say it'll heal. The doctor told me that your quick action saved me from being much sicker than I am. I want to thank you again."

"No problem. I'm glad it isn't worse. Do you think I could speak with Beth for a minute?"

"Sure, hang on."

He put down the handset, which picked up music in the background—Backstreet Boys singing "I Want It That Way"—which was interrupted by Beth's voice after about thirty seconds.

"Hey, Dagny, thanks for calling."

"Hey, Beth. I called to see how things went this morning, but I take it they went okay. Philip sounds good."

"It went just fine. I got my sister to drive me out to Cynthia's to get the car. They both insisted on coming with me to the hospital, so we caravanned over. Philip had three women fussing over him, dripping with sympathy. I think he'd do it all over again just for that."

She made a small laughing sound, and I heard a faint "not on your life" in the background.

"Sounds like he wouldn't," I said, smiling, "but do you remember our conversation last night? I have my client's permission to purchase the tapes you told me about."

"Well, good, I can help you with that, like I said."

"Also, a friend of mine suggested that maybe I could hire one of your programmers as a consultant. Is that a possibility? I wouldn't want to create a conflict."

"I don't see any reason why not. Let me think. There's one guy, KC Fu, who's a bit of a workaholic. He's accrued maximum vacation and needs to take some time off. And, he's familiar with the tapes and the database. I'll get the two of you together. Could you come to the DMV building on the corner of Scarboro and Morton at eleven tomorrow?"

"Sure, I know where it is. How do I find you?"

"There is just one entrance with a big DMV on a sign outside it. Come through the double glass doors into the lobby and ask for me at the receptionist's desk. You can park behind the building. I'll help you with buying the tapes, too."

"That's great, Beth. I really appreciate it. I'll see you tomorrow."

CHAPTER 7

The lack of solid clues in the Ashley Bloodworth case forced me to make guesses so that I could get off the spot, as it were. John called them "working hypotheses" in his book. One guess was that the belt buckle owner had some connection to Marquis University. Another guess was that the first names of the three men were in fact Tom, Dick, and Harry. A third guess was that one of them owned the van.

I met Beth at the DMV's main building at the appointed time. Looking sharp in a starchy light gray pants suit, Beth was the antithesis of the T-shirted, pot-smoking girl I had met barely two days earlier. She took me over to the clerk who dealt with the purchase of the data tapes and helped me fill out the forms. She suggested I write "Mail order sales" under "Purpose." The cost was $26,750. The state charged sales tax on their product, which seemed a tad unfair. Next thing, they'll be putting a sales tax on vehicle registration. Or worse—I thought inanely—a sales tax on the sales tax, and who knows what kind of state that would put us in? The good part was that if I returned with the cashier's check by five o'clock, I could have the tapes by noon the next day.

Beth led me through a labyrinth of corridors to a cubicle with the nameplate K.C. Fu. Inside was a diminutive Chinese man of no more than twenty-five, who wore wide, thick-rimmed glasses that covered half his face. He stood up when we appeared and I doubt he reached five foot two. The crotch of his baggy Bermuda shorts drooped below his knees and his Hawaiian shirt size was an excessive XXXL. A receding hairline left behind a high forehead that made his head seem far too large for his body. I knew a smart computer geek when I saw one.

After introductions, I told him what I needed while Beth listened in. He left me impressed with his capabilities. I didn't even have to persuade him to work for me because at the right moment Beth pitched in and said, "KC, things are slow around here now. You need to take some vacation days or you'll lose them at the year's end. Work for Dagny for a few days and earn some extra money. Maybe you can treat yourself to a short holiday afterwards. Why not?"

KC didn't look as though he'd know what to do with a holiday of any length, but he wasn't about to argue with the big boss.

Beth looked at her watch. "It's nearly time for lunch. Why don't we go down to the cafeteria before it gets crowded—my treat. I'll need to leave early and you two can talk business."

At lunch Beth brought me up to date on Philip, which was that he felt like shit and his foot hurt but his doctor expected him to recover fully. Under the guise of polite curiosity, I asked how they met and when they got married and similar things. I didn't have much of a profile of Fatboy, apart from his body type and the missing toe, but from what Beth said about Philip it didn't seem likely that he was a sadistic rapist. I didn't ask outright, but I could tell that they weren't overly religious people. Philip would not be the type to wear an ostentatious crucifix. I couldn't cross him off the list—hell, he was the only one on the list—but I was about convinced that the missing toe was one of life's cruel coincidences.

KC had grown up in Hong Kong, speaking both Chinese and English—his English had the bare traces of an accent. His parents had moved to North Carolina when he was a teenager, and he'd gotten his master's degree in computer science at State. I asked him if he'd work for me. I figured he must earn around $50,000 a year, or $25 an hour. I offered him $50. He agreed on the spot as long as it was okay with his manager, but since Beth was his manager's boss, I didn't foresee a problem.

I gave him the names of the two computer companies that Lily had given me the day before. He said his cousin owned a company in Chapel Hill that could do the work for a fair price, if it was all the same to me, which it was. He even agreed to collect the tapes from the DMV if I'd give him the check for payment.

"Basically, I'll need, like, one or two days to get the data copied onto a drive. After that, you can tell me basically exactly what you want."

We exchanged phone numbers, and then as an afterthought I said, "Why don't you come with me to the bank now, if you have the time? I think it's within walking distance. They should be able to cut the check while we wait."

"Okay, I can do that. Basically, I don't have too much to do this afternoon."

There was a branch of SB&T two blocks from the DMV building. I presented my credit card and asked the woman behind the counter for a cashier's check made out to the North Carolina Department of Motor Vehicles for $26,750. She screwed her face into a question mark the way bank tellers do when you try to cash check number 0000.

"Excuse me, I'll have to show your card to the branch manager."

People behind me moved to other lines. KC stood patiently by, squinting every few seconds at the alien quality of life off of the computer screen. The branch manager was a crusty, slow-talking southerner who asked for a picture ID, studied it, studied me, studied the credit card, and then studied it all again. Finally satisfied, he turned on what charm he could muster and apologized for the delay. He ordered the teller to print the check while he waited to sign it, so as "not to inconvenience Ms. Jamison any further."

We walked back to the DMV building together. At the door I handed the check to KC, reminded him to keep track of his hours, and asked him to call me when he got the data transferred. He disappeared into the lobby with a small wave of goodbye.

In my car, I called the number at Marquis University that Ashley had given me. A voice answered: "President Jenkins' office, Sophia speaking."

"My name is Dagny Jamison and I—"

"Oh, Ms. Jamison. I've been expecting your call. I'm afraid Dr. Jenkins is in a meeting. She told me to help you with anything you need."

"That's very kind of you. If it's possible, could I get a list of all students who were attending Marquis in March 1990?"

"That shouldn't be a problem. You need to speak with the Registrar of Records, Dr. Downey Bryan. Let me call him first. May I put you on hold for a moment?"

After a short wait Sophia transferred me to Dr. Bryan, who suggested I come to his offices on campus and said he'd assign someone to help me.

Marquis University was once outside the city limits amidst Marquis Forest, a tract of unspoiled woods and streams owned by the Marquis family. They had endowed it as a seminary in the nineteenth century. Its mission expanded over the years to encompass more general goals than simply the training of clergy, and it grew to become one of the nation's fine private universities.

Though some of Marquis Forest remains unspoiled, much of it was lost to libraries, dorms, gyms, labs, athletic fields and parking lots. Still, the planners left many acres of parks and gardens on the campus, so the school has a countrified ambiance.

Marquis describes itself this way in its PR pamphlet:

Our architecture is above all eclectic. It ranges from a Gothic cathedral called Marquis Chapel, much beloved and photographed, to an ultramodern glass and metal edifice that houses the school of business. Every building on our campus has both form and function, regardless of the style, and in no period of history were the architects bound by the need for a "foolish consistency."

The registrar's office is in a building with a stone façade on the same quad as the famous chapel. Parking is nonexistent so near to central campus and visitors can expect a long trek from the metered parking at the fringes. Still, the campus fascinates. One catches up on the current college fashions by observing the students who loll about on the grassy plots and benches when the weather is clement. And in autumn it's a pleasure to see the trees and shrubs changing from cool shades of green to warmer reds and oranges, contrary to the seasonal temperature changes.

A systems programmer named Ellis was assigned to assist me. He looked as though he had stepped out of the 1960s, what with his hair lapping over his ears and collar, and his bellbottomed trousers. I asked for a list of students enrolled in March 1990, with the first names of Tom, Thomas, Dick, Richard, or Harry. I wanted dates of birth, addresses, major subjects and any personal information in the records.

"Man, you must have a major in with the old lady," said Ellis. "I mean, I can promise you, we don't do this for just anybody. I guess they gave you the bit about confidentiality, commercial use, all that. But that's not my job. I'll need about an hour to offload and print the data, if you don't mind waiting."

It's a pleasure to wile away an hour on Marquis's beautiful campus. The cathedral and the popular Marquis Gardens are tourist attractions, with the latter noted for its spectacular horticultural displays that span every season except winter. Both places are trendy sites for weddings.

I opted to wait in the chapel, which was close by. Its stained-glass windows, marble columns, carved pews, finely wrought artifacts, and stupendous pipe organ make it an exotic place to visit. On that day an organ concert rehearsal added to the pleasure and made the time pass swiftly.

When I returned to Ellis's office, he was waiting for me. "You got 33 records of first name Harry, 81 records of first name Richard or Dick, and 216 records of first name Thomas or Tom. Each record's got the student's complete personal information, but confidential stuff like whether they got caught cheating or using drugs is withheld. If that sounds okay, I'll go ahead and print them out."

"If you wouldn't mind. I really appreciate this."

"No problem."

He sat down at his computer and tap-tapped away while I watched over his shoulder. "This will take around ten minutes. If there's anything else I can help you with, Dr. Bryan says I'm to give your requests priority."

"That's really great, but it looks like I have enough for now. If I think of something later, can I call you?"

He encouraged me to do so. We made small talk for a few minutes. He didn't ask why I wanted the data, so I didn't have to make up a story. The printout amounted to more than a ream of paper.

I drove home with my prize. The stack of printouts looked even larger on my desk than it had in Ellis's office. I poured a glass of white wine, carried it to my desk, took a sip for courage, and drew the pile toward me. I went through the records and set aside those of freshmen, sophomores, anyone 20 years old or under, anyone 30 years old or over (yes, there were several), and women (one named Thomasina). I noticed with some annoyance that I had records in which the middle name, when fully spelled out, was one of the key names. I put those aside too. That got the Toms down to 90, the Dicks to 31 and the Harrys to 17.

The Harrys were the most manageable, so I picked one up and studied it. I was relying on a part of my mind I didn't fully control but trusted to alert me to noteworthy items. I didn't have to wait long. The records were alphabetized by last name, and the first record I picked up was that of a Harry Angelica. Two red flags went up. His major subject was film and video; his permanent address was in Plainfield, New Jersey. That would account for the camera equipment that Ashley saw, and she thought Strong might have had a New York or New Jersey accent.

By the afternoon of the next day, Tuesday, I'd examined all 138 records. A Thomas Horton and a Thomas Bienvenu were also listed as film and video majors, along with a Richard Sydnor. Horton's permanent address was a street in Raleigh that I didn't recognize. Bienvenu was from Greensboro and had come to Marquis as a junior, having already done two years at a local college. Richard Sydnor's record placed his family in Richmond, Virginia.

Narrowing down to film and video majors had given me a scant harvest: two Toms, a Dick, and a Harry. These were slim pickings indeed, but I was starved for clues and had to take what meager bounty the data put forth.

CHAPTER 8

I looked Thomas Horton's street up in my map book of Raleigh. It was about two miles south of my house, on the other side of the Capital. A phone call would have been more efficient, but the stack of printouts had cooped me up all day and I needed some air and some exercise. Another mild, clear day of Carolina blue skies and low humidity further beckoned me outdoors. I chose to walk across town and pay a personal call.

The house at the address given in Thomas Horton's school record was located in a neighborhood of diverse race and income. It was one of the nicer homes on the block. The lawn in the small front yard was green and close-cropped, and the beds of flowers and shrubs appeared to be well tended. The dwelling itself was a recently painted off-white two-story, with clapboard siding and faux shutters on the windows. A small front porch contained two well-worn, comfortable-looking chairs. Between them stood a table large enough to hold three or four glasses or drink cans. The mailbox in the front showed an address but no name.

I don't much like walking up to unfamiliar houses and knocking on the door. It reminds me too much of religion peddlers, who by now have almost entirely displaced the Fuller Brush Man. It's also unwise for a lone woman to do so for obvious reasons—witness the case I was working on—though I can keep one hand in my handbag around the butt of my automatic if I sense danger.

Nobody was to be seen on the street, and inside the house the occupants had drawn the curtains. I chanced a peek in the mailbox. They hadn't taken in their mail and I glimpsed the name "Horton" on an L.L. Bean catalog. I walked briskly up the driveway and then across a short cement walkway that led to the front porch and door. I slipped my left hand into my handbag, and with the right pressed the ringer button. I heard a loud buzz inside the house.

There was a stirring inside and the curtain on the window by the door parted, affording the person behind the glass a look at me, and vice versa. A man of color in his fifties opened the door and politely asked me what I wanted. I'd prepared a small lie.

"Excuse me for bothering you, sir, but I was told at Marquis University that Mr. Thomas Horton lived here and that he was in the business of making video tapes."

"Well, miss, they told you wrong. Thomas is an actor and an assistant director."

"Oh, dear. I seem to have wasted a trip. Wasn't he a film and video major at Marquis?"

"He was, but that includes acting, directing, producing and all of it."

"And he doesn't make videotapes for advertising?"

"No ma'am, he sure don't."

"Oh, pity!" I said with a little stamp of my foot. "Anyway, you must be very proud of your, uh, son—is it?—for graduating from Marquis. That's a fine university."

He softened at that and, more significantly, didn't balk at the supposition. I wanted to make sure I had the right Thomas Horton.

"Thomas worked hard to earn his scholarship, because there was no way we could've had the money to send him there, no way with three other children."

A late-model car turned into the driveway, parked, and a sharply dressed woman of African descent, also about 50 years of age, stepped out.

"I'm very sorry to have disturbed you, sir. I'll just be on my way," I said to Mr. Horton. To the woman whose expression was somewhat leery, I said, "You must be Mrs. Horton, Thomas's mother."

She nodded.

"I mistakenly thought he made videotapes but Mr. Horton tells me he's a director. Isn't it wonderful that after all this time the folks at Marquis still recommend him?"

"Yes, I suppose it is," she said, as we squeezed past each other on the narrow walkway.

"Y'all have a good evening, then," I said. "It was nice to meet you both."

It had been successful outing. I'd gotten some exercise on a splendid day, and I had eliminated one of the Toms. All of Ashley's attackers were Caucasians.

I called Thomas Bienvenu's home phone number as given in his student record. A man with some kind of accent answered. He confirmed that it was the Bienvenu residence, and when I asked for Thomas he said he was Thomas. My heartbeat notched up when I thought I recognized the accent to be French. Wasn't one of those men called Frenchy?

Always prepared though never a Girl Scout, I pretended to be a fundraiser from Marquis. "Good to catch you home, Thomas. This is Nan calling from the Marquis University alumni office. Are you the Thomas Bienvenu who graduated with a major in film and video in 1990?"

"Yes I am, but you people, you called last week. I already made the pledge."

"Yes, well, I'm awfully sorry to bother you again but I'm afraid your address was misplaced. Would you mind giving it to me so I can send you your, uh, pledge package?"

He grumbled about how he'd been receiving mail from Marquis for ten years and it seemed to him awfully careless to lose the address of people who promised them money, but in the end he gave it to me. I really wanted to hear him speak enough to be sure of the French accent. It was not strong but it was distinctive.

I had good reason for making sure of his current address. While Ashley hadn't mentioned a foreign accent, if I asked her specifically and she recalled one, then Monsieur Bienvenu would merit further investigation. This Thomas wasn't as easily eliminated as Thomas Horton.

There were no Sydnors at the Sydnor's phone number supplied by Marquis. I punched in 4-1-1, asked for Richmond, Virginia, the number for a Richard or a Dick Sydnor, S-y-d-n-o-r. A human voice thanked me and an automated voice gave me the number for a Dick, and even dialed it for me. A man picked up on the second ring. I introduced myself as Susan Radford. Susan attended Marquis about ten years ago and remembered that a certain Dick Sydnor was a film and video major. Susan wondered if this was that same Dick, and if he was still making videos—if so, she had a job for him.

I half expected him to say "Huh?", as Susan tends toward a stream of consciousness style of speaking. Instead, he said, "Well, this is Dick, but actually, all I do now is editing. That keeps me pretty much busy fulltime. I'm sorry but I don't think I can be of much help." His tone of voice reflected an inner battle in which politeness barely won over skepticism.

I said, "That gives me an idea. I have several old videotapes that I once used for advertising. What are the chances of editing them into something new? That might be less expensive than starting from scratch."

"I'm not sure about that. I certainly can't give you an answer over the phone. If you want to ship the tapes to me, I'll take a look at them. I'll have to charge you for my time."

"What if I brought them to you? I have to be in the Richmond area anyway. I have no problem paying your fee."

He agreed to the arrangement with a reluctant "I can only give you half an hour," and gave me directions to his studio in Richmond where we could meet the next day.

I was on a roll with these phone calls and I didn't want to quit. I called Harry Angelica's number in Plainfield, New Jersey. An elderly sounding lady answered who claimed she didn't know any Angelicas, in response to my inquiry. I tried the local number in Raleigh, the one Harry had had when he was a student. An answering machine speaking for Laurie, Suzie and Katie said none of them could come to the phone. That was far too long of a long shot anyway.

Three Angelicas—Annie, Michael and the Angelica Bakery—were coughed up by directory services for Plainfield. I dutifully copied down the numbers and—surprise, surprise!—Annie's was the one in Plainfield I'd already called: Harry's "permanent" number from his school record. I contemplated this oddity. Electronic phone books are nearly always current and do not become gradually outdated like paper ones. The possibility that someone had moved into the house and kept the Angelicas' phone number seemed remote. And even if they had, why would they deny knowing the family? It didn't add up.

I considered calling back and confronting whoever answered. Maybe that would coax out information about Harry Angelica. It might have the opposite effect, too. I was going to have to sleep on it. I had Dick Sydnor to check out, in any event.

I didn't fancy driving to Richmond and back in one day. It's two and a half to three hours one way, depending on traffic. But I needed to meet Dick Sydnor in person to see if he fit any of the thinly described assaulters of Ashley. He spoke the flat kind of English that met Ashley's description of Little's speech.

In case he was a candidate, I needed work for him so I could follow up. My brother John advertised his private investigation firm in Santa Barbara on late-night television. I had copies of his tapes from the past several years. I'd ask Sydnor if he could edit them into something that would suit my business in Raleigh.

The next morning I drove to Richmond. Dick Sydnor lived in the Huguenot suburb northwest of the downtown area. I found his house with no difficulty. Per his directions, I followed the driveway around to the back where his studio stood.

A modest sign hung above the half-open door: Sydnor Video Edit, Inc. I parked and keyed off. John's videotapes were on the passenger seat. I grabbed them and got out of the car. I was stretching and yawning away the effects of the long drive when a twisted little man in an electric wheelchair rolled out of the studio.

"Hello. You must be Susan Radford."

"And you're Mr. Sydnor, I believe," I said, trying to hold the pitch of my voice steady and contain my surprise.

We shook hands. He had the full use of his right arm and his grip was strong. The left arm lay motionless on the armrest of the chair. I couldn't see his legs but I imagined they were atrophied. His torso was somehow off-center vis-à-vis his head and neck, giving the contorted appearance. He invited me into the studio. It was ingeniously outfitted so that he could reach every bit of electronic hardware from his chair. It was as clever an arrangement as I'd ever seen. He noticed my awe.

"My wife and I designed the layout," he said with undisguised pride. "When I was at Marquis learning to produce and edit videos, I couldn't reach the equipment. This was a breach of the Americans with Disabilities Act and other statutes. Rather than sue over it, I asked them to let me refit the lab to make it wheelchair accessible. They loved the idea. I collaborated with a woman majoring in design, now my wife, and we tried out all sorts of configurations. Some worked and some didn't. I was the guinea pig and ultimate arbiter. We came up with many innovations and we both wrote our master's degree theses on the topic. What you see here is the quintessence of our work."

Of course that settled it for me and my hidden agenda, but I was so impressed with his setup that I thought I'd see what he could do with the tapes anyway. I explained, truthfully, that I worked for John during the summer months. Then not so truthfully, that John had asked me to have several years' worth of video advertising coalesced into one brilliant 60-second spot. Actually, if Sydnor could do it then I'd have a surprise birthday present for my elder bro'.

Meeting a person who had overcome extreme adversity put me in a good mood for the long drive home. I used the time to ponder the strange call to Harry Angelica's supposed address of ten years ago. I needed to find the underlying cause of the funny business in Plainfield. I couldn't afford to let a single thread slip, as I had so few. Curiouser and curiouser, I thought, repeating Alice's words about Wonderland, long remembered from my childhood reading. But this wasn't Wonderland; it was New Jersey, and curious matters were suspect.

I was just inside the Raleigh city limits when my mobile chimed. It was KC. He had good news and bad news. Good was that he'd already transferred the data from tape to hard drive. It had run overnight. Bad was that there were well over a thousand dark-blue Dodge vans registered in 1990 between two and five years old.

"Basically, I didn't print anything because I wanted to know if you could, like, narrow the search," said KC.

I could make a stab at it. "KC, how long would it take to see if one of the owners was named Harry Angelica, that's A-n-g-e-l-i-c-a?"

"No problemo. I'll call you back in ten minutes."

When the phone chimed precisely ten minutes later, it was with an anticipatory shiver of excitement that I pressed the talk button. This time KC had only good news.

"You hit the jackpot, Dagny. Angelica was the owner of record of a 1987 Dodge van."

CHAPTER 9

Harry Angelica had both owned a Dodge van and been a film and video major at Marquis University. I had the name of one of Ashley's rapists and I was hungry like a wolf to have the man.

I remained in an excited state for several minutes before the cold rain of reason dampened my parade. The identification of Harry Angelica was circumstantial. It was based on four inferences. First, that the men were Marquis students—inferred from the belt buckle. Second, that one of them was a film and video major—inferred from the photographic gear that Ashley had observed in the van. Third, that one of them had owned a dark-blue Dodge van, as opposed to having rented, borrowed, or stolen it. Fourth, that the name was Tom, Dick, or Harry. The deductions were consistent with the hypothesis that Harry Angelica was one of the men, but they didn't prove it. Brother John had something to say about this in *How to be a Private Eye*:

> Good detection is like good science. Once you have your working hypothesis, you seek evidence that supports it, and, with equal vigor, evidence that discredits it. The importance of the latter is often overlooked. The failure of every attempt to falsify a hypothesis ultimately lends strength to the likelihood of its verity.

I called KC back and asked him to find out if Angelica had ever had a North Carolina driver's license, and if so, to get me his age, height, weight, eye and hair color, and race, from the record. KC was also to check to make sure that the van was dark blue in color.

"I'll walk over to the driver's license division tomorrow morning. Basically, they'll give me any information I ask for. I'll call you tomorrow."

The next day I rose impatient and edgy. After a run in my neighborhood, I thought I might as well call the house in Plainfield. The same woman answered.

In my friendliest voice, I said, "Hello, I'm very sorry to bother you. Am I speaking with Mrs. Annie Angelica?" There was silence on the other end, then the faint clicks that precede a return to dial tone. She had wordlessly hung up on me.

I dialed again, expecting either a busy signal or endless ringing. But she picked up. In my most pleading voice, I said, "Please, please don't hang up. Let me please tell you that I'm not selling anything and I'm not a bill collector. I only want to speak with Annie Angelica about Harry." I held my breath. She was thinking because there were no clicking sounds. Finally she spoke.

"What about Harry?"

"Is this Mrs. Angelica?"

"No. I'm Mrs. Palmer. I keep house for Mrs. Angelica."

"Thank you for speaking with me, Mrs. Palmer. My name is Dagny Jamison. I'm trying to reach Harry Angelica."

"So are many people. I cannot help you."

"Is there any way you'd let me speak with Annie Angelica? I assume that's his mother."

"Mrs. Angelica cannot come to the telephone."

"Please, Mrs. Palmer, may I ask why?"

"She wouldn't know what to do with a telephone. Now if you'll excuse me, I have to get on with my work. There's nothing I can do for you."

She hung up on me again. That was vexing. My only definite lead was misbehaving.

While waiting for KC's call I decided to surf the Internet for clues to Harry's existence and whereabouts. I tried Google, Yahoo and all the other available search engines, but nothing turned up, if you discount the various Harry Angelicas from Idaho, Samoa and the Canary Islands, none of whom were the right age or right race. I was starting to hope that my Harry Angelica would turn out to be a five-foot three Mongolian and save me this aggravation, when the phone finally rang. I grabbed it on the first ring.

KC at last. He'd had a buddy pull the license record. Harry Angelica was six-feet one-inch tall with blond hair and blue eyes. That was consistent with how Ashley perceived Strong, but Strong was not the driver. Little was the driver. Or did Ashley assume that because Little wasn't one of the two men who had grabbed her, he must have been driving? One expects the owner to be the driver, but I wasn't going to get hung up over that. My hypothesis stood up to those facts. I was going after Harry Angelica.

After another frustrating hour at the computer I recalled yet another bit from John's book:

Computers often help to find a person, but sometimes eyes, ears and personal presence are superior to bits, bytes and blinding speed.

I used the Internet to book a late afternoon flight to Newark and a hotel in Plainfield, New Jersey. There was no time to engage Janet, my usual dog-sitter, and it was a sad pair of greyhounds that checked into the nearby doggie hotel.

The flight to Newark was uneventful. The line at the rental-car counter tried my patience, but at least the agency had my reservation and, ironically, a dark-blue Dodge sedan when I was finally served. They also had a computer that printed out directions from the airport to wherever you wanted to go. I typed in the name of my hotel in Plainfield and received a sheet with instructions on how to get there.

Within an hour I was checking in. The desk clerk gave me a map of the city and directions to the Angelicas' street. The next morning I dressed in a conservative skirt, blouse, and sweater, and made myself up to look businesslike. I checked to make sure I had a chunk of one-hundred dollar bills in my handbag. When Ashley had hinted at the use of bribery I'd been somewhat put off, but if a few C-notes would loosen Mrs. Palmer's tongue, I'd go for it.

I followed my map to an older, elegant upper-middle-class section of the city. The homes were large, mostly two- and even three-story. Despite their size they were close together, separated from each other by narrow strips of grass or garden, and from the curb by small front yards. The Angelica's house was on a corner and stood out from the rest. It was double the size of those around it, with spacious lawns on two sides.

The house was not in good repair. The paint around the windows was chipped and peeling, and several roof gutters had slipped off their bolts and would no longer catch water. The grounds, too, which seemed to have been well groomed once, had become seedy from lack of care. It makes me sad to see plants dying from neglect but I shoved that emotion aside. I had a purpose and I focused on it.

At the front door I had a choice of a doorbell or a huge brass knocker. I rang the bell, and tapped lightly with the knocker for good measure. A moment later I heard footsteps. A deadbolt snapped back and the door opened five inches, held by a chain. A woman with a craggy face appeared in the crack and asked what I wanted." You must be Mrs. Palmer," I cooed. "I'm Dagny Jamison. We spoke on the phone. I know I'm not welcome, but I've come all the way from North Carolina because I'm desperate and don't know where to turn. I'm here to beg for your help. Please hear me out."

I resisted the temptation to insert my foot in the door, which I feared she was about to slam in my face. Mrs. Palmer paused, her face filled with uncertainty, which made it look even craggier. Whether out of sympathy for my plea, or simply because she was in a good mood, or maybe just bored, she gently closed the door to release the chain, then opened it wide to let me in. Before she could have second thoughts, I swished past her with several giant steps and nary a Mother May I.

My first impressions were of genteel wealth. There were tapestries and oil paintings on every wall. Columns of purple velvet draperies surrounded the windows. The substantial dark-wooded chairs and sofas, which would put your back out if you tried to move them, were plush and elegantly upholstered. But a closer examination revealed old wealth that no one was renewing. The handsomely sewn cushion covers were threadbare at the seams, the edges of the velvet frayed, and the once luxurious carpets stained with time.

Mrs. Palmer signaled me to follow her. She led me through a dining room to the kitchen. At the far end of the kitchen was a breakfast nook with an oriel window facing south. In the nook stood a massive, square table of dark oak supported by five sturdy legs on casters, with the fifth leg supporting the center of the table. Mrs. Palmer gestured for me to sit at this table. Had I not spoken with her previously I might have thought her incapable of speech. She remained silent and stood as if waiting on me. I broke the rapidly thickening ice with the spiel I'd concocted as we walked through the house.

"Thank you very much for letting me in. I'm very sorry to inconvenience you. I went to Marquis University with Harry Angelica. We were both film majors and we made a video together that was highly praised by the professor. He recently described our work to an executive at a large studio, who wants to see it. I'm the only one of us the professor could find, but I had lost my copy of the tape. I'm hoping that Harry still has one. There may be a lot of money in it for us. That's why I want to get in touch with him so badly."

"How much money?" said Mrs. Palmer, finally.

It wasn't a question I'd expected. Not right away. But if it was a matter of money, then I was willing to flaunt it. After all, Ashley had spent considerable thousands to get me this far, so we were definitely "in for a penny, in for a pound." I reached in my bag and pulled out the wad of C-notes.

"The studio is so interested that they financed my trip up here and gave me an advance of two thousand dollars. We could make some very big bucks if they like the work."

Mrs. Palmer sighed and asked if she might sit down. It seemed a peculiar request since I was the supplicant. On the other hand, she was the housekeeper and a servant; I was a guest, welcome or unwelcome. In her eyes I had social status. I said kindly, with a tinge of authority, "Please do sit down, Mrs. Palmer. I appreciate your speaking with me."

CHAPTER 10

She sat in the chair facing the window and squinted in the morning brightness. The thumb of her right hand massaged her left palm nervously. She wasn't a hostile person, but she was troubled.

"Miss Jamison—if I got the name right—the Angelicas, they're a very private family. They don't welcome outsiders. I shouldn'a' let you in. I only did it because you come from so far away. Now you want to know where Master Harry is and that's the problem."

"I don't understand. Is it a problem because you can't tell me, or a problem because you don't know?"

"Mr. Angelica, when he knew he was going to die, he left everything to Master Harry. He's the executioner of the estate. You see, Mrs. Angelica, she's not well. I mean, she's not right in the head. She's got that Alzheimer's disease."

"I'd like to see her. Would she speak with me?"

"No, no, no. You can't do that. It'd just confuse her. She has a sister come to visit two or three times a week, but sometimes she don't even know her—her own sister! Her brother used to come, too. He's Tommy's dad. But he passed away last year. And Mrs. Riley, she's the neighbor from a few doors away. They knew each other for twenty years but now Mrs. Riley don't come anymore because when she used to come and Mrs. A. just stared at her, she'd start to cry, it upset her so."

"Does Mrs. Angelica have a nurse?"

"Someone comes from the county three times a week. They don't do much. They feel her pulse and blood pressure. They check with me to see if she's taking her medicine. Maybe they talk to her a little if Mrs. A. is feeling good. If she's sick, I take her to the hospital. She has one of those HMOs."

"Does her son Harry ever visit?"

"You see, Master Harry, he used to visit. When he came over, Mrs. A. got all emotional and teary. She'd hug him and cry and want to know why couldn't he move back into the house with her, and why didn't he visit her more often. Even if he visited yesterday, she wouldn't remember and would scold him for being away so long. She'd sing songs to him but he didn't like that. Sometimes when he came over, he'd take her out for lunch. She liked that. I'd go with them to help out. One time she acted real strange in the restaurant. She whispered to the waitress it was Harry's birthday and made her bring over cake and ice cream and a candle. She sang "Happy Birthday." But it wasn't his birthday and he was real put out with her. He wouldn't take her out anymore, but she started to get much worse after that anyway."

Mrs. Palmer had gone from zero to garrulous in under a minute, and while much of what she said was rambling, I was happy to have the data to pick through. "How long ago did Mr. Angelica die?" I asked, hoping to encourage her to talk and not retreat into her former silence.

"I remember that. He died the same week that Princess Diana was killed. He was too sick to know about it. I don't think it mattered to him."

"If Harry doesn't live here, who takes care of the house and pays the bills?"

"I take care of the house," she said proudly. "Except for the outside. We have a service come in for that."

I persisted. "But can you tell me, how do they get paid?"

"Master Harry pays all the bills. Every month I send him them. But the last two months they come back 'return to sender.'"

"What about groceries or small expenses?"

"Mostly I pay with Mrs. A.'s credit card. The merchants are used to that. I get cash with the card at the bank for taxicabs or if they don't accept credit cards." She was looking down and wringing her hands now. "You see, that's the problem. The machine at the bank won't give me cash. It says there's no money."

"Has this ever happened before?"

"Once or twice, but Master Harry always calls and says he's sorry. He says he's been so busy he forgot. And then it gets fixed."

"Look, Mrs. Palmer, why don't you let me help you find Harry? I could tell him that you need him to pay the bills and take care of his mother and yourself and the house. Just tell me where you send the bills, even though they're returned."

"Oh, I can't do that. Master Harry, he made me promise, made me swear to God, to keep his address secret. He said he had private business and nobody could be allowed to bother him. But, you see, I'm afraid maybe he's lost his money and that's why he isn't taking care of us. And you said maybe you had a way for him to make money. So I don't know what to do."

Just as Mrs. Palmer was weakening, an ancient voice from far away interrupted us. "Sarah," it croaked. "Sarah, I hear someone. Who is there?"

"She's calling me. I have to go. I think you should leave. I really shouldn'a' let you in."

"May I speak with Mrs. Angelica? I've come all this way. I'd like to meet her."

"No, ma'am. I told you. She's just an old lady, crazy, out of her head. I couldn't let you."

The voice sounded again, this time with a note of pleading. "Sarah, is that the nurse? I want to know who's there."

I put a note of authority into my voice. "Mrs. Palmer, I think if your employer wants to know who is here, you should tell her. She doesn't sound crazy to me. I hope you're not spreading stories about her."

"No, I'm not. Mostly, she don't know nothin'. Then, sometimes, she remembers things, mostly things from years ago. She don't care who you are."

The voice sounded again. I had a split second to make a bold decision. "I'm coming, Mrs. Angelica," I cried. "I'll be right there."

Mrs. Palmer's eyes widened but she didn't try to stop me. I followed the voice to a wide, carpeted staircase. I bounded up the stairs, afraid that Mrs. Palmer would try to bar my way if I hesitated. I'd have been reluctant to use force.

Once upstairs, I could follow my nose, literally. The malodor of confinement is distinctive: a mixture of body odors, stale food, and mustiness. It led me to Mrs. Angelica's bedroom. I stopped before her door to calm myself. I needed to present a tranquil façade.

She was in a dimly lit master bedroom richly appointed with sturdy old mahogany and cherry wood furniture. Lush draperies dressed the windows, and oil paintings and watercolors hung in artistically placed groups on every wall. On one wall there was a life-size upper-body portrait of a woman of robust frame and stately bearing. She appeared to be about 40 years of age. Against the opposite wall stood a four-poster bed. Instead of holding up a canopy, the posts supported guardrails. In the bed was the woman in the portrait, easily recognizable though at least three decades older.

"Mrs. Angelica, I'm——"

"Are you new here?" interrupted the old lady.

"Yes ma'am, my name is Dagny. I've come to visit you."

"Visit me?" The notion seemed to amuse her. "Nobody visits me. They come to stick me or make me swallow pills."

"I've just come to talk with you."

"Well, what do you want me to say? I can sing 'Happy Birthday.'"

She began humming the familiar tune, keeping time with feeble movements of her wrist.

"Is it someone's birthday today?" I asked.

She didn't answer but the humming became singing, "...happy birthday my darling, happy birthday to you."

"That was very pretty."

"Would you like to hear 'Over the Rainbow'?" Without waiting for my answer, she resumed singing, shyly at first, then with feeling. She knew all the words.

About halfway through the song, I heard a whispering through clenched teeth. Mrs. Palmer was standing behind my right ear.

"You see what I mean?" she hissed. "She's balmy. It's best to leave her be."

I didn't want to argue, but it seemed that Annie Angelica was enjoying herself. I saw no harm in my presence. When her singing ended, I applauded lightly. She nodded, looking pleased for the moment, but in the next moment her features resumed the vacant look that she wore when I'd first peered into the room.

"Can you tell me about Harry? About your son, Harry?"

No response. I looked about the room. On her dressing table were several photographs of a man that fit Harry's description. There were also photographs of a baby, a toddler, a young child—all of Harry at various stages. I picked up the photograph of the baby and showed it to her.

"Is this your son?"

She looked at it, cocked her head one way, then the other, but didn't say anything.

I tried a different approach. I showed her the most recent photograph. "This is Harry, your son," I said firmly. "Do you remember Harry?"

She reached out toward the baby picture instead. I handed it to her. She stared at it and began to sing again, this time "Rock-a-Bye Baby." She cradled the photograph in her hands, rocking it back and forth to the rhythm of the music. A big tear formed in the corner of her right eye, broke, and tracked down her cheek.

When she had finished the song the sound stopped, but her mouth moved silently as if she was trying to form thoughts into words. At last she said, "He was a big baby. It hurt so much. I was too old to have a baby. I was almost forty-five." She beckoned me closer. When she saw Mrs. Palmer come closer too she said, "Go away, Sarah. I'll call you when I need you." Mrs. Palmer balked, but she was too used to being subservient to argue, and backed out of the room.

"Harry was a good baby, a good little boy. He was an only child, a lonely child. He had just one friend growing up, my sister's son, Tommy. They always played together by themselves. One day when Tommy didn't come he did a very naughty thing." She lowered her voice to a conspiratorial whisper. "He didn't think I saw him but I did. I told him that God would take away his thingy."

"Do you know where Harry is now?" I whispered.

"Maybe he's in his room or playing with Tommy. I don't know." She brightened. "Would you like to hear 'America, the Beautiful'?"

"Of course I would, Annie."

She sang it, but toward the end her voice broke and "from sea to shining sea" came out as a squawk. She had slipped into the dull-eyed neutrality of extreme senescence and nothing I could do or say touched her. Her moment of lucidity had passed, and who knew how long it would be until the next one.

I had a more leisurely look around the room, starting with the vanity. On its top stood a number of photographs in a haphazard variety of frames, all of a single subject—Harry at different stages of his life. I looked carefully at the most recent one. Harry appeared to be in his mid-twenties. He fit Ashley's description of Strong perfectly, to the extent that she'd seen him. He had dark blond hair which he wore combed straight back. His thick blond brows and cover-boy eyelashes compensated for rheumy eyes of washed-out blue. A strong, square jaw contrasted with his effeminate forehead and accentuated the thinness of his lips and nose. I slipped the photo out of its frame and into my handbag. I hid the frame in a drawer. Annie didn't stir.

A glassed-in wedding invitation was hung above one of the low dressers. It read:

Mr. and Mrs. Thompson Samuel Beck
invite you to join them to celebrate the marriage
of their daughter
Annie Flora Leigh Beck
to
Mr. Lawrence Harold Angelica

I hastily jotted down the essentials. It wouldn't be right to steal it. I was just putting my notepad away when I noticed Mrs. Palmer at the door giving me as evil a stare as she could muster. Her eyes were bulging and she was motioning frantically for me to leave.

"Thank you, Mrs. Palmer, for being patient. I believe Mrs. Angelica has gone back to sleep. I trust she enjoyed our little chat."

I followed her downstairs. The way to the front door was through a small room that appeared to serve as Mrs. Palmer's office. As we passed the desk, I noticed a manila envelope, in the upper left-hand corner of which was the red finger of undelivered mail. Suddenly, I slumped to the ground with a terrible moan. I bent over double, clutching my abdomen, mewling like a half-slaughtered lamb.

Mrs. Palmer, whose favor I'd certainly not earned, instinctively came to my aid. "Oh dear. Are you all right?"

"Cramps," I gasped. "I get these terrible cramps. It's my endometriosis. I'll be okay in a moment. Please, may I have a glass of ice water?" I threw in an extra moan.

She hurried off for the water, fearful, I conjectured, that anyone with an illness as horrid-sounding as endometriosis might end up in her care for the rest of the month.

I sprang to the envelope. How I wanted to steal it. I imagined it was plump with succulent delights such as phone bills, bank statements, and any number of means of directing me to Master Harry. I couldn't filch it with the impunity with which I'd filched the snapshot. Its disappearance would point to me as the thief.

I checked to see if it was open. I wasn't beyond purloining an item or two of its contents, but it was sealed and taped over. The best I could do was to observe the address on the front. The envelope had been mailed to a hotel in Orlando, Florida. I memorized the name of the hotel and its address. I shut my eyes and visualized the data, locking it into my memory.

I heard ice clinking in a glass as Mrs. Palmer returned. I got back on the floor and propped myself up against the front of a fat leather armchair. I screwed up my face in mock pain. I drank the water slowly and tried not to look at the desk. Finally, I permitted Mrs. Palmer to help me to my feet.

"You're very kind to minister to an unwelcome guest. I wish you'd let me help you find Harry. I promise if I find him, he'll never know you helped me. I'd make up some story."

She shook her head sadly.

At the door I made my plea again but Mrs. Palmer was adamant. I left my phone number in case she changed her mind.

I had scarcely been aware of the oppressive atmosphere of the house when I entered it, so intent had I been on my purpose. But when I returned to the crisp autumn air and the bright daylight, the contrast between inside and outside struck me. Except for the sunny breakfast nook, the house was dully lit and in perpetual twilight. The withering mind of the matriarch, the waning spirit of the faithful housekeeper, and the apparent indifference of the son created an atmosphere of Gothic malaise.

As I walked pensively to my car, I saw the name "Riley" on a mailbox. A woman of about 70, tanned and bony and, as they say, well preserved, was on her hands and knees pulling weeds.

"Hullo," I said. "Beautiful day, isn't it?"

She looked up and smiled, nodding her head in agreement. "I don't believe I know you, young lady."

"I'm not from around here. Actually, I went to college with Harry Angelica. I happened to be in Plainfield and I remembered that he grew up here. I still had his address after ten years, would you believe it? It's the house on the corner. On the off-chance he was around, I went and knocked on his door."

Her eyes looked at me doubtfully but her mouth continued the smile. "Harry hasn't stayed there for a long while. He's always away somewhere making movies. Only his mother and a housekeeper live in that big house, and Annie, I mean Mrs. Angelica, isn't well. She has Alzheimer's disease. Did you know that?"

"I'm afraid the housekeeper was somewhat reticent. She said that Harry didn't live there and she didn't know where he was."

"Hmm, that's strange. I thought he was managing his mother's affairs. Oh well, it's none of my business. I used to visit Annie every couple of days. Some days she wouldn't even know who I was, but sometimes she seemed happy to see me. Then one day Sarah, that's the housekeeper, said I shouldn't come anymore. That it made her too upset. Truth is, I was the one getting upset."

"It must be hard. Had you been friends with the Angelicas for long?"

"About 20 years. That's when they bought the big house. It was through Harry that we ultimately became friendly, though it was a rocky start. When they moved here Harry was around 10. He and his fat cousin Tommy Beck loved to do mischief. They'd throw stones at people's pets and kick trashcans over. One time they pushed all my clay pots off the shelf in my back yard. Broke every one but at least I was able to save the plants. That was too much. I hadn't complained before, but this time I just walked right up to the front door and told my story. The Angelicas were horrified. They sent the cousin home and Mr. Angelica said that if I waited right by the door I'd hear him give Harry a good strapping. Well, I didn't want that and I don't think Annie did either. I suggested that they make the child earn money to pay for the pots. They asked me how much they were. It wasn't much in those days, maybe 50 cents a pot for six pots. They made me take the three dollars. As I walked away I could hear Harry wailing from one of the upstairs rooms. That's how we were first acquainted, strangely enough. Harry never could bring himself to speak with me afterwards. I guess he was embarrassed or mad. I'm glad he grew up and is making something of himself." She looked at her watch. "My goodness, I'm turning into a gabby old gossip."

"Not at all. I've only known Harry as an adult, myself. It's interesting to hear about his childhood. If I ever see him I'll remind him of your story."

"Don't you dare tell him I told you. I still don't think he likes me and, who knows, sooner or later he may be my neighbor again."

"Mum's the word, ma'am. You have a nice day."

CHAPTER 11

When I got home I called Ashley and briefed her on recent happenings. She had an idea.

"I want that photo of Harry. I'm going to see if I recognize it under hypnosis."

"I'll scan it into my computer and e-mail you a copy. You'll have it in twenty minutes. Can you download and print it?"

"Yes, of course. I'm going to call Dr. Brodsky in Chicago. If he's in town he'll see me tonight," said Ashley.

"I doubt you'll get on a flight to Chicago tonight. It's the weekend, you know."

She made one of those hrumphing sounds that the very rich reserve for us whose poverty of cash begets a poverty of imagination.

"If Dr. Brodsky is available, I'll take the company jet to Midway Airport. Why don't you accompany me? There should be great visibility and smooth flying."

"Well, I was planning to catch the early flight to Orlando. I need to pick up Harry's trail, if there is a trail."

"A few hours one way or the other aren't going to matter. Plan your Florida trip for tomorrow. I want to hear every detail of your investigation and this is a fine opportunity. I'm not eager to drive to Raleigh again."

"Okay, you're the boss. What do I do?"

"I still want you to transmit the photograph. We should have electronic backups. By the time you've done that, I should know about Dr. Brodsky. I'll call you and we'll proceed from there."

I scanned the photograph into a .jpg file, connected to the Internet and e-mailed the image to Ashley. I logged onto my travel site. There were several direct flights to Orlando, starting at six in the morning. As usual at the last minute, everything was booked except the high-priced seats in first class. I bought a ticket for the flight departing at 4:05 in the afternoon with an open return, using the Bloodworth credit card. There were links to all of the car rental agencies. I reserved a mid-sized sedan.

I searched on "Sans Souci," the name of the hotel in Orlando that was on the envelope. It would be the obvious place to stay. The hotel had an elaborate Web site where they proclaimed their many facilities, their proximity to the major amusement parks, and their package deals. I could reserve a room online. It was a busy season for Orlando now that the excessively hot Florida weather was past, and northerners were already trying to escape the cold. All that was available was a suite. I booked it for five days. My mobile phone chimed just as the confirmation from the Sans Souci flashed on the screen.

"This is Ashley. Are you able to meet me at the airport one hour from now?"

I said I could and jotted down the directions she gave me. After only one wrong turn, I found the area that Ashley had directed me to. It was at the far end of the airport away from the passenger terminals. Two armed guards controlled a sliding chain link gate at the entrance. The name "Bloodworth" sufficed as a password, and the guards admitted me with a salute. Before me was an airport within an airport. Dozens of small and medium-sized airplanes sat in neat rows on a tarmac. Wide-mouthed hangars housed others. I parked, locked my car, and walked toward a flat-roofed building on the skirt of the taxiway, which served as a terminal for privately owned aircraft.

I stopped halfway to watch a helicopter swoop gracefully down and alight on a nearby pad. A familiar figure emerged, her flowing blond hair gorgon-like under the wash of the swishing blades. She got clear, shook her head to make her hair fall tidily in place, and waved to the pilot. He waved back and adjusted the pitch of the rotor blades so that they bit the air and drew the craft skyward. It rotated 180 degrees and sped away to the southeast.

Ashley entered the little building from one side as I entered from the other. She was dressed in a black pants suit of a matte fabric that might be worn by a Ninja assassin, so stealth-like a quality did it impart to its wearer. On Ashley, it accented the luster of her hair and the brightness of her straight white teeth. Though she could probably afford the best, I never saw Ashley wear jewelry other than a unisex Timex and ear studs. The effect was to make her look younger than her years. Nothing adds age to a woman's appearance more persuasively than a jewel-encrusted gewgaw.

"Ah, Dagny. Perfect timing. This is Brad," she said, gesturing toward a clean-shaven man about our age, wearing a blue denim shirt and brown corduroy trousers. "He's our pilot. Shall we go?"

The three of us walked out the door that Ashley had just entered and turned toward a row of hangars. Brad waved to a man on a tractor and we all converged on hangar H102. As we drew near, automatic doors retracted from the center outward, exposing the interior. A sleek, silver airplane, delicate and avian, shone in the gap. The tractor driver attached a towing bar to the nose wheel strut, and gently tugged the shimmering craft onto the tarmac and into the red light of the setting sun.

Ashley walked up and stroked its nose as if it was an animal she wished to befriend. She ran her hand along a wing and, unseen by Brad, inserted a bobby pin under a small, loose metal flap that protruded from the wing's leading edge.

The man in the tractor disconnected and drove off with a wave. Brad went to work immediately. He began with an external inspection of the aircraft: nose, wings, fuselage and tail, including the various antennas, lights and other unknown-to-me protrusions. He studied the landing gear as if it bore weighty inscriptions. He stooped under each wing to drain condensed water from the fuel tanks. Finished at last, he invited us to board.

There is no graceful way to climb into a small airplane, even a jet-propelled one that costs two million dollars and cruises at 400 knots. The vital thing is to avoid stepping on places stenciled NO STEP in large red letters; less important is whether you look like a newborn fawn getting on its feet for the first time. Ashley managed it quite well, perhaps owing to the practice of slithering in and out of the Lotus. I followed her inside far less gracefully, nearly splitting a seam, and falling into Ashley's lap. Brad was last in, pulling the door shut behind him and taking charge of the flight deck.

For its size, the jet accommodated five passengers in surprising comfort. The bucket seats were well upholstered and covered in soft leather. They provided ampler legroom than the typical airliner. Each seat could be fitted with a table to support a computer. On the middle armrests were power supplies and jacks for Internet connections.

Brad began to work his way through a lengthy checklist, reading gauges and toggling switches. About halfway through it he donned earphones. He set his radio frequencies and flipped a switch that ignited the engine. It was remarkably quiet and free of vibration, unlike the small prop planes I'd flown in when I was in the army, which deafened you and rattled the fillings in your teeth.

He still had a bevy of gauges to check now that the engine was running, and another five minutes passed. He offered earphones with mouth mikes to Ashley and me. They would permit us to listen to the control tower, and talk among ourselves without having to raise our voices.

We put on our earphones and Brad showed us how to switch between internal and external communications. Making it seem like an afterthought, he reached straight back over his shoulder and handed Ashley's bobby pin to her at the same time as he said through the earphones, "Nice try, Miss Bloodworth. I suppose turnabout's fair play."

Ashley rounded her lips into a pretend moue and gave Brad a friendly whack on the shoulder. Later she explained to me that Brad gave her flying lessons, an important part of which is the pre-flight external inspection. He'd set subtle traps for her, such as loosening the oil cap. If she didn't catch it, she got an extra hour of ground school homework. Ashley had jammed one of the stall detectors, which is the function of the metal flap. It warns the pilot when the angle of the wing is too steep to maintain lift. Had Brad not found the bobby pin, Ashley would have scored a point in the time-honored student game of one-upping one's teacher.

Ground control cleared us to the taxiway. As we rolled out, they gave us the altimeter setting and wind conditions, and assigned us to a runway. We were seventh in line for takeoff in a queue of commercial airliners. Our jet was a Lilliputian in the land of giants. We watched each monster accelerate down the runway, rotate into a wheelie, then break contact with the ground and ascend toward the red flush in the western sky.

When our turn came, the tower ordered Brad to "taxi into position and hold." When all danger to our small craft from the wake turbulence of our predecessors was past, the tower cleared us for takeoff. Our takeoff run was short compared to that of the airliners. In a few seconds we were airborne, and for some few seconds more we flew directly over the two-mile long runway.

Air traffic control vectored us out of the area and gave us an altitude and magnetic heading for the first leg of our flight to Chicago. As we climbed toward our assigned altitude, a helicopter belonging to a local TV station flew beneath us, our relative motions making the chopper appear to be flying sideways.

It was, as Ashley had predicted, gorgeous weather for flying, with visibility to the horizon in every direction. Other aircraft were in view for most of the flight, crisscrossing the skies at various altitudes. Brad pointed out landmarks of interest such as the Ohio River, a dark meandering serpent whose tail brushed past Cincinnati, the lights of which twinkled in the distance off the starboard wing. All too soon, for I was thoroughly enchanted by the experience, we began our descent into Chicago's airspace, which ended with a feathery touchdown at Midway Airport.

The flight had taken just over two hours, and since we gained an hour by flying west, it was still early evening. Brad taxied to the private owner sector where he could park the little jet and tie it down. He powered off and let us out while he completed yet another checklist. A limousine was waiting for us next to the small terminal that served the personal and corporate aircraft that fly in and out of Midway every day.

The limo was furnished with fresh sandwiches, a stocked bar including champagne on ice, a television set, a stereo and a small library. Ashley was to meet with Dr. Brodsky at his home in Hyde Park, about twenty-five minutes from the airport. When we got there she asked me to wait for her, promising not to be longer than an hour. "I've done this many times. Unless we have to unearth something new, this should go quickly. Drive around if you'd like. This is a fairly nice part of Chicago."

"Fairly nice" was an understatement. We'd driven past sundry mansions before pulling up to Dr. Brodsky's home. Six Greek columns fronted the doctor's house. They supported a second-story roof that overhung a broad porch with decorative benches, statues and urns. Floodlights on the roof illuminated the grounds and façade of the house. The architecture dwarfed Ashley as she mounted the steps to the porch. The front door was thrown wide open before she reached it. A bespectacled man in a black turtleneck greeted her. The two of them exchanged hugs and European-style kisses: first one cheek, then the other, then the first. The door closed.

The driver asked me if I wanted to sightsee, but I didn't. I was content to sip champagne, eat a sandwich, and peruse one of those Harry Potter books that all the kids were dotty about, and that I found in the limo's library.

I was soon drowsing, the result of a long day full of flying, not to mention the champagne and the coziness of the limo. I put down the book, slipped off my shoes and tucked my feet under me, and put a CD in the player. Appropriately, I had grabbed a disk of Chopin nocturnes— night music for the piano—and I was as mesmerized by the music as I imagined Ashley to be by Dr. Brodsky's undulating pocket watch.

The next thing I knew, the door opened and Ashley slid into one of the seats. Her face was ashen and she'd been crying. She found a bottle of VSOP brandy in the bar and poured herself two-fingers worth. When she had drunk half of it, she lit a cigarette with a snap of the harp-shaped lighter. After a deep drag she was sufficiently composed to order the driver to return to the airport. I let her speak first.

"It's him, Strong." She waved the photograph. "He came around the rear of the van and grabbed me from the front. Fatboy grabbed me from behind. Before seeing his picture, the face was a blur in my memory. Once my mind had something substantial to relate to, Dr. Brodsky could bring me to the exact moment that I first saw him."

She paused to finish the brandy, her hand still shaky.

"God, I can't do this any more. You may not know, but hypnotism brings back emotional memory even more vividly than sensory memory. So you suffer the emotional trauma of the sensory event."

Slowly, Ashley regained her composure and the color returned to her face. She turned to me and said, "Tomorrow you will go to Orlando to see if this Harry Angelica can be found. There is some resemblance between him and Jeanne-Renée. I want a DNA test."

The return flight to Raleigh was every bit as lovely as the flight up. Visibility remained perfect and the night sky was a splendor. Brad pointed out more landmarks, such as the oval-shaped Indianapolis Motor Speedway.

It was midnight in Raleigh when we touched down. I'd done about as much flying in one day as an airline professional, but without doing the work. It was exhausting nonetheless and it raised my opinion of the men and women who fill those jobs. Ashley's helicopter was waiting for her. She reminded me to stay in touch and wished me luck in Orlando. I stayed to watch her soar away. What a life! What a tortured soul!

CHAPTER 12

I was home again. Although it was nearly one o'clock in the morning, there was an unusual amount of activity. Cars sped by, stereos pounding, screaming young heads hanging out the windows. The city was up late, for State had won an upset victory over a hated football rival. Nothing including an Elvis sighting or the return of The Grateful Dead would fuel this level of excitement among the city's striplings. And nothing including the risk of alcohol poisoning would dampen their spirits faster than the siren call of the blue-lighted squad car that raced past my front door.

Thankfully, festivities soon ended. I dropped into bed, exhausted, missing my dogs for the brief moments that preceded sleep. I slept dreamlessly and awoke in time for my Saturday morning martial arts class at nearby State College.

I'd forgotten about yesterday's game but there were plenty of signs on campus to remind me of it. Rolls of toilet paper draped the trees and bushes. An extraterrestrial botanist would have marveled that plants would bear so utilitarian a fruit. Revelers had spray painted the upset score, 10-3 apparently, on the asphalt roads and parking lots. Crews were already at work removing the vast numbers of empty containers scattered everywhere.

The gym was open and the usual folks were there. I didn't have any particular friends among them, but they were familiar faces and it was agreeable to see them. The autumn day was so splendid that the instructor had us bring mats outdoors for the morning workout. We warmed up with a one-mile jog and it was sheer joy to breathe the oaky air and feel the cool breeze. Class that morning focused on defense against being grabbed. The lesson taught us to respond swiftly before being lifted off the ground, mainly by the judicious and violent use of the elbow.

Post-workout ablutions complete, I went immediately to bail out Hank and Midas, who were at first happy to see me, but then remembered to sulk at their unfair treatment. I cheered them up with some playtime and then broke the "good news, bad news." The bad news is I was off again; the good news was that Janet, known to the hounds as "Auntie Janet," would mind them while I was away this time.

After dropping them off at Janet's, where they willingly and happily go, I returned home to pack for Orlando. At four o'clock I was sitting in my first-class seat sipping orange juice as the coach passengers boarded; I felt somewhat sheepish about my temporary elevation in social class.

I'd downloaded information about the hotel that I was going to, and where Harry Angelica had lived at some point, and perhaps was still living. The Sans Souci hotel is one of the five hotels on International Crescent. The others are the Mirabelle, the Tierra Verde, the Alcazar, and the Raphael. They're all different, each following the architectural traditions of Germany, France, Spain, Moorish Spain, and Italy. Sans Souci is the name of a Prussian palace in Potsdam, Germany. Its Orlando namesake had a duplicate of its formal colonnade to mark its entrance.

The lobby was huge, reaching out in various directions towards the pools, the restaurants, the rooms, and the shops. There was a long line at the check-in counter but as there were eight stations for the newcomers, it moved quickly. Children of all ages were underfoot, bouncing off each other and entangling innocent bystanders. It seemed like I was the only one in the hotel not bound for a major entertainment site with a passel of kids. But then, what the hell was Harry doing here, and living here long enough to have it as his mailing address?

Because nearly every man in the lobby was part of a family, the square-jawed man with a crew cut stood out. Like me, he was alone, and he was measuring me up as though I might make a comrade-in-arms against the family hordes. I didn't much feel like being hit on, and directed my gaze at my feet. I half expected a tap on the shoulder, but when I chanced to look up, he was gone.

The clerk that checked me in couldn't believe that I didn't have at least one child with me. After all, how many single people are willing to pay for a suite? I assured her I was alone and didn't mind paying the same price I'd pay if accompanied by the residents of an orphanage. I did, however, put in a request for a more modest room if one came open. She handed me my key and a gazillion flyers hawking specials, bargains, discounts, rebates and markdowns. I told her I was meeting a colleague named Harry Angelica, and wondered if I could leave him a message.

She sent me to the message desk where I queued up and repeated my request when my turn came. There was neither a Harry Angelica in residence nor a reservation in that name. To my question of whether a Harry Angelica had ever stayed in the hotel, I was politely informed that hotel policy did not permit the handing out of such information.

My suite was laughably large. My Bösendorfer at home would have fit in the "living room" after a minor rearrangement of furniture. The suite was on the second of three floors in one of the many detached annexes of the hotel. I could come and go inconspicuously, although I didn't see the need for stealth at the time.

I unpacked, washed my hands and face, reapplied a little eyeliner and a tad of blusher, tucked a map of the grounds into my bag, and went to find a quiet place to eat. "Quiet" is a relative term in a hotel whose clientele have come to play at the greatest entertainment complex on earth. I settled for a Mexican-theme bar with a small menu. It at least had the benefit that the background clatter was an adult din in lieu of screaming children. I ordered a margarita without salt and a chicken fajita.

I had the snapshot of Harry with me and there wasn't any reason not to go right to work. After eating I moved to the bar and ordered another drink. It was peak time and people had stored up big thirsts bustling about all day under the Florida sun. The bartender, a whirling dervish of mix-shake-pour, struggled to keep up with demand, and it was an hour before I could show her the photo of Harry. She didn't recognize him.

There were three other bars in the hotel. I repeated the scenario in each, leaving untouched drinks behind, and suffering similar results. Maybe Harry didn't drink, he drank in his room, or he patronized other bars in other hotels.

It's easy to find the main building of the hotel from one of the outbuildings, but on the return trip you find yourself in a maze of swimming pools, shuffle board courts, ping-pong tables, Jacuzzis, fountains and refreshment stands. The grounds appear different at night than in the day on account of artful lighting that is pretty to look at but not helpful for navigation. I was by now on the grounds of the Tierra Verde and hopelessly astray. I dug the map out of my handbag.

I was standing under a light turning the map to align it with the territory when a man addressed me. "Can I help you find something? I know my way around this place pretty good."

I looked up and nearly swallowed my tongue. It was Harry. He had even said "dis place," in a New Jersey accent. He was with another man—a hulking figure—and two very pretty kids in their late teens, a boy and a girl.

This was both good luck and bad luck. Good in that I'd found him and no longer needed to make inquiries, which I was fearful he'd discover—I didn't want him to be on his guard. Bad, because I couldn't hide behind a screen of anonymity in my effort to get the DNA sample.

The one thing in my favor was that my back was to the light, so I could see him and his entourage more clearly than they could see me.

I reacted as quickly as my wits would allow. "No thank you," I squeaked, "I see where to go."

I spun around and walked briskly away. It was a natural reaction for a young woman alone at night when approached by two men, and I doubted that it would raise suspicions. I kept walking, not daring to look back. I took a slight turn so I could see behind me out of the corner of my eye. There was no one there. I consulted the map again, and once I got oriented easily found my building.

I called the other four hotels in the morning and asked for Harry Angelica, with negative results. Either he was staying elsewhere or he'd checked in under a different name. I assumed that he was in one of the five hotels, using an alias. I planned to look for him without revealing myself. I took the clothes I'd had on when he saw me and put them away, for they were not to be worn again. My short-cropped blond hair and my pale face made me stand out among the tanned, long-haired women who frequented the hotels. I would have to remedy that.

I could do little until the stores opened Monday. I spent Sunday exploring the grounds. I wore a scarf over my hair and baggy clothes that I padded with throw pillows from the couch in my suite. I looked like the Michelin Man's girlfriend. As I wandered around, I kept a sharp eye out for Harry and his friends.

The five hotels stand on the perimeter of a horseshoe-shaped park bordered by a fresh water pond that snakes around the entire horseshoe save for the open side. Various aquatic creatures inhabit the pond, including swans, ducks, turtles and frogs. Several bridges link the walking paths that are on both sides of the water. The paths converge beyond the pond's end and become a hiking trail, after passing under a highway and leaving the developed area.

The grounds of the hotels blend into one another, and it's not always clear whose property you're on, not that it seemed to matter. By repeatedly walking from the Sans Souci at one end of the horseshoe, to the Raphael at the other end, and back, I obtained a good sense of the area's layout. The Raphael was nearly half a mile away from the Sans Souci if you took the circular route, but you could halve the trip by crossing from one tip of the horseshoe to the other using the bridges.

Because everything appeared different at night, I repeated my explorations after dark. I must have walked five miles all told that day, not that the exercise wasn't welcome. In the end I was able to find my way between the five hotels and their recreation areas with unerring accuracy.

On Monday morning I drove to Orlando where, with a little help from the Yellow Pages and much getting lost, I found a shop that sold wigs. I was about to experience life as a brunette. A brief stop at a mall served up a pair of wide-lens Ray-Bans to embellish the disguise. Though Florida is the right place to acquire a tan, I bought some tan-in-a-bottle to hasten the appearance of one.

Back in my room, I soon learned that it's frustratingly difficult to apply tanning lotion to your own skin and come out looking like anything other than an exotic piebald creature. Oh well, so much the better the disguise, I supposed. I donned the wig and the Ray-Bans, and thus camouflaged, walked to the pool at the Tierra Verde to start on a natural tan, and to watch for Harry.

Days by the pool, nights in the bars, all on an expense account. This might be some people's concept of paradise. To me, it was work. Surveillance is mind numbing. Mostly nothing happens, but you must remain alert. I invented game after game to stay focused. I counted the number of people who walked by a certain point, to see how long it took to reach one hundred. I repeated this while keeping track of females versus males. Then adults versus children. Once I thought I saw the boy that had been with Harry that night, but I wasn't sure. After two days of no results at the Tierra Verde, I moved the daylight operation to the Alcazar.

At night I circulated randomly among the various bars in the five hotels, careful not to visit any one bar often enough to stand out. I wore a different outfit every night, buying them in the morning when the hotel shops opened, and never patronizing the same shop twice.

In this manner several days passed. I worried that Harry had only been visiting the night he spoke to me, and wasn't residing in any of the hotels. Or perhaps he'd already moved on. I was taking sun at the Raphael by this time, and my tan was genuine. I threw the bottled stuff in the trash.

As shadows overtook the pool area on Thursday afternoon, I gathered my possessions to return to my suite. I had one last look around and bingo! there was a head of dark blond hair with the rest of Harry under it. He was alone, walking toward the main building of the hotel. I pulled my straw hat down over my ears, put on my three-quarter-length terrycloth robe, and trailed after him.

Harry went directly to an elevator with an open door. I didn't dare follow. Instead, I timed how long it took his elevator to return. Forty seconds, and it came back empty.

Since the other three elevators sat idle on the ground floor, there was a good chance that Harry's elevator had gone up and come back unused by anyone except him.

I got in the same elevator, checked my watch, and mashed (that's how we say it in the South) the top button. The elevator mounted to the eighth floor. The door opened, closed, and returned to the ground floor in fifty seconds. But damn! I'd forgotten a crucial measurement. I repeated the experiment, noting that it took about two and one-half seconds for the elevator to pass between floors. Since the eighth floor roundtrip was ten seconds longer, Harry's trip had to have been to the sixth floor. Hah! And my ninth grade math teacher had thought I was hopeless.

A bellhop noticed that I'd been up and down twice in the same elevator. He was an older man with graying sideburns. He asked me, speaking with a foreign accent, if I needed help.

"I just realized I'm in the wrong hotel," I said. "I'm staying at the Alcazar, not the Raphael. I always get those Italian painters mixed up." While he pondered that inanity, I escaped back to the pool area.

The Raphael didn't appear to be sold out. I called from my room and asked if they had a vacancy and if so, might I be on the sixth floor, as I'd stayed there last year and was partial to the view.

"Let me check that for you, madam," said the voice on the other end. After a lengthy pause, he came back on. "I do have a room available. I must advise you that it isn't the quietest room in the hotel. It's across the hall from our corporate suite, which is occupied by the owner of a movie company. He has people in every night and they do tend to stay up late. There've been complaints."

"That's not a problem for me. I'm very much of a night owl myself."

"The hotel will discount your room twenty-five percent," the nice man said.

I arranged to check in the next day.

That night I went back to the Raphael and was rewarded with a sighting. In a bar called "The Bellini," I spotted Harry and his large friend sitting at a long table with a slew of good-looking boys and girls whose drinking ages were doubtful.

I found a stool at the bar, which afforded me a view of his table. The place swarmed with newly arrived weekend revelers. I could spy on

Harry's group surreptitiously, shrouded by clusters of people and the smoky thickness of the air. I'd done everything to make myself unnoticeable. My mousy wig, ill-fitting clothes, and rounded shoulders as I hunched over my drink did not inspire second looks. From time to time I had to suppress my vanity, for I prefer to look attractive.

I waited for Harry to leave. At his table some kids came, some went, but he and his large buddy, the only two seeming adults, showed little inclination to budge. By midnight there were too few people to shield me. I was about to pay the bill and leave when his whole table arose and moved toward the exit. I ordered a fresh drink and said I was going to the "little girl's room." I followed Harry and company at a safe distance. The young adults had even younger friends whom they met up with, and the entire party crowded into an elevator and disappeared.

I'd been tipping the bartender well all evening and now, with business winding down, it was time for a girl-to-girl talk. "Excuse me, but do you know who the blond-headed chap is who was sitting over there at the large table? I thought he looked a bit like Nick Nolte, the movie star."

"He ain't no movie star, I don't think, but I hear he's been hired by Disney to make TV spots. Kids are all hanging around him, trying out for parts, I guess. We've had to be real careful with the IDs. What, you like him?"

"No, just curious. I thought, you know, he might be someone famous."

"I tell you, we don't get famous people here. If they come, they stay in the Disney World Hotel. Last year some Arab came and leased a whole floor for a week. Brought his wives and kids for a holiday. Each wife had her own suite, so they said. They said the tab was half a million."

"Wow, really! So you never see anyone famous? I thought that was part of the fun of tending bar."

"Aw, once in a while I see someone I recognize from the soaps, but never no one real famous."

I got up to leave. "Enjoyed the evening. See you again."

"I'm not sure what you enjoyed. You didn't talk to anyone."

"I like watching people. I know I'm a little shy, but I'll be back tomorrow night."

"His name his Harry. Hari-kari, no, just kidding. It's Harry Beck. Just in case you want to know." She gave me a girl-to-girl all-knowing wink.

CHAPTER 13

The next morning I checked out of the Sans Souci and into the Raphael. The same bellhop who saw me in the elevator the day before helped me with my suitcase, now well stuffed with all the clothes I'd bought. He bowed me into the elevator. When I reached toward the panel of buttons, he murmured, "Permit me, madam," and promptly pressed six.

Opposite the elevator on the sixth floor was room 600. It had double doors and a brass plate that read Executive Suite. The old bellhop had me exit before him, perhaps concerned that I'd ride up and down a few times before getting off. My room, number 606, was down the hall a short bit on the opposite side. He let me in and showed me how to lock the door, unlock the minibar, adjust the A/C and turn the TV set on and off. He apologized that there was no turndown service and prepared to leave. I had nothing smaller than a ten and I didn't want to stiff him.

He took the bill without looking at it and with great sincerity said, "Thank you madam. And if madam will permit, regarding yesterday's encounter—I am from Italy, and there are no Italian painters named Alcazar."

"I'll make a note of that," I assured him, endeavoring to be equally sincere.

I unpacked and surveyed my new digs. It was not a room with a view, unless you like parking lots. However, I was far more interested in the vista as seen through my door's peephole. The Executive Suite was just out of range to the left; time for some reengineering. The peephole was held in place by four tiny screws that yielded easily to my Swiss Army Knife. I removed the entire unit and shook the lens free. I shimmed the right side of the lens encasement with some bits of cardboard. I reinserted the lens, which now was biased to look left. I reinstalled the whole unit. Harry's residence, or so I hoped it was, was now in sight.

A wearisome vigil ensued. "Keeping one's eye to the peephole" replaced "putting one's nose to the grindstone" as a metaphor for tedium. The traffic to and from the Executive Suite included Harry, his wide-bodied friend, and an assortment of the young pretties that hung out with them. A woman I hadn't seen enter emerged carrying a sleeping girl of around nine or ten clad in skimpy pajamas. There were gaps in my surveillance for meals from room service and bathroom breaks. I napped in the late afternoon and early evening when I figured activity would be least.

By the next morning I knew who had come and who had gone. When the room cleaners began their rounds just after midday, I was certain that the suite was empty. I showered, shaved my legs, put on a very short skirt, heels, and a midriff-exposing, dove-gray halter-top. I made up my face to look young and cheap and eschewed the wig for my own short, blonde hair. The cleaners soon got to the suite, and as was their habit, they used their cart to prop open the door while they were cleaning inside.

When they had been in the suite for about five minutes, I slipped out of my room and walked boldly in. "Oh hi, I'm looking for Harry. He said to meet him here at two. Oh, wow! What a cool place!"

It was indeed a deluxe suite. I found myself in a spacious room with plush furniture, an executive desk of polished cherry wood, and a long table that had been moved aside for meetings. Atop the table and around the room was video equipment of all kinds: cameras, lights, screens, microphones, and a bevy of electronic gear whose functions were unknown to me. The wall art was typical of upscale hotel suites: high quality prints of landscapes, bowls of fruit, and Roman urns, all in ornate frames. At the end of the room was a balcony with French doors; it overlooked the pool area.

"Uh, ma'am, you shouldn't be in here," said one of the cleaning crew.

"Oh, it's okay. Mr. Beck and I are old friends. Oh, what a cool view." While the cleaners were trying to figure out what to do with the floozy blonde that was upsetting their routine, I plunged across the room to admire the scenery, and furtively unlocked the French doors.

"Please, ma'am," she pleaded, "we could get into trouble."

"Oh, for goodness sake, I'll wait for Harry outside." I backed away from the balcony, still looking around. "Say, are those bedrooms in there?" Neither woman answered, but a male voice did.

"Why so interested in bedrooms?" asked Harry Angelica, alias Harry Beck.

That was the second time his voice had startled me, and this time I had to keep my cool. Escape would not be quite as easy as bolting away into the dark.

"Oh, Mr. Beck, you said, I mean someone said, that you might have a part for me in one of your films."

"Do I know you? You look vaguely familiar," he said, as he looked me up and down.

"Yes, I mean no. One of the girls in the bar said you might need someone to help out."

"Who was that?"

"I didn't get her name, actually. It's one of the barkeeps—you know, the one with the white waiter's shirt and a black bow tie."

"Really, so what's your name anyway?" he asked, more kindly.

"Susan. Susan Radford." I gave my head a little toss. My knees had stabilized.

"Well, Susan Radford, we don't shoot on weekends. Why don't you meet my friends and I in the Bellini bar tonight? We'll talk it over."

"Okay, I'll be there," I said eagerly. I brushed past him to leave and nearly ran into his size EEE shadow, a cretinous, thick-jawed man with yellowed teeth and mismatched ears.

"This is Ernest. He'll be there tonight, eh, Ernie?"

"Sure, boss."

As I edged past and walked away, I overheard him say, "Where'd the bird come from? Nice stuff."

I took the stairs at the end of the hall down six flights to a fire exit at the rear of the building, which I propped ajar. I circled around to the front where, partially concealed by a potted cypress tree, I could observe the balconies on the sixth floor. Harry's was easy to spot because it was twice as large as the others, and abutted its neighbors on both sides.

I returned to the back door and climbed to the sixth floor. The hallway was empty and Harry's door was closed. I crept unseen into my room. I donned my dumpy brunette costume once again and returned to the lobby to speak with the desk clerk.

"I'm in 606 but do you think it might be possible for me to have a room with a view of something other than the parking lot? The rooms across the hall look out onto the pools. I wouldn't mind paying the difference."

Luck was with me. Because the hotel had had complaints about noise in the Executive Suite, they had left the rooms on either side to be the last filled. After warning me, they let me move to room 601 next door. This meant I didn't need to clamber across other people's balconies to get to Harry's. It was all a matter of timing now.

That evening I was me except for the cheap makeup job, and sat on the same barstool that bewigged, piggy me had sat on two nights earlier.

I'd dressed in a sharp silk blouse of nearly translucent material and tight lime-green flat-front pants. I wore platform shoes to exaggerate my movie-starlet worthiness by making me seem taller and thinner. The bartender with whom I'd had the girl-to-girl bonding showed no signs of recognition.

Harry's tables were vacant but had "reserved" signs on them. I ordered a drink. A few quick sips helped settle my nerves and calm the fidgetiness that made me want to pace. I concentrated on observing the people trickling in, attempting through powers of observation to deduce facts about them. One of them was the square-jawed man with a crew cut that I'd seen when I checked in. If he recognized me from the lobby, he didn't let on. I watched him out of the corner of my eye as he pretended to be looking for someone that he didn't find and left.

After a while Harry, Ernest and a small band of youths arrived, shoved the tables together, and took their places. I hid behind my compact and made final adjustments to my face. They didn't notice me. When they were settled in, or as close to it as they would get, for there were constant arrivals and departures, I paid my tab and sauntered over.

Harry looked glad to see me. Ernest, apelike, just looked. Harry stood up and presented me to all as "Susan, who might be helping out with a shoot." The pretty couple I'd encountered earlier had twin names, Jamie and Jamie; they might almost have been twins, too.

Most of the talk was about moviemaking, movie stars, and movie careers. Susan's persona had dropped out of college to try to break into Hollywood. She'd been unsuccessful there and so had come to Wilmington, North Carolina, where more and more studios were setting up shop. She hoped to get something in television. As for Orlando, she was taking a short vacation, but she was always open to opportunity.

Because I'd lived in southern California for some years when I attended UCLA, I knew enough about Hollywood to make Susan's tale plausible. The youngsters immediately accepted her as one of the crowd. Ernest seemed capable only of staring lasciviously, a glassy-eyed, angry ape. Harry's face was friendly, but inscrutable. By listening carefully, I figured out that only Harry and Ernest actually lived in the suite, though evidently others crashed there from time to time. They shot footage in the suite but I couldn't gather exactly of what. When I thought that Harry was fully engaged with his guests, I excused myself to go to the powder room.

I hurried to room 600 and knocked loudly and waited. No one responded. In my own room, I stepped out of the platforms, stripped and put on the wig, the dumpy clothes and black tennies. I turned out all the lights and went out on my balcony, closing the door behind me. I listened for sounds coming from the suite. There were none. I climbed up on my balcony wall, maintaining a low crouch for balance. There was a two-foot gap between our balconies, the effect of which was magnified by the 70-foot drop to the ground below. I vaulted across, landing lightly on my feet. I peered through the French doors. The room was empty. With a "c'mon baby," I tried the handle I'd unlocked earlier. It turned. The door yielded to a push and I was inside, amid the mélange of moviemaking apparatus. I left the door open for a quick getaway in case someone came through the front.

The apartment had four bedrooms, but only two appeared to be occupied, presumably by Harry and Ernest. Determining which was which was easy. Harry was a sharp dresser and a glance into the respective closets was a giveaway. I also saw luggage in the one room with the initials H.A.—Harry Angelica—to remove all doubt.

My plan was to steal Harry's toothbrush. Cells from inside his mouth would cling to it and that was enough for a DNA analysis. As a backup, I intended to steal some dirty laundry, perhaps a shirt with hair on it. But I found something far better in the bathroom: Harry's electric razor, which he had obligingly failed to clean since his last shave. I slipped it and his toothbrush into the pockets of my baggy jeans.

Never satisfied, always curious, I continued to look around the bedroom. There was a small desk in one corner and on it was a laptop computer. I unlatched the screen and turned it on. While it was booting up, I checked out the drawers of the bureau and the closet. Nothing there for me, but the computer screen was a different story. It contained a "Palm Desktop" icon. I double-clicked on it and up came Harry's address book. This was too valuable to leave behind, though I was already gone too long, even for a floozy in a powder room. There were several diskettes on the desk. I chose one without a label and inserted it into the A-drive. I "exported" the contents of the address book to the diskette, which I pocketed. I shut down the computer, and just as it made its final ta-da sound I heard the key in the slot of the front door.

I rushed out of the bedroom and in my haste turned the wrong way. I spun around just as a meaty hand grabbed my hair. The wig came off, and in his surprise Ernest lost his balance. He tumbled forward, towards the balcony, and I reversed direction again and leapt to the front door. I pulled it open and dashed into the enveloping arms of Harry.

I spun quickly round and launched an elbow to his solar plexus. He went "whoof" and loosened his grip as he folded forward. I got him with my other elbow on the side of his neck and had broken loose, but before I could get out the door a Mack truck with license plate E-R-N-E-S-T hit me. Ernest had proved somewhat more agile than I'd have predicted, and before I could make good my escape he piled into me. I was stunned into a moment's unconsciousness, and when I recovered, I found myself under the one-eyed gaze of a .45 caliber semiautomatic.

"Well, well, Susan. I had a feeling there was more to you than met the eye," said Harry. "Do tell me what you're up to, or should I have Ernie here toss you over the side? It happens when you've had too much to drink and lose your balance, you know."

Knowing what Harry had done to Ashley, I didn't think scruples would stand in the way. The truth, of course, was out of the question. His crime against Ashley was capital in North Carolina.

"Okay, you're on to me. I confess. I'm a thief, and you've got some mighty valuable shit." I swept my hand around the room. "One of those cameras to the pawnshop. It's a week's pay. Just let me go. I'll be out of your hair in a sec. You'll never see me again."

"No can do, boss," said Ernest. "We don't know what she's been into."

"I ain't been into anything, I swear. I didn't even have time to grab a camera before ape man here tried to pull my hair out."

"Fuck, she's a sassy cunt. Let me teach her somethin', boss.

"Not here. You got to get rid of her. We can't take any chances. You know what to do, just like…you know."

"Aw, boss. Lemme poke her before I do it."

"Listen, get her out of here. I'd throw her over the fucking rail myself but I don't want the goddamn cops all over the place. I don't care what you do to her, but in the end she has a very…nasty…fatal…accident. And for Chrissake, don't botch it."

"Hey, I ain't never botched no job yet. We'll just take her along for a little ride."

"Not we. You. I can't leave here. I've got an all-night shoot at the farm."

"Jesus, boss, I can't drive and watch her both."

"Make her drive your car. If she won't, shoot her with this." Harry brandished another handgun, fitted sharply with a silencer. "Start with a foot. She'll cooperate. Here, get cozy."

He withdrew a pair of handcuffs from a drawer and cuffed me to Ernest, right hand to left. He dropped the key into Ernest's jacket pocket and handed him the silenced pistol. "Now go," he commanded. "Use the back stairs."

Ernest jerked my handcuffed arm, leaving a deep scrape on my wrist. Pain shot through my shoulder. He grasped my hand in his, as if we were boyfriend and girlfriend, and half dragged me to the back stairs.

In the stairwell he held the gun under my nose and said, "You heard Mr. Beck. We're taking a ride and you're the driver. You be good, I'll make it quick. You don't, you'll still be alive when I got one bullet left."

On the way to the car Ernest stuck the gun in his coat and replaced it with a half-pint bottle of Old Grand-Dad, which he withdrew from an inside pocket. He unscrewed the cap and took a healthy pull. When we reached his car, he had us get in the passenger side and then pushed me across into the driver's seat. He removed his half of the handcuffs and attached it to the steering wheel. He put the key in the ignition and started the engine.

"Drive, birdie!" he said. "I'll direct you."

We exited the parking area onto International Crescent, leaving the hotels behind. After a few turns he put us on an entrance ramp of the westbound I-4 and said, "Step on it."

Ernest was getting drunk, swigging bourbon every few minutes. His looks in my direction became increasingly lewd as the alcohol went to his brain. His judgment lapsed to the point where he offered me the bottle.

"I don't drink and drive," I said. "Somebody might get hurt." He found this hilarious and guffawed, showing dingy teeth, until it was time for his next swallow.

The length of the drive permitted me to calm myself by repeating the mantra of my namesake: "I am, therefore I think." I was going to become "am not" if I couldn't think my way out of this. There had to be a way to capitalize on his drunken state. If I hadn't had one arm cuffed to the steering wheel, I might have jammed on the brakes, fishtailed, and leaped out of the car. By the time he'd gotten the gun out of his jacket pocket I'd have been out of range, and if not, I doubt he could have shot straight. But this was an idle thought. Such an option, cuffed as I was, was not open to me.

My torn-up wrist hurt and demanded attention. I blew on it to relieve the smarting. Ernest had a better idea; he poured whisky on it. I squealed in pain, which he found amusing.

"Oh, so sorry, let me make nice." He reached over to grab my breast, but he didn't find much. "Jesus, you're a flat-chested little sparrow."

He splashed more whisky on my wound. I bit my lower lip hard to keep from crying out. I wouldn't give him the satisfaction, but he saw my eyes tear up.

"Quit crying, bitch. You wouldn't want an infection, would you?" The guffawing began again.

A look at the handcuffed wrist made it clear that there was no way of sliding it over my hand: the cuff was fixed securely. My gaze went to the steering wheel hub and alighted on the words "SRS AIRBAG." I let my eyes drift casually to the dash in front of Ernest. I saw no such letters. This was an early '90s model, before passenger airbags were required.

Ernest was singing to himself. "I'm gonna have some fun, toniiigght; I'm gonna get my kicks, toniiiiiggghht." He looked at my reflection in the rearview mirror, then directly at my face, then the rest of my body. The dumpy clothes of my disguise together with my flat-chestedness must have dampened his ardor for the moment, so that he didn't molest me again.

I thought of the busty babes I was once jealous of, including the one who stole my professor boyfriend. They would have fared poorly in my place, for if Ernest was aroused there was no telling what he might do. Score one for small-breasted women.

After some 40 miles, he ordered me off the Interstate onto a secondary four-lane highway. We drove two or three more miles and he had me turn right at a BP station onto a two-lane, unlighted county road.

There was no traffic in front or behind. A forest rose up on both sides of the road, pressing in nearly to the edge of the asphalt. The darkness was profound, giving ground grudgingly to the headlights and instantly closing in behind us. I saw only black in my mirrors.

Out of machismo, and ultimately fatal stupidity, Ernest had not put on his seat belt, but he had made me attach mine as a further, though unnecessary, restraint. I thought of Princess Diana's accident of just over two years ago. The lone survivor, a bodyguard, was the only one wearing a seat belt. Ironic, I thought, that I had been reminded of her death by Mrs. Palmer's reference to that event with respect to the death of Harry's father.

Ernest was becoming excited in anticipation of his fantasized fun-and-games with Susan. I sensed we were nearing the place where he intended to torture, rape and murder me. He drained the bottle and exchanged it for the pistol in his jacket pocket. He took a final drag from his cigarette and stubbed it out on the floor in front of him.

If Harry hadn't been so specific about having me killed, I doubt I'd have conceived the reckless plan now gelling in my brain. My adrenaline levels rose, my breathing became shallow and frequent. I felt my heart pound in my ears and hoped, mindlessly, that Ernest couldn't hear it and be forewarned. The nearness of death and the lust for life combine to free the mind to navigate black and foreboding waters. On such a dark sea was I now afloat.

Ernest pointed up the road. "Pull over to the side."

"But screw your courage to the sticking place," I exhorted myself, the only line kids ever remember from the reading of *Macbeth* forced on eleventh graders; who'd have thought it would pop into my head at such a moment? I depressed the accelerator. The car shot forward. This caught him by surprise.

"Slow up, goddammit."

I pushed it to 80.

He yelled, "Did you hear me, cunt? Slow the fuck up! I'll kill you."

I tighten my seat belt with my free hand, white-knuckling the wheel with the other. I nudge the car up to 90, focusing intently on the road, ignoring the pistol that Ernest is waving in my face. Even drunk, he isn't stupid enough to shoot the driver at this speed. He's screaming something unintelligible. I can see the reflection of his jaw pumping up and down in the mirror. We're approaching a bend to the left. I flick to high beams. A sign warns drivers to slow to 35 miles per hour. I hold at 90. The forest is now in front of me, with the road curving away before it. A large tree looms into view straight ahead.

Ernest is all at once desperately afraid. He reaches for the ignition keys. I harden my grip on the steering wheel with my cuffed hand, and holding steady, I make a tight fist of my other hand and snap a left cross into his left eye. Reflexively, his hands come up to his face. The steering wheel jerks a smidgen and I nearly lose control of the speeding vehicle. If I roll the car at this speed, we both will die.

I aim at the tree, my hands hold fast in a death grip on the wheel, my right foot pressed doggedly on the gas pedal under a trembling knee. As my nerve begins to fail, I close my eyes, tense my body, hold my breath, and wish for a deeper belief in God.

My last glimpse of Ernest before slamming my eyes shut was of him trying to shoot me in the leg. Booze and fear conspire against him. Before he can get off a shot, it's too late.

CHAPTER 14

A bomb detonated. A colossal marshmallow sprang from nowhere to receive my hurtling body. I bounced off the rubbery confection, slammed backwards into my seat, and twisted about pivoting on my shackled right arm. The unyielding metal of the handcuff lacerated my wrist and hand to the bone. I fainted.

When I regained my senses, all was quiet except for the last few gurgling sounds of life abandoning Ernest's body, and the plop, plop of a thick fluid dripping onto a metallic surface.

There was a dim light coming from behind. By some quirky electrical miracle, the trunk light was on and shone through a rent in the rear seat. The car had accordioned. I could nearly reach the hood ornament. The force of the collision had crushed the doors to half their former length. Every window was shattered.

My right arm was bleeding fearfully. Though dazed, I knew it wasn't an artery, for the blood flowed rather than spurted. But it would all flow out if I didn't do something. Forgetting the handcuff, I pulled my hand toward me to bury in my shirt. The action produced a sharp, horrific pain. My eyes filled with tears and I started to cry.

Between sobs, I'd begun to remove my shirt with my free hand so as to use it as a bandage, when I remembered the key. Harry had dropped it in Ernest's pocket. I was so concerned about my predicament I hadn't looked at him.

I looked and instantly turned away in revulsion. I gained control of myself and looked again. I've seen gruesome sights. As a corpsman in the army, I was supposed to be inured to torn-up bodies, but Ernest's was beyond the pale. The same mega-g force that had buckled the steel frame of the Buick had crushed and compressed his torso. His head and chest had smashed through the windshield and jutted upward, supported by the crumpled hood. He looked not unlike a carved figure on the prow of a Viking ship. The glass had guillotined his throat and neck, forcing the half-severed head to tilt back at a hideous angle. Blood dripped steadily from the appalling cavity, and dribbled away in the channels of the wrinkled metal.

Movement was painful. The impact wrenched my shoulder and back, and my right arm throbbed to the beat of my pulse. I released my seatbelt and reached across my chest to Ernest with my left arm. With a painful lunge, I grabbed on to his jacket and pulled it, and him, towards me. I turned away again, retching, and tried not to vomit on myself.

I counted to ten and went back to it. I groped in his jacket pocket, whimpering with relief when my hand closed around the precious key. I was trembling uncontrollably. I couldn't risk dropping it. I tried to bring about a spell of calmness by taking steady, shallow Lamaze breaths, disregarding the fact that every moment I was losing precious blood.

My eyes had adjusted to the dim light. When my left hand stopped shaking, it became possible, taking ever so much care, to unlock the cuffs. I removed them from both my wrist and the steering wheel and put them in my pocket. I took off my shirt and the T-shirt under it. I tied the T-shirt tightly over my lacerations and re-dressed myself.

Now I faced a grim task. I pulled Ernest down into the passenger's seat and propped him up in the corner. His head bobbled precariously, blood dribbling everywhere. I threw my left shoulder into the driver's door. It gave, but just a tad, and pain flashed through my left side. I turned gingerly and, despite the overwhelming abhorrence that I felt, leaned my back against Ernest for leverage. I drew up my legs and kicked the door hard. I recoiled against the corpse and I could swear it groaned, but it was the sound of the door yielding with reluctance. I repeated the kicks until I inched it open enough to squeeze through.

Ignoring protesting muscles, I reached back in and grabbed Ernest by the legs. Bit by bit, his head lolling dreadfully, I pulled him into the driver's position, with his upper body lying on the passenger's seat. He now appeared as though he'd been driving, and had thrown himself down on the seat at the last moment, missing the protection of the airbag, and thereby sustaining his terrible injuries.

I used a part of the T-shirt-cum-bandage to wipe my fingerprints off the steering wheel and anything else I could think of. The odor of bourbon would bear silent witness to Ernest's tragic drunk-driving accident. I was sure his blood, if he had any left, would also bear testament to the foolhardiness of mixing speed with alcohol.

I stood up and surveyed the scene in what dim light was available. The crumpled Buick had slid back from the tree a couple of feet. Any resemblance between the wreck before my eyes and the finished product of a Detroit assembly line was purely coincidental.

The odor of gasoline was in the air. Fuel was seeping out of the ruptured gas tank and trickling down the side of the road in a small stream. If I'd considered the high possibility of a conflagration, I might have shrunk away from the action I took. I'd have survived the impact only to die a far worse death by fire, trapped as I was.

Another vehicle could be along at any moment. I didn't want to be seen. Fortunately, in the dark, approaching headlights would be visible in ample time for me to duck into the woods that so closely bordered the road. I began walking in the direction that we had come from. I remembered the service station and minimart, and if I thought up a good story I might get a ride to Orlando.

My appearance was problematic. My clothes were blood-spattered and my wrist looked like so much raw hamburger, though the bleeding had subsided. When I had walked well away from the demolished Buick, I stepped into the woods, stripped to my underwear, turned my clothes inside out, and put them back on. The overlarge, unattractive dungarees and man's work shirt looked no worse one way than the other, but the bloodstains now looked vague and more generic. Hell, if some rap star did this, half the teens in the country would be wearing their clothes inside out.

Inevitably, a car came. I hid, but I knew that soon after the driver saw the wreck, the place would be swarming with emergency vehicles. I was within a quarter mile of the service station and I could see a little by its ambient light. I untied the bloody T-shirt and tore it into strips. This made my arm throb and sent waves of nausea through me. With the least bloody of the strips, I bandaged the wounded limb as neatly as I could with left hand and teeth. I resisted the temptation to jog the last stretch to the highway. I didn't need to begin bleeding again. Instead, I marched quickly and deliberately. Shades of army boot camp.

A mud-caked Ford Explorer stood at the pumps of the BP station. One guy was gassing up while exploring the inside of a nostril with the little finger of his left hand. His passenger was chugging from a tall can of Coors. I walked up to the gas pump and addressed the driver, who flicked his little finger behind him when he saw me. He was a ruddy-faced youth with dirty fingernails and pimples. His attire was barely less gross than mine, though unlike me, he was trying to look good, this being Saturday night and all.

"Hi," I said shyly. "I want to ask you to do me a really big favor. I just had a really big fight with my boyfriend, you know, and I jumped out of the car, and about fucking killed myself. Do you think you and your friend could give me a lift? I'd be glad to pay you."

I reached into a back pocket, now an inside back pocket, where I'd sequestered a few one-hundred-dollar bills. I brandished one of them.

"Aw, you don't hafta pay me, ma'am. Chucky 'n' me'd be happy to help a dame in distress."

"Look, I'm from Orlando, okay, and that's pretty far to go. I'd feel better if you'd just take the money. I'm just so happy just to have a ride." I pushed the C-note into his shirt pocket.

"That's right nice o' you. Go ahead 'n' hop in the back seat. Say, ain't yer clothes on backward, or some'n'."

"Yeah, well, I had to dress in a hurry," I said, looking embarrassed. It embarrassed him too and the matter was dropped.

He topped off and went inside to pay. He gave the clerk my hundred and she was holding it up to the light, clearly doubting that the likes of him could have that much genuine cash. The bill survived scrutiny and she doled out change. A moment later he was in the cab cranking the engine. Before shifting into gear, he turned to say he was Lionel and his bud was Chucky.

I didn't want to be Susan since it could be argued that she had murdered a man. I introduced myself as Norma, another one of my multiple personalities. Norma is not the sharpest tack in the box, and her mother dresses her funny.

While the introductions were taking place, a wail of sirens and a constellation of twinkling blue, red and orange lights grabbed our attention.

A veritable parade of government vehicles had stopped tentatively on the highway by the road from which I'd just come. There were two sheriffs' cars, two highway patrol cruisers, an ambulance, and a fire engine bringing up the rear. The boys in the front seat found this a circus not to be missed. Lionel asked if I wouldn't mind a small delay while they fell in behind the troop to see what was up. Demurring would be ungrateful, if not suspicious.

They stayed well behind until the caravan came upon the hulk of the Buick. The first sheriff's car stopped on the berm a few car lengths back from the wreck. The others lined up behind it. Lionel caught up to them and happily drove his four-wheeler as far into the forest as it would go, on the opposite side of the road. He backed and turned to give us a bird's-eye view of the scene.

A stout deputy sheriff got slowly out of the first vehicle. His ankles showed white under his hitched-up uniform trousers, and his belly lapped over his belt. He walked toward the wreck in the light of his cruiser's headlamps. A lit cigarette dangled from his lips. As I watched, he grabbed it between his thumb and forefinger and flipped it onto the side of the road.

A stream of fire surged to the ruined car. The deputy barely had time to turn his back when the gas tank blew, enveloping the wreckage in a swath of flame. This elicited a rousing "fucking A" from my two companions. It made their night, and they hadn't even gotten laid.

The crew on the fire truck, who up to now must have felt fairly dispensable, leaped into action. They drove the truck alongside the flaming wreckage and proceeded to hose it down. When the fire was under control, they finished it off with copious amounts of foam. At the same time, the EMTs from the ambulance ministered to the hapless deputy, who appeared shaken but not seriously injured. The brunt of the explosion expended itself in hurtling the vehicle onto its side.

For me, this was an unbelievably lucky turn of events. Despite my efforts to reposition Ernest, the nature of his injuries was not consistent with the scene I'd left behind. I'd had to hope for carelessness or naiveté on the part of the officers sent to the accident. A good forensic analyst would have seen straight through the ruse. Then questions would be raised that might ultimately put me in jeopardy with the law. The explosion annihilated any evidence that Ernest was not the driver.

With the fire out, and the first deputy safely in the ambulance, the second deputy approached the charred wreckage with a broom, swept away a mass of foam, and shone his flashlight inside. He did not like what he saw. He jerked back and looked to his companions for support.

A convocation of law enforcement, fire-fighting and medical personnel took place in the middle of the road. When it concluded, they all returned to their own vehicles. I half expected them to drive away, leaving the mess to be rediscovered after their shifts were over. Instead, the fire truck pulled up close once again. One of the crew attached a cable to the driver's door and winched it wide open.

The medical team came up to the wreck with a stretcher and body bag. They were preparing to remove Ernest's corpse when I noticed one of the state troopers walking in our direction. My heart leaped into my throat and my wrist began to throb in synch with my accelerating pulse. He played the light of his flashlight first on the car, then on us. I held my breath. I didn't have any ID on me and my explanation for my presence wouldn't fly with the cops.

He seemed to know my new friends, however. Instead of hassling them, as I expected, he waved them on with the flashlight. "Okay, boys, you've had your fun, now get the fuck outta here. And goddammit,

Chucky, don't litter," he said as he stepped on an empty Coors can. Chucky apologized sheepishly and hopped out to retrieve the crushed can.

The boys drove slowly away, Chucky craning for a glimpse of the body.

"I guess you know the trooper, huh?" I asked, curiosity getting the better of me.

"Yeah, he's me uncle," said Chucky. "He's pretty fuckin' cool for a copper."

I had them drive me to the hotel complex. I thanked them again and gave each a left-armed hug and a kiss on the cheek, which elicited a couple of aw, shuckses. They were nice boys.

It was the wee hours and there were few people out. I made my way cautiously to the center of the horseshoe. I looked up to find Harry's suite in the Raphael. It was dark, as I had hoped. Harry had said he was going someplace: the ranch, the farm, I couldn't remember. Best not to run into him.

I wondered if Harry knew that I had a room next door. It would compromise me if he returned the favor and searched it. But then I realized that the last thing on earth he wanted was any association with me, the person whose murder he had ordered. He'd think that if he was perchance found in my room, the charge might be a great deal more severe than trespassing.

I wasn't keen on walking through the lobby. I tried all the other doors, which ordinarily are locked at night. My luck held and I found one that Security had overlooked. I had to stop several times to catch my breath while climbing to the sixth floor, I was so exhausted. As soon as my heart rate rose, the throbbing began again in my right arm.

The hall was clear. As quietly as I could, I staggered to my room, unlocked the door and slipped inside, fearful even of switching on a light. I stripped and went into the bathroom. With the bathroom door closed, the light was safe.

I removed the makeshift bandages from my hand and wrist. I sucked in my breath at the sight of the caked blood intermingled with torn skin and flesh. Carefully, with many a grimace, I washed the injury until the entire site was clean. Blood had begun oozing from several places. I made a fresh bandage from a washcloth, which I held in place with elastic bands. I held my arm over my head and stepped into the shower. I washed as best I could with one hand. When I finished, the bleeding had stopped and the arm no longer throbbed. I replaced the blood-soaked washcloth with a clean one, doused the light, and crawled naked into bed to await the dawn.

Though I'd slept only three hours, I felt rejuvenated when the first rays of the morning sun shone in. The bandage was dry and I managed to change it without causing more bleeding. I kept my hand elevated at shoulder level as I dressed and packed. I used automatic checkout through the TV set and, after one final survey of the room, slipped softly into the hall. Next door was quiet. I had no idea whether Harry had returned. I summoned the elevator.

In the lobby, two uniformed police officers stood at the check-in counter having an animated conversation with the clerk. The janitorial staff had been hard at work overnight. They had polished the floor anew, dusted the furniture and vacuumed the upholstery. The sand in the freestanding ashtrays was sifted smooth and left with an imprint of an ornate capital "R." The louvered windows were open and drafts of morning air had driven away the odor of stale tobacco and alcohol. Despite my injuries, I felt renewed, resurrected, and so full of life as to be euphoric.

The security guard watched as I pulled my rolling bag across the lobby toward the exit. The automatic doors retracted and I stepped outside into the fresh morning and took in this new day of life. A squirrel skipped across the branches of a nearby tree. I became aware of the liquid song of a bird high in that tree, singing its own sweet carol of thankfulness to be alive on this morning.

The rising sun cast long shadows. One of those shadows was moving toward me. I thought I recognized the silhouette and turned my head to see Harry. He was gaping at me, slack-jawed, a look of disbelief on his face. The sight of him gave me an adrenaline rush. My arm throbbed in response to my pounding heart. We stared at each other for a few seconds. With regained composure, I passed close to him and hissed, "Tell your next goon not to drink and drive—somebody might get hurt."

I didn't think he'd shoot me in the back that Sunday morning. It wasn't bird season.

BOOK TWO

TOM

CHAPTER 15

It felt strange to be driving again. I had to keep looking at my right hand to make sure it wasn't chained to the steering wheel. The stunt I'd pulled the previous night wouldn't have worked in my rental car. Both driver and passenger seats had airbags.

I drove to the Orlando airport with added caution. My earlier recklessness had had a rebound effect and had made me timid. I'd used up a lot of luck in the past 24 hours and now I was taking no chances. The morning flight to Raleigh was only half filled. I had no trouble getting a seat on my open return. My mood swung between the euphoric feeling I'd had in the hotel lobby and anxiety about the next stage of the investigation.

When I got home, I called Ashley to report success. The hair in the razor would be more than ample for the DNA test. The toothbrush, if it had enough cells on it, would provide confirmation against the outside chance that Ernest had used the razor. Ashley said that a courier would call for the items within two hours.

In response to her questions about the week's activities, I told the whole truth with the exception of my run-in with Ernest. As far as she knew, I'd committed a successful burglary of Harry's room, obtained the desired items, and brought them home. I didn't like the gap in my report because, as my client, Ashley was entitled to know what I did while in her employ. I excused myself from this obligation on the basis that the law might construe my actions as murder, though in my mind it was justifiable homicide. In any event, I didn't want to make Ashley an accessory.

Ashley moved quickly on to the topic of finding the other two men— presumably Tom and Dick—who had also assaulted her. I assured her that I'd expend every effort to pursue them, and that I had "some leads." What I really wanted at that moment was some time off. I was spent to the core and my arm was feeling worse every moment. I ended our conversation with a promise to get back to her when I had something solid.

Immediately upon hanging up I went into the bathroom to change dressings. The wound had an angry look and spidery red streaks stretched up my forearm. This was a sure sign of infection. I needed professional help immediately. I was annoyed with myself for having called Ashley first, for now I had to await the courier.

I prepared the razor and toothbrush for shipping. The bloodstained clothes went into the wash—cold water, to be sure—with plenty of detergent. The house needed cleaning, which task I performed left-handed, holding my right hand in a makeshift sling. That done and still no courier, I got out a book of piano music for the left hand alone. I'd received it for a birthday gift one time and had kept it around out of curiosity. Now I actually had need of it, and the quaintness of playing—or trying to play, in any case—the one-handed music helped wile away the time.

The courier finally showed up. He was an off-duty state trooper with flinty eyes behind wire-framed glasses, and a service automatic on his hip. There was paperwork to be filled out. We both averred and avowed that our intentions were honest. I indemnified the courier's company against everything from flat tires to epidemics. When I went to sign, I became aware of how stiff my right hand had become. My signature was cramped and unnatural. He left at last with the precious cargo in hand.

I drove to the emergency room immediately after the courier had departed. I took plenty of reading material, for there is no place on earth outside of the army where one hurries up and waits so much. When I showed the duty-nurse my arm, however, her eyebrows twitched. For the cool-headed emergency room personnel this is the equivalent of a gasp.

Within five minutes I was in an examining room. Another five and the ER doctor rapped twice and let himself in. He asked difficult questions, like "How did this happen?" and "Why didn't you go to the hospital in Orlando?"

My answers were plausible lies. "I caught my arm in an electric car window and panicked. I didn't want to miss my flight. I trust the doctors in Raleigh because I'm from here," a piece of flattery that misfired since, as I learned later, he was a native Floridian.

Tetanus and penicillin shots promptly followed. He volunteered to call a plastic surgeon to stitch the wounds properly to minimize scarring. I'd have to wait a few hours, but as he noted wryly, I'd already waited far too long.

The plastic surgeon was unmoved by the injury. She was a middle-aged woman whose hair was just beginning to gray. She wore no makeup and exuded self-confidence without egoism. I liked her immediately.

"You're going to take about 100 stitches," she said. "I'm going to have to tear all this apart and sew it in place. I'm afraid you didn't get it all put back right."

She numbed the area with repeated injections. The first one stung like hell but the numbness soon took over. She aimed each subsequent shot through a desensitized area so that the entire process was pain-free after the first injection.

Now she went to work on the injured tissues. She peeled back the flaps of skin to reveal the pulpy flesh beneath. She probed repeatedly to ensure that there was no structural damage.

"You're extremely lucky not to have cut any tendons, honey. You destroyed several small veins in your wrist, but that shouldn't matter. It'll be swollen for months, and perhaps always be slightly larger than your other wrist, but you'll be the only one to notice."

The nurse who was assisting her flooded the area with an antiseptic, dried it thoroughly, and dusted it with steroidal powder. The surgeon repositioned the flaps and trimmed their ragged edges with surgical scissors. She sewed the flaps in place with a sickle-shaped needle. Each tiny stitch adjoined the next in a solid line of black that traced the boundaries of each wound. When she had finished, my arm looked like a Balkanized region on an atlas. I mentioned that to her and she laughed and said she'd never thought of herself as a cartographer. But indeed, with a little imagination, I could identify Bosnia, Croatia and Yugoslavia.

The doctor sent me home with antibiotics and pain medication, and strict instructions to rest for the next forty-eight hours. I barely took time to brush my teeth before crawling into bed. I remained there until the following afternoon.

When I awoke, I felt well enough to walk over to see Janet and reclaim my two greyhounds. They nearly jumped out of their skins with pleasure when I walked through the door. We went back home and played in the yard for a bit. Then it was back to work.

I needed Palm Pilot software to read the purloined file of names and addresses that I had gotten from Harry's computer. I called next door and got Lily on the line. She was sure someone there had the software and offered to come over and get the diskette. Ten minutes later she was back with a complete printout of Harry's address book.

I highlighted all the entries with the T-names and the D-names: Tom, Thomas, Thompson, Tommy, Initial-T, Richard, Rich, Richie, Dick, and so on. There were quite a few marked entries when I'd finished, but one stood out above the rest: Tommy Beck. Beck was the surname that Harry had employed as an alias. It had to be more than coincidence.

I got out the stacks of records from Marquis. There were no Becks in the working pile of Toms, but I'd excluded records of freshmen, sophomores, and people not between the ages of 20 and 30. There were no Becks there either and my disappointment mounted.

But wait, there was one more stack to search: the one with matching middle names. My last coin in the slot machine spun up three bars in a row in the form of the name of Jay Thompson Beck. I'd been annoyed with Ellis for giving me middle names. I mouthed a silent apology.

Beck was a philosophy and religion major in the Divinity School. That piqued some memory cells in my head. I got out my laptop and examined my database. Ashley had noticed an exceptionally large crucifix on Fatboy's clothes. And there were references to someone named J.T. or J.D. during Ashley's ordeal. The clincher was that Harry's mother's maiden name was Beck. What I now knew dovetailed neatly. Jay Thompson Beck was Harry's cousin Tommy, a.k.a. Fatboy.

I considered whether Ernest might actually have been Beck. He was more or less the right size, according to Ashley's description. I wouldn't describe him as fat the way Ashley had, but in ten years his build could have changed. It would be a pity if they were the same person. I'd been bathed in the man's DNA, all of which had gone down the drain in the wash.

I had Ellis's phone number at Marquis. It was nearly five and I hated to bother him near quitting time. If he was annoyed at my call his voice didn't reveal it. I got the "anything for you, Ms. Jamison" treatment. Would the whole world were of that persuasion. I asked him for all of the information on Jay Thompson Beck he could find. He promised it by ten the next morning.

A short nap before supper seemed like a good idea. Sometimes the more you sleep the more you want to sleep, but it's self-limiting. One of the hounds got me up around midnight—I'd neglected to let them out before my "nap." By the time they had gone out and come back in, I found myself wide-awake, a victim of self-induced jetlag. I decided to ring up Charles.

Charles Cranston Clarke is my boyfriend. We live together for three months every summer in his house in Santa Barbara, California. During that time, I work for my brother John. The remainder of the year we spend flying across the country to see each other, often meeting in romantic places between our two cities such as New Orleans. We're experts at finding cheap airfares. We talk openly about marriage but we value our independence and are tied to our respective cities through our professions.

Charles is an assistant medical examiner. He's an Englishman, educated at Oxford, and a graduate of the New London Medical College. He speaks uncannily like James Bond. He's one of the smartest people I know, one of the kindest, and one of the most resourceful. Admittedly, I'm prejudiced.

We met by chance when a client hired me to investigate her friend's apparent suicide. My client suspected foul play, and Charles, who did the autopsy, found irregularities enough to persuade me that my client might be right.

Boldly for me, for I was still traumatized by my bout with cancer, I asked Charles out the evening of the day that I met him. We hit it off and he became entangled in my investigation when we combined a vacation to San Francisco with my pursuit of the circumstances surrounding the questionable death.

Eventually we found the central cohesive clue in the case on a corpse that had been buried for twenty years—Charles and I exhumed the body early one eerie morning, and he found that the remains bore marks identical to those on the apparent suicide. Thanks to Charles, I cleared up the matter, though not without some additional mayhem, and added to the renown of John's firm, and, according to Ashley, to my own renown.

Charles answered on the second ring.

I said "Chaaahhles," imitating his accent.

He said "Daaahhlink," imitating an east coast accent.

"I love you."

"I love you, too. I miss you, Dag. What's happening? How are you?

"How much time do you have?"

I hadn't spoken with Charles since taking Ashley's case. He was at a pathologists' convention in Hawaii for a week, and of course I was in Orlando, and we kept missing each other. I told him of my adventures, careful to keep everyone anonymous so as not to invade my client's privacy.

"Bloody hell!" he exclaimed when I got to the passing of Ernest. "You purposely rammed a ruddy tree at 90 miles per hour! Fawking junipers! You put a lot of faith in that fawking airbag. You know, Dagny, I study these scenarios. Above 60 miles per hour we see fatalities even with seatbelts and airbags. At 90 you had a 50 percent chance of being killed. You could've done at 60 and taken your man out. Good God, your stories give me gray hairs."

"You'd look quite handsome with a few gray hairs. And anyway, I couldn't exactly call you from the car to get the optimum speed, could I?"

"Hmm, I suppose I'm uncommonly lucky not to hear you say you bit off this man's finger to get a DNA sample, aren't I?"

"What a great idea. I'll consider it next time. I still need to find two more of these creeps."

We talked until two in the morning when I became sleepy again. With promises to meet as soon as Ashley's case had moved forward, we rang off. I little knew then how soon the whole business would bring us together.

The next morning I felt normal. My injury wasn't bothering me at all. I thought that maybe a half-jog would only half violate doctor's orders. I padded into the bathroom and washed my uninjured hand and my face, careful to keep bandaged hand and wrist dry. I stood naked in front of the mirror and had a good look at myself. The scars on my chest, once fiery and angry, had faded to tamer pinks, grays, and whites. They'd be joined by new scars now incubating under the bandages. Add to those a bullet wound, a knife wound, and a nasty burn, and I was favored to compete well in a Raggedy Anne contest.

My face was slightly bruised. There was a perceptible swelling around the eyes and the flesh was discolored. I hadn't noticed it before because I was focused on the mangled arm. Diagonally across my body, from left shoulder to right hip, was a faint outline of the seat belt I'd been wearing. After having heard Charles recite the statistics on survival, I counted myself more than fortunate to have only these small reminders of the horrific impact. I swore I had more lines radiating from the corners of my eyes than before Orlando, but who's counting?

It was time for a haircut. I keep my hair close-cropped to prevent assholes like Ernest from dragging me around by it, but it was getting a bit unruly. I snipped away at several of the more errant strands, but doing this left-handed was even riskier than my usual right-handed hack job, and I soon decided to await professional treatment. My body hadn't been as tanned since I was a teenager, and I had to admit that I liked the look. It made my teeth whiter—those straight white teeth that had cost my parents the price of a used car in orthodontic fees. Too bad I was so fearful of more cancer. I couldn't see myself maintaining this shade for long.

I managed a mile and a half before my arm started to throb, and I stopped immediately. The greyhounds were surprised at the short duration of our outing but it turned out for the best. I'd only been home for a moment when the phone rang. It was Ellis getting back to me early

J. Thompson Beck was now Dr. J. Thompson Beck, Doctor of Divinity. He had graduated from Marquis with his bachelor's degree the same year as the attack on Ashley. He was accepted into graduate school and received his D.D. four years later. His last biographical sketch in the Marquis Alumni Magazine stated that he was the director of an orphanage and adoption agency in Istanbul, Turkey. The article credited him with rescuing hundreds of homeless children, many of whom found adoptive homes in the United States and elsewhere. It also mentioned that he was in the "Friends" category of donors, meaning that he gave Marquis at least $1,000 per year.

I asked Ellis to fax everything to me. Two points had become certain. First, Ernest was not Fatboy/Tommy. He was too lowlife and ignorant for a Marquis graduate, or *even* for a Marquis graduate as my friends from State might say. Besides, if the bio was correct, Tommy wouldn't be in the country, let alone have nothing better to do than act as Harry's bouncer, or bodyguard, or whatever Ernest was. Finally, I reasoned, Harry wouldn't have used "Beck" as an alias if an actual Beck was with him.

Second, I could happily eliminate Beth's husband Philip Martin. His missing toe had me going for a while, but his life story and Tommy's life story were on divergent paths.

Of all the foreign countries Fatboy might be in, Turkey was both unexpected and welcomed. I'd lived in Turkey for years on the military base where my father served. I could speak and understand Turkish fairly well for a foreigner, and I thought I understood the customs and values of the Turkish Islamic community.

This would be duck soup, thought I. Fly to Istanbul, find Dr. Beck, bribe an employee to bring me his hairbrush or whatnot, visit old friends for a few days, and fly home. Not once did I suspect how soon I would be the duck in the soup.

CHAPTER 16

I reported to Ashley. She was pleased but hardly thrilled. She could see that the identification of Fatboy was circumstantial. "Convincing, but not conclusive," she said. "Make sure he fits the physical description. Try to get a look at his feet."

The real Fatboy was missing a toe, if Ashley's memory under hypnosis was correct. I envisioned Fatboy living among the upper class, as most westerners do who reside in Turkey. He'd be likely to have domestic services. Turkey is a poor country, and what some might term "bribery" is often taken to be a fair means of persuasion between the haves and the have-nots. With my knowledge of the language and culture, I was sure I'd have access to Fatboy through his servants. Obtaining a toe count should be easy.

The first order of business was a plane reservation. I prefer to fly Turkish Airlines to Turkey. I can begin right away to speak Turkish and readapt myself to the culture. I telephoned the airline directly—it was too late to buy a ticket online—and was able to book a seat in business class with the return left open.

It was noon in Raleigh, making it early evening in Istanbul—still time to reserve a hotel room for the next day. I called the Basilica Hotel, my favorite place to stay when in Istanbul. Speaking Turkish, I asked the clerk who answered the telephone for Mr. Oktalmus, the owner. I wasn't being pushy. Husnu Oktalmus was "Uncle Husnu" when I was growing up; he was our family's close friend. I was under strict orders to ask for him whenever I called the hotel.

He came on the line.

"Uncle, it's Dagny, how are you?"

"Dagny, my sweet little lamb, it's so good to hear your voice. When are you coming to see me?"

I don't think he expected me to say, "Tomorrow, Uncle. I have the Hava Yollari"—Turkish Airlines—"flight from New York."

"Oh my, oh my. That's wonderful, darling. I'm going to put you in the penthouse."

"Please, Uncle, I'm coming on business and I need to be invisible."
He chuckled. I had said "invisible" in Turkish when I meant
"inconspicuous."

"You're such a skinny little lamb, you *are* nearly invisible, but I
can see we have to work on your Turkish. You shall have a room at the
end of a nice quiet corridor by the cistern door. None of the nearby
rooms is hired. It's as peaceful as the lap of Allah"

"That's fine, Uncle. And you must let me pay because it's
business. Please tell the clerks, okay?"

Everything was agreed upon. I looked forward to seeing Uncle
Husnu, not only because he was a dear man and a dear friend, but
because he knew everything that went on inside Istanbul, in the sky
above, in the mud below. I'd need help finding Beck. Harry's electronic
address book had no information about him other than a defunct post
office box number in the zip code of Marquis University.

Back went the dogs to Janet's, out came the suitcase, and off I
went in a Raleigh cab to the airport. Exactly fourteen hours later I
emerged from the Atatürk International Airport. It was shortly after 11
a.m. Turkish time, which was shortly after 4 a.m. Dagny time. I'd
managed a few hours of fitful sleep during the overnight flight. I wasn't
sufficiently inured to jetlag to escape feeling as though I'd been knocked
down again by the late Ernest.

Atatürk Airport is never short on taxicabs. There must have been
two hundred of them queued up in their own parking lot by the
international terminal. The drivers at the end of the queue are often
asleep in the back seat of their cabs. Some of them, I'm almost positive,
live in their cabs 24/7. My driver was a burly, mustachioed man with
brown hair, tobacco-stained teeth to match, and breath to stun a camel.

He was delighted, as Turks always are, when I spoke to him in
Turkish. He had me sit up front so he could bring me up to date on all
the "real" news, not the "pap one reads in the papers." He spoke a mile a
minute and gesticulated wildly with both hands as we raced through
morning traffic. I tightened my seat belt. It would be too ironic if I ended
up like Ernest. Turkish taxis do not have airbags.

My constant requests to him to repeat what he said due to the
rapidity of his speech tempered his talkativeness. By the time we were
cruising alongside the Sea of Marmara, heading for downtown Istanbul,
both his speech and his driving had slowed. I had a few moments to
absorb the beautiful vista of this inland sea, dotted with commercial
vessels from all over the world.

We turned off the highway and drove directly to the Basilica Hotel. The hotel is so named because it sits over the Cistern Basilica, a sixth-century underground reservoir. It's a wondrously eerie place to explore, dimly lit and dripping with mystery. Its roof is supported by hundreds of floor-to-ceiling columns that seem to fade away to infinity in the murkiness. This imparts a labyrinthine feeling to the place, and a sense of vastness that belies its mere two acres. It still contains water, so one must stay on raised walkways or ride in a shallow-bottomed dory to explore its fringes. Many people have unwittingly seen the Cistern Basilica. It was an on-location site in the James Bond movie "From Russia with Love." There is a little known access to the cistern from the hotel, and the staff provides private tours after hours to privileged guests.

Uncle Husnu was there to greet me. He took me into his private office and sent for tea, the traditional daytime drink that always accompanies business and social meetings throughout Turkey. We talked until the afternoon call to prayer floated through a window and intruded on our conversation. Uncle showed me to my room which was, as he had said, at the end of a quiet corridor, and left to fulfill his religious duty.

The highly amplified recorded chanting—the call to prayer—that summons the faithful to cleanse, face Mecca, and worship Allah, often startles the first-time visitor. The sound is distorted and discordant, and has a sinister air about it. To the unaccustomed ear it sounds like caterwauling, and one is unable to distinguish the individual words: "God is great! There is no deity but God, and Muhammad is his Prophet." It's very much a part of the exotic atmosphere that surrounds the foreign visitor to Istanbul.

In my room I stripped, showered, unpacked and crawled between the sheets to catch up on lost sleep. Uncle insisted that I dine with him that night. That would be a treat for he knew the best bistros in Istanbul. I'd asked him to find out what he could about Dr. J. Thompson Beck and his orphanage-cum-adoption agency. He promised to report to me over dinner.

I awoke, still a bit groggy, in the late afternoon. I didn't feel like jogging but the mild October sunshine beckoned me outside. The hotel is just a few hundred yards from the Hippodrome, a one-acre plaza that was the center of the city's life for 1400 years. It still contains impressive statues and obelisks despite most of its treasures having been looted over the centuries. Many a popular uprising had its start in the Hippodrome, which had also been the site of grisly executions, including crucifixions, over the ages.

I jogged around the Hippodrome toward The Blue Mosque—so-called because of the striking blue tiles of the interior. Ordinarily, its tier upon tier of domes, culminating in the colossal main dome, appears to be a glory to the architects and the God they worshipped. On this occasion, in the dwindling daylight, the mosque seemed to float ominously above the ground, dwarfing the people around it, and promising terrible retribution to the sinner.

The call to prayer at dusk interrupted my darkening thoughts. A great bustle arose as the devout converged on the mosque for their ablutions and prayer. I walked back to the hotel to dress for dinner.

Uncle had one of the hotel staff drive us to Istiklal Avenue, a popular pedestrians-only street of shops, restaurants, jazz bars and late-night tavernas. There we got out and made our way through a fifty-fifty mix of tourists and locals to a building with a jewelry store on the ground floor and a restaurant on the floor above.

The maître d' knew Uncle, of course, and sat us at a table where we could look down at the bustling crowd below, while enjoying the quiet elegance and filtered air of a dining establishment that claimed to date back to the days of the Ottoman Empire. Uncle ordered a bottle of raki, an anise-flavored brandy. This was a surprise.

"Uncle Husnu, I can't drink a bottle of raki by myself."

"Dear child, it's not all for you. I will drink raki tonight."

I expressed my surprise, for as long as I'd known Uncle he had obeyed the Islamic stricture against the use of alcohol.

"My sweet lambkin"—this is my best translation of the Turkish—"it's true that I'm a Muslim, and I believe that Allah is God and Muhammad his sole messenger. But I'm also a Turk, and raki is the national elixir of Turkey. And you, my precious one, you are an honorary Turk and like a daughter to me, so together we must drink raki."

And so we did. The raki is poured into a narrow glass over two cubes of ice. Water is added to produce a milky drink with a distinct licorice flavor. It's best to go easy with it. Its effect is summed up by an adage often seen imprinted on T-shirts generally worn by the young: "Raki is the answer" says the front; and, "if only I remembered the question," says the back of the garment.

The food was superb, as I knew it would be. Uncle is somewhat of a gourmet and he did the ordering, emphasizing variety over quantity. We ate and chatted and it wasn't until dessert that we'd finished talking about family, friends and politics. I was somewhat antsy to hear about

Beck, but politeness and custom must reign, and the raki helped me to nurture my patience.

"You're a patient little doe," said Uncle. "Most Americans want always to go straight to the point. You must come to Turkey and become a Muslim and marry a wealthy Turkish businessman." With that, he sat back in his chair, crossed his arms, and beamed at me.

"Uncle, you're teasing me. Really rich Turkish men marry European actresses, isn't that so?"

"Not always true, my lovely little dove. I could marry you by the next new moon to a man who would worship the ground you walk on, and give you a bank account as big as my belly," he said, thumping said part of his anatomy with both his hands.

"Perhaps, Uncle Husnu, if you'd help me finish my business here I'd have time to meet one of your Turkish Adonises."

"Yes, yes, you're right, my charming raptor. I'll help you find this man Beck. Is he a dangerous criminal? Will you devour him? Or will he devour you?"

"Uncle, you're too dramatic. I have a client who wants to know where this man is, and beyond that I cannot say more. So will you be a good Uncle Husnu and tell your little lambie pie what you found out?"

Over the last of the raki, Uncle Husnu told me that Beck did, in fact, run an orphanage called "Angel Wings Home for Children." It was located on the Asian side of the Bosporus Strait, about five miles northeast of downtown Istanbul. Adoption agencies in Orlando and Los Angeles were active in placing the children with American families. There was controversy about the Home. Muslim clerics were concerned that the children weren't receiving an Islamic education.

Back at the hotel, Uncle gave me a week-old newspaper to read with some articles about Angel Wings. Conservatives had picketed the orphanage and demanded that the government close it, or at the very least ensure that Islamic law was being obeyed on its premises. Dr. Beck said that the orphanage operated under the aegis of the secular Turkish government, and was therefore itself a secular institution.

One writer argued that the children, while awaiting adoption, were given "Christian exposure." He went on to note that Dr. Beck was a "doctor of Christianity" and could hardly be indifferent to religion.

Another pundit observed that the orphanage removed homeless children from the streets and provided them with food and shelter at no cost to the government. He congratulated Dr. Beck for his "good works for the Turkish people and the poorest of poor children." He further noted that because Dr. Beck was a Christian minister, he'd see to it that the children went to homes of believers in God, and in the end that was what mattered.

There had been violence, and the orphanage was now under an around-the-clock police guard.

I slept poorly, in part owing to jetlag, and in part because I'd drunk a bit more raki than was good for me. At breakfast I choked down a cup and a half of instant coffee, adored by the Turks for some mysterious reason, and ordered a cab to take me to the Angel Wings Home for Children.

Uncle had told me that the Home was a converted hundred-year-old palazzo once owned by an Italian count. The count's fortune collapsed along with the Ottoman Empire at the end of the First World War. The estate was eventually bought "for a melody"—Uncle was practicing his English—by a council of churches, who used it as a rest stop for Christian pilgrims on their way to the Holy Land. When air travel made such a stopover unnecessary, the once splendid palazzo became a humble orphanage.

Most of Turkey is in Asia, or "Asia Minor" as my social studies teacher called it, prompting me to ask where is "Asia Major," a question that earned me an hour of detention. The piece of Turkey that is in Europe is roughly the size of New Jersey and comprises but two percent of the whole. That two percent, however, contains the ancient city of Constantinople—now part of Istanbul—and its world-famous antiquities. Istanbul itself is a reflection of the country as a whole, being also divided geographically into European and Asian sectors. The airport, the commercial centers, and the major hotels, including Uncle's, are in Europe. The sprawling Asian sector is far more residential, and is poorer and rougher than its European counterpart.

The Bosporus Strait is an eighteen-mile-long waterway that separates the two continents, as well as dividing the city of Istanbul into its European and Asian halves. Travel between the two parts of the city is usually by ferry, though a few miles up the Bosporus toward the Black Sea, where the waterway narrows, are a couple of bridges. The orphanage was close to a bridge, so I told the taxi driver to cross to the Asian sector that way.

In bygone days, high walls surrounded the nobleman's palazzo to keep out the rabble. The walls, though crumbling in many places and riven by tremendous cracks, nevertheless afforded the orphanage a degree of privacy and some protection from the current tumult. I had the taxi driver circle the compound so I could get a feel for the place. Access to the property was via a front gate for foot traffic, and double-doors in the rear for vehicles. Two police officers patrolled each of these locations, and four more sat in a police van across the street from the front entrance. All of them cradled Uzi submachine guns. Policing is serious business in Turkey.

Hanging around waiting to meet someone who worked at the orphanage would raise suspicions. I'd have to get creative. I had the taxi drop me near the front and asked the driver to wait. A patrolman, or really a patrolboy, for he couldn't have been more than eighteen, challenged me at the front gate. I smiled and asked in English if he spoke English. He shook his head wistfully and attempted a sexy gaze that merely made him look sleepy. He livened up when I switched to Turkish. I apologized for my terrible accent, explained that I'd come all the way from America to see the great Dr. Beck, whose charitable deeds were admired by God. Would he be so kind as to announce me?

The other officer heard me and came over. After answering a bunch of flirtatious questions of the "what's a nice girl like you doing in a place like this?" variety, they let me through the gate. I rang the doorbell of a massive front door. There was a stirring within and a woman's voice cried out in Turkish that she was in the toilet, or cleaning the toilet, or maybe fixing the toilet for all I could tell. A man's voice said something muted and I heard him stride toward the door. Several dead bolts were thrown back and finally the heavy door opened slowly inward.

CHAPTER 17

Standing before me was a porcine man in his early thirties. He was clearly a westerner. He was too light-skinned to be Turkish and he was clean-shaven. Moustaches are *de rigueur* for Turkish men. He wore western-style slacks and an open-collared shirt. A large silver cross hung from his neck and rested against his breastbone. Light from the morning sun glinted off its surface. It fit Ashley's description of Fatboy's crucifix to a tee.

I said, "May I please speak with Dr. Beck?"

He peered over my shoulder to make sure I wasn't the vanguard of an unwelcome mob. When he saw that I was alone, he beckoned me in and closed the door.

"I'm Dr. Beck. To what do I owe the pleasure of a visit from so lovely a young lady?" He spoke with the lilt of the American South on every vowel. The flattery and touch of sarcasm were unnerving, and it didn't help to have the heavy door shut behind me, the deadbolt thrown with a clack.

For a brief moment I thought of blurting out, "Please remove your shoes and socks so I can count your toes, and if you have nine or less kindly favor me with a lock of your hair." This, of course, was out of the question, but it was what ran through my mind.

However, it was in the persona of Violet Williams that I confronted J.T. Beck, and my job was to play out the part.

"My name is Violet Williams," I said. "I heard that you're the head of an adoption agency. I'm childless but I want a child very much. My life feels incomplete without my having any children, but it's so hard to adopt when you're single. I have Turkish friends back in the States that I admire a lot. I want to adopt a Turkish child, and I've come here personally in the hopes that you'll help me."

My "acting" had genuine feelings behind it because I had thought more than once about having a child, and had even discussed it with Charles, who was sweetly sympathetic but counseled me—us, really—to wait a little longer.

Beck replied, "I'm sorry, Violet, but you must know that the adoption laws are very, very strict. You must follow them to the letter. I could get into trouble just for talking to you about this. You must go through an accredited agency."

"I've tried the agencies. They're too, too…difficult. Couldn't you tell me what agencies you work with? Then if I showed you that I'd be a good parent, maybe you could put in a word for me."

"I'm sorry, I'm not permitted to even mention the agencies I work with. There's a great deal of competition for adoption and the protocols are very strict, as you know."

I opened my mouth to protest but he continued in an oily voice.

"But tell me, you're young and healthy. I imagine that hundreds of men would like to father your child. Perhaps you haven't found the right man. I myself would be proud to be your partner except…." He fingered the crucifix as if to say "…except for my religious convictions."

"Thank you for your kind words. My problem is my own medical condition. The doctors say I can't ever have a baby. It's very personal, but I'm telling you so perhaps you'll help me," I said, choking back a sob.

"Come, let us talk further."

We walked through the hall to a pleasantly furnished sitting room with a bay window overlooking the front garden. Beck waved me to a sofa and took the plush chair diagonally opposite to it. He clapped his hands twice, sharply, and within moments a woman came in carrying a tray with two tulip-shaped glasses of tea, a sugar bowl and tongs, and two tiny spoons. She set the tray down on the small, round table beside the sofa. Beck added some lumps to both our glasses, stirred, and invited me to partake, tipping his glass toward mine in a distinctly non-Turkish gesture.

We sipped in silence for a short time. Then he leaned forward, so that his knees touched my legs, and spoke in a low voice.

"I could lose my position here by violating the rules. The children are my life's work. If I could be sure, I mean, if I really knew you much better, you know…." He tailed off, then restarted. "I'd be taking a big risk." He placed a hand on my knee.

I patted his hand and allowed it to remain for a moment before removing it with a wan smile.

"I have a résumé that I could send you. It explains that I can afford to raise a child, that I have a good job and live in a nice part of Santa Barbara, California."

"Oh, anybody can type a résumé. I go by my instincts. If I get to know you and I see that you're a good person, that would go a long way. Do you see what I mean?"

The hand returned to the knee.

I saw clearly what he meant and was thankful that I didn't truly need a favor from the swine. I was frantically trying to figure out what my next step should be when he saved me the trouble.

"I have a suggestion. This isn't a good place to get to know each other. Tomorrow night, when the Muslim Sabbath ends, there's a grand soirée at Topkapi Palace. It's by invitation only, but the mayor happens to be a good friend of mine and he's invited me. Why don't you accompany me? I'll have my car pick you up at your hotel."

"That's very kind. I'd love to go but I don't think I should. I sort of have a boyfriend back home."

"My dear Violet, this is not a date. Surely I'm no threat to your boyfriend? This is an opportunity for you to meet some very important people in Istanbul, and after we've gotten better acquainted, I'll be better able to evaluate your special request. I may even take the liberty of asking you to discuss the matter with a friend of mine who's an excellent judge of character. So you see, you should take me up on my invitation."

"I do need your help very much. If I go to this event, could I come on my own? I'd rather not be picked up. My hotel is near the palace and I won't have any trouble getting there. I'm sure you understand."

"Ah, I'll bet you're here with a 'friend.' I don't want to cause you embarrassment. Let's meet at eight o'clock tomorrow night. Do you know the ticket booth in the Court of the Janissaries, the park between the Topkapi Palace and the Sofia Mosque?"

"Well, I suppose I could find it. I've been to Topkapi as a tourist. Is that where you want to meet?"

"Yes, I'll need to accompany you inside. The party is in the Third Court, the one beside the Harem Quarters. And by the way, it's quite formal. I'll be wearing a tuxedo. Did you bring any dressy clothes?"

"No, not really. I didn't expect to go anywhere fancy. This will be an excuse to go shopping in the New City."

"Let me help you, my dear. God has been generous with me, or I should say He's smiled on my investments." He stood up and pulled a wad of bills from his pocket. He peeled off ten 10,000,000 lira notes and pressed them into my hand.

"Oh no, Dr. Beck, I couldn't possibly accept money."

"Now, Violet," he said, pressing the money to my palm, "tonight I'll be doing a bit of schmoozing, looking for donors to help the orphanage. Since you'll be with me, you'll be helping me. So please don't be shy about a small gift to put towards a beautiful dress. I want you to look lovely."

"Please, Dr. Beck, I'd rather have your help with the adoption."

"Take the one, and if all goes well, you shall have the other," he said, forcing my fingers to close around the money.

I winced when he squeezed, for it was the injured hand, barely half-healed.

He looked closely and saw the stitches.

"Oh, heaven forgive me, I'm terribly sorry. I didn't mean to hurt you, you poor girl. How did you injure yourself? I shall surely include you in my prayers tonight."

"My hand got caught in an electric car window," I lied, figuring that if the plastic surgeon bought the story, Beck would. "It's much better now, but it still hurts to the touch."

"Well then, I shall hold only the other hand," he said gallantly, and reached out to give my left hand an affectionate squeeze. His attentions had diverted my effort to return the money, and I stood there holding it. He took my elbow and guided me to the door.

"There, it's understood. You shall be my helpmeet for one night and we will convince the rich bankers to part with a few billions for the homeless children. It's fun raising money in Turkish liras. The numbers are so impressively large."

There was some irony here. Ashley was paying me to find Fatboy and get up close and personal enough to collect a DNA sample. Fatboy was paying me for more or less the same thing, though I don't think he thought of it in genetic terms. The easiest route was to take the money graciously. I thanked him profusely and gave my word of honor to meet him at the appointed time and place. To his offer of a car to take me back to the city, I pointed out my waiting taxi through the bay window.

I asked the driver to take me to the foot of Istiklal Avenue close to where Uncle and I had disembarked the previous night. Beyond that point, traffic rules permitted only pedestrians and the small, rubber-wheeled trolleys that plied the shops for the mile-long outdoor mall. I walked in and out of half a dozen boutiques without finding anything I could wear. Finally, I ran across a women's clothier I liked, whose name in Turkish, as best I could translate, meant The Elegant Peach.

It was upscale, with prices comparable to those in the U.S. I consulted the proprietress with regard to the social event at Topkapi Palace. She advised a conservative approach. "The arms and legs must be covered, madam. The young men will be disappointed but they will still admire you, and you will deflect criticism and unwanted attention."

Dark colors with reddish ocher aspects were apparently in season. I tried on an ankle-length, full-sleeved cocktail dress, the color of which would be called chestnut if it were on a horse. It had a slit up one side just high enough to suggest provocativeness without actually being provocative. It was a bit large on me but I bought it anyway. I could have it taken in back home if I continued to like it. My purchase so pleased the owner that she took me to a nearby shoe store managed by her friend, to ensure that I bought the right shoes for the dress. Once I had the "right" shoes—I'd stressed comfort over style, to the chagrin of my fashion advisors—the two of them accompanied me to a shop where I could purchase a matching bag.

I now had three counselors of couture, and they were considering the best type of hat for me to wear when I drew the line. Each of them hugged me and kissed me on both cheeks. I returned the hugs, and with many a "God go with you" I made my escape.

I returned to the Old City by taxi. The vast quantity of pollution from the day's traffic hung low to the ground, creating a cancerous-looking haze. The steady breezes of yesterday, which had cleansed the air for jogging, hadn't yet begun to blow. What might have been an ozone alert in an American city, however, didn't deter the Turks from coming out. Everywhere were last minute shoppers making purchases for observing Friday, the holy day of the Islamic religion. Workers were scouring the grounds of the city's mosques to prepare for the next day's onslaught of worshippers.

Back in my room, I showered and lay down naked on the bed for a short rest. The seven-hour time difference wreaks havoc with the body's clock. My "interview" with Beck had effectively taken place in the wee hours of the morning. Now, though it was dinnertime, I felt like a noontime nap. That, I knew, would worsen the situation, so I forced myself out of bed and got dressed.

The sun had slipped below the Sea of Marmara, and with its departure the breezes finally came, making the air more breathable. It was cool enough for jeans and a sweater, and that was my attire when I walked to the Medusa's Head Café, a favorite of mine, with both indoor and outdoor seating. I took an outside table near the sidewalk where I could watch passersby, and ordered a beer.

I perused with fondness a menu unchanged since my last visit several years ago. Although I was feeling slightly nauseated and out of sorts, the stomach-settling effect of the carbonated pilsner, and the thought of a good solid Turkish meal, revived my appetite. I ordered the "tas kebap," lamb stew. It was as delicious as I remembered and it bolstered my flagging spirits.

Mary, the cat, sat by my leg as I ate dinner. She was the only living being at the Medusa's Head that I recognized from past years. This was her territory and she was tolerated by customers and staff alike. I used to eat there with a group of American friends. When the cat had scored a morsel of meat, we'd sing "Mary had a little lamb." This produced hilarity at our table, and baffled looks from other patrons. One time a Turkish lady at a nearby table, who obviously knew quite a bit of English, asked us, "Do you have white fleas in America?" It was our turn to be baffled until we realized that "whose fleece was white as snow," sounded pretty much like, "whose fleas were white as snow." We set the record straight, though not without a nauseating digression into the color of lice.

I shared some bits of lamb with Mary and silently sang the song to myself, causing tears to well up in my eyes. I was stressed and lonely—blue, as my mom would say. I thought of the thousands of homeless dogs and cats throughout Istanbul. Many live among the ruins of the city, hiding in the depths by day and foraging at night. The dogs, wretched and starving, are taken away and dispatched when caught. The cats are not so easily disposed of. Many of them are adept at working the outdoor cafés for scraps. Some will sit politely by your table waiting for a handout. The more aggressive ones will paw your pant cuff or mew pathetically with a wide-eyed, hungry look. Mary included all these tricks in her repertoire, and she appraised her mark carefully before deciding which one to use.

On my way back to the hotel, I took the street that passed by the public entrance to the Cistern Basilica to see if it was open. On the occasional evening, there would be chamber music or singing in the underground cavern. It was as unlikely a place for a concert as you can imagine, yet it was effective. The brightness of the music contrasted with the gloomy menace of the dark recesses, creating a tension that accentuated both the music's beauty and the cavern's mystery.

To my surprise the entrance was barricaded with an iron grill. A sign in both Turkish and English announced that the Cistern Basilica was closed for repairs. This was a disappointment. I always looked forward to escaping the noisy bustle of the Old City for the eerie, echoing ambience of the underground reservoir. I'd hoped to spend a meditative hour or two down there, but the best laid plans…

As I was caught up in this contemplation, three young men and a young woman came unsteadily toward me. They were speaking and singing in what I took to be Scottish-accented English, since the song exalted the heathery hills of bonny Scotland. They had almost undoubtedly discovered raki. When they reached me, they stopped and asked if I spoke English. I said that I did.

"We're lost," said the girl, a petite brunette who was half the size of her largest companion, who looked every bit the rugby player.

"Yeah, we lost our sodding map, bugger it!" said one of the guys.

"Chill it, Clyde, you'll scare the lady," exclaimed the girl. "I'm Dotty," she said, holding out a hand. "I mean," she giggled, "my name is Dotty. I must be crazy to drink with these savages. You don't by any chance have a map we could look at, do you?"

"I don't," I replied, "but I know this area fairly well. Where are you staying?"

They named a pension I knew; it was tucked away in a quiet corner behind the Sofia Mosque. It was difficult to give precise directions, so I volunteered to walk with them. They were, as I had guessed, from Scotland, here on holiday. I aimed them up the right street toward their hotel. Dotty invited me to join them the next night. She said she needed another female "to keep these brutes in line." Regretfully, I had to decline. Their company would have been far preferable to Fatboy's.

I watched them walk unsteadily up the cobble-pebbled road, stumbling occasionally on the uneven surface. As they receded into the gloom a feeling of desolation came over me. I had an urge to follow them, a desire for companionship. The Sofia Mosque loomed darkly, its shadow smothering what little light came from the feeble street lamps. Two cats—was it a mother and her kitten?—sat on a low wall of stone and mortar, pupils wide open, mewing hungrily. I had nothing for them.

CHAPTER 18

The next morning, Uncle Husnu joined me for breakfast. "Dagny, darling, you look as fresh as a daisy. How was your meeting with Dr. Beck?"

"Fine. I thought it went well," I said noncommittally. "He asked me to a party at the Topkapi Palace."

Uncle looked both impressed and disapproving.

"Is there something wrong?" I asked

"These parties are for the elite and powerful of Istanbul. Perhaps my little she-wolf will meet her Turkish, how did you call it, 'Adonis.' I don't think I know that word."

"It means 'a very handsome man.' In mythology, Adonis was the lover of Venus."

"Ah, so my precious honeybee is comparing herself with the goddess of love?"

"Hardly that, Uncle. Anyway, why the frown when I mentioned the party?"

"Rich men take beautiful women to such parties with the intention of seducing them. You will be careful, no?"

"Uncle, you're holding something back. You know perfectly well that men take women everywhere with the intention of seducing them. What's special?"

"My innocent little heifer, what do you know about Dr. Beck?"

This was not a question to which I could reply candidly.

"Dear Uncle, I cannot answer you except to say that I have a professional interest. I know he directs the orphanage and helps disadvantaged children get adopted. He was polite to me and I believe he found me attractive, so he asked me out."

"And you will accompany him because of this 'professional interest'?"

"Yes, Uncle. Please don't worry about me."

"Do you wonder, my lamb, how such a man as your Dr. Beck is invited to the palace where great Sultans once lived? Especially so controversial a man, a man accused of stealing children from Islam? I will tell you. He's very, very rich. And how does this American become so rich?"

"I can't say."

"The rumor is that he accepts large payments for, how do you say, 'greasing the skids,' for wealthy Americans who want a fast adoption with niminal red tape. Is that what you're here to investigate?"

"That's 'minimal,' Uncle, and no, it has nothing to do with that. If everyone knows that he's breaking the law, why isn't he arrested or deported?"

"For two reasons. One, he's rich and can afford to be generous to those in power. Two, from our point of view, from Turkey's point of view, he's saving poor street children, and rescuing orphans, and finding them homes with good families. Some think it's bad that they won't be raised Muslims. But Turkey is a secular country and many are happy for them to be removed from poverty."

"How do you feel about it, Uncle?"

He pressed his lips together in thought. "I do not approve of corruption for any purpose. Deserving families may be denied the privilege of adoption because they cannot pay the bribe. As for the religion, as long as they are brought up to believe in God, then it's good. This is why I worry about you, my little imp of Satan."

"Uncle! I have little to do with God or Satan. They leave me alone; I leave them alone. You mustn't worry about me. We agreed, once."

"I struggle every day with the thought that good people who do not believe in Allah may nonetheless receive his blessing. It goes against Islam and the beliefs that my parents and the Koran taught me. Ah, but the world is changing so. Perhaps you'll find God in your heart one day. I pray for it."

After breakfast I returned to my room to work at my computer. I brought my files for the case up to date, including a tabulation of everything about Beck I'd learned since my arrival in Istanbul. That Beck the doctor of divinity and Fatboy the rapist were the same person seemed highly probable, though I had to admit that the evidence was circumstantial. It hung from the threads of Ashley's observations made while she was terrified and blindfolded. Making matters even more tenuous was the fact that Ashley's recollections were pried from her under hypnosis.

I was acquainted with the recent history of repressed memories, one of the topics of the Psychology of Memory class that I took at UCLA in my senior year. After first hearing Ashley's story I dug out of my school files some notes on the subject that the professor had handed out to the class. I wanted to refresh my own memory. They began with the chronicles of Bridey Murphy:

> Bridey Murphy was a middle-aged Irish woman who "remembered" previous lives while hypnotized. She had been undergoing repressed-memory therapy through "age regression." The therapist led her backward through time, stopping her at various ages to describe the images and feelings of her youth. This information would be used to help treat her current mental problems.
>
> Bridey's therapist did something unusual and experimental. He regressed her past age zero. To his surprise she became a different person, living in a previous era, and capable of describing scenes from the past. Over the months he regressed this predecessor-Bridey through zero and discovered yet a different, more ancient being.
>
> These "memories" were remarkable because they contained details that could be known only to the persons who Bridey was. Her recollections had information about the distant past that a 1950s middle-aged, middle-class Irish woman couldn't possibly know.
>
> Medical personnel and representatives from the media witnessed the hypnotic sessions. They attested that she spoke spontaneously without suggestion or prompting. She took on different speech characteristics as she regressed through the various personas that were she in an earlier time.
>
> Historians, antiquarians, sociologists and linguists were asked to authenticate Bridey's remembrances. Through her precursory avatars she revealed social customs of the past long since unused, forgotten and unknowable to the layman. She had access to petty political information that was important in its time, but no longer regarded. She knew expressions from the obscure dialects spoken by her pre-Bridey incarnations that only a linguist might be aware of.
>
> The tabloids in both Britain and America had a field day. Not a week went by without a feature article that further validated Bridey's pre-birth experiences. Amateur hypnotists regressed their friends relentlessly through bygone millennia. All had led previous lives in Ancient Greece, Troy, Rome or the Isle of Atlantis. Not a one had the misfortune of having been a wretched Greenlander or half-starved Russian serf. It was said that if everyone who claimed to be a princess from Atlantis in a previous life truly was, the island would surely have sunk under the sheer weight of royalty.
>
> The competition for attention to one's previous lives was fierce. Faded movie stars tried to make comebacks through their pre-birth personas. Religious leaders on the fringe found themselves to be rebirths of religious leaders who were central in yesteryears. Purveyors of séances nimbly switched to channelers of previous embodiments. Bridey's imitators were legion, and for years they strutted their hour upon the stage and then were heard no more. None was able to maintain the verisimilitude that Bridey managed.

> When it was revealed that the Bridey Murphy chronicles were a carefully planned hoax, the concept of previous lives retreated to the seedy outposts of pseudoscience, where it dwells to this day.
>
> But something important remained. Having been bamboozled by swindlers, and being once bitten, twice shy, psychologists began to look askance at the verity of repressed memories. A book was published in the mid 1990s that showed that recollections revealed under hypnosis may be right, wrong in minor detail, wrong in major detail, or entirely fictional. Much depended on the personality of the patient, the methods of the analyst, hidden or even subconscious motives, and the synergism amongst them.

Rereading the notes planted questions in my own mind as to how reliable Ashley's recovered memories were. I had to take them at face value when I took the case. I needed something solid on which to base the investigation. When Harry/Strong fit the picture I felt more sanguine about Ashley's recollections. Even so, the identification was not rock solid in my mind and I eagerly awaited the results of the DNA test. While I wouldn't wish that bastard to be anybody's father, a positive result would ease many of my misgivings.

I spent the afternoon in my room brainstorming ways of obtaining a DNA sample from Fatboy. I wrote down every idea I thought of, irrespective of how outré it was. I managed to come up with a list of seventeen items. Some were clearly unacceptable, but it's important to suspend judgment when brainstorming. One can cull later.

My ideas ranged from the sexual to the sublime. Any sample of his semen would suffice, however obtained. This I could contemplate but not do. On the sublime side, I might tell him that feet turned me on and offer to give him a pedicure. Of course I'd steal some clippings. That idea had the virtue of confirming his identification. A manicure would work, too, DNA-wise. Also on the list was running my hand through his hair when we got friendly, which I was sure we would, and extract one or two strands. The same result might be achieved by obtaining a skin scraping from his back by means of pretended passion, though kissing the man was at the outer limits of what I would do to achieve this goal.

An hour before I had to leave, I showered, put on a minimal amount of makeup, and donned my new outfit. I transferred a few essentials, including nail clippers, to the small, matching bag. I hadn't brought my handgun to Turkey. The law forbids it and a conviction means jail time. I was missing it now. There's nothing like a loaded automatic to give heft to the handbag and confidence to its bearer.

I opted to go on foot to the appointed meeting place. It was under half a mile from my hotel. The walk gave me time to calm myself and review my stratagems. I was glad I'd chosen more or less comfortable shoes. This wouldn't have worked in spike heels.

The park in front of the Topkapi Palace, called the Court of the Janissaries, was full of families enjoying the mild autumn weather and celebrating the end of the Sabbath, for the sun had officially set a while ago. A few elegantly dressed men and women were making their way across the park toward the entrance to the palace. I assumed they were my fellow partygoers.

Beck was standing by the ticket booth talking to a tall, thin, bald man wearing wire-rimmed glasses and dressed, like Beck, in a tuxedo. As soon as Beck saw me he waved and, keeping one hand on his companion's shoulder, reached out the other arm to sweep me in.

"There, didn't I tell you this was my lucky night with the ladies?" he beamed.

"Thank you for inviting me, Dr. Beck," I said shyly.

"You look utterly ravishing, Violet, and please call me Thompson. My congratulations on a successful shopping venture. Let me introduce you to Alan Beeman. He's the president of IKX Corporation, the biggest importer of American machinery in Turkey. Alan, this is my friend Violet Williams."

We shook hands. The men finished their conversation and Beeman excused himself, leaving us alone.

Beck stepped up to the window of the ticket booth, showed his ID and, after a conversation I couldn't hear, appeared to hand over some American currency. In return he received two engraved invitations that would admit us. I was becoming an ever more costly date.

The palace proper begins with the Second Court, which we now entered through the awesome Gate of Greeting. On the left side of the courtyard stood several guards, their side arms purposefully conspicuous. Rooms containing precious artifacts, as well as the entrance to the Harem, bordered the Second Court on this side. Naturally, all were off-limits to the attendees. Light-fingeredness is a character flaw shared by rich and poor alike.

The Gate of Felicity admitted us to the Third Court, the locus of the party and formerly the sultan's private domain. This courtyard was populated with partygoers, sprinkled among whom were palace guards dressed up to be inconspicuous, never mind that the .45 caliber bulge in their dinner jackets cried out "I'm a cop." Along the wall on the right side was an eight- or nine-piece band. They played both Turkish and

Western music, the musicians shifting effortlessly between the two modalities. Two belly dancers sat languidly in the corner waiting for a later hour to show their talent.

Tables of food backed by starched servers in white were arranged along the far end of the courtyard. All sorts of kebabs, stews, salads, vegetables, fruits, and the ubiquitous döner—spit-roasted leg-of-lamb— were freshly prepared and abundant. The dessert table was the only concession to Western cuisine. It was covered with French pastries.

On either side of the tables of food, in the far left and right corners of the courtyard, arranged under canopies so as to be not readily noticeable, were fully stocked bars with bartenders. It was toward one of these that we ambled. Beck stopped to talk with various people as we slowly made our way across the Third Court. He was polite and genteel, and introduced me with great courtesy to civic leaders, business executives and foreign dignitaries. I was surprised, though I tried to conceal it, when I heard him speak Turkish, albeit dreadfully accented, with some of his acquaintances.

When we reached the bar Beck said, "You must try our national drink. If you're going to raise a Turkish child, you must be like a Turk." He greeted the bartender in Turkish, inquired after his family, and accompanied by a wink asked him to make me a very strong raki.

"This is raki," pronounced Beck, when the two glasses were set before us. "It has a licorice flavor but it's smooth and not very strong. Let's drink a toast, Violet, to the changes about to happen in your life."

I sipped the milky liquid. It was a bomb.

"How do you find it?" asked Beck.

"It's okay. I think I once drank some with my Turkish friends. It's like ouzo, isn't it?"

"Yes, my dear, only better, smoother. Isn't that right, Hussein?" he said to a man who had just come up to the bar. Hussein agreed, and after ordering an American whisky took Beck by the arm to introduce him to his companions. As soon as Beck turned his back, I said to the bartender in Turkish that as sure as God was great and Muhammad his prophet he must serve me only the weakest possible drink. I shoved my glass toward him and he replaced it with one that contained just enough raki to make the milky white color.

Beck returned, urged me to down my drink so we could have another. I did so and he ordered two more from the bartender, who was true to his word. Another toast hinted at my successful adoption. We downed those drinks and I began to act slightly tipsy.

The band was playing American oldies. "I'm in the Mood for Love" inspired Beck to ask me to dance. As we held each other, I could feel the layers of blubber that were concealed under his clothing. He held me close and tight. I remained impassive. When his right hand slid down to my ass I moved it up. The same hand attempted to caress my breast. I removed it. I wanted neither to lead him on nor reject him outright so that he wouldn't see me again.

I put my left hand behind his neck and felt the hair on the back of his head. It had been washed and was slicked down with some kind of a non-greasy styling gel. I stroked it and made subtle attempts to extract a strand but it didn't work.

Beck responded to this mildly amorous act by squeezing me yet closer to his body. He thrust his hips forward and I could feel that he had an erection. His hand dropped once more to my ass.

"Thompson," I giggled, "please stop that."

He resisted my efforts to relocate his hand.

I was relieved when the music ended and the band switched to the Turkish mode, which is much less conducive to the cheek-to-cheek style of dance. Beck looked somewhat flushed. He still played the gentleman, complimenting me on my dancing. He suggested another round of drinks.

"Do you know there is a Fourth Court?" he said, when we had our fresh glasses of raki. "It's behind the food tables. Let's see if we can have a peek."

With drinks in hand, he led us around the tables and through a corridor. I was sure we'd be stopped or I wouldn't have followed him. We found ourselves in an open area.

"Down there," continued Beck, "is the tulip garden. It's quite lovely, though not as lovely as you. I'd like to show you it."

He took my hand and led me down a short flight of stairs into a lowered terrace. The spring-flowering tulips were missing, but the garden was replete with other flowering plants. Beck rightly knew this would be a romantic spot. We walked across the garden toward a canopied area.

"This is where the sultans took breakfast," explained Beck. "And here," he indicated an archway, "was the Circumcision Room. That room was used for the ritual that admits Muslim boys to manhood. The circumcision occurs when the boy is nine or ten years old. It's the principal rite of passage of Muslim males."

He spoke with a prurient tone as he related these facts to me, but I wasn't sure if it was brought on by thinking of the boys or by thinking of me. Whatever it was, it made me shudder.

"Shall we have a peek?" said Beck. "There are some beautiful tiled walls."

Before I could answer he pulled me inside. The room was the size of a large American bedroom, furnished with two divans, several chairs and a table. There was only one way in and out. It dawned on me that we hadn't seen another soul in the garden and that we probably shouldn't be there. The low level of lighting reinforced the impression that visitors were not expected. The first seep of adrenaline made me flush.

No sooner had we entered than Beck pulled me toward him and tried to kiss me. I resisted.

"It's okay, Violet, no one will come. It's private here. We have our little understanding, don't we? I've been nice to you, so now you be nice to me. So come, just a little kiss to show you like me."

"Really, Thompson, I don't think we're supposed to be here. Please take me back."

"You know that I'll work with the agencies for you. I can just about guarantee you an adoption. Just give me one small kiss."

I shook my head. I wanted a piece of Beck's body but not the piece he was offering.

"I really think we should leave. I hardly know you. I need some time to think about this."

Beck had positioned himself between the door and me. He grabbed my injured wrist and squeezed hard.

I yelped and tried to free myself.

With one hand tight around the stitched lacerations, and the other on my neck, he began pushing me back in the room toward one of the divans.

"Let's sit down and talk about it, then," he said in a menacing tone.

I protested once more and this time both his hands slid up around my throat. He growled, "You can cooperate and we'll be friends, or you can have your neck wrung like a chicken. The choice is yours, my dear."

CHAPTER 19

When I didn't answer him he began to squeeze harder. I was beginning to black out. I knew what I had to do, though it repulsed me.

"Okay, okay," I gasped, sobbing. "Please don't hurt me anymore. I'll cooperate. Let's at least do it right. I don't want a zipless fuck. Get undressed."

He shoved me in a corner so I couldn't make a dash for it. He removed his cummerbund and trousers. My sobs had aroused him to a fever pitch. He was wide-eyed and flushed, and his licorice breath came in short, shallow spurts. His bulbous, hairy belly ballooned out from under the formal white shirt. His erection bulged through his underpants.

"Take off your shoes and socks. I'm not fucking a man with his shoes on."

He looked annoyed and for a moment I thought he was going to come at me again, but he commanded me to get on the divan, then sat down and removed his footwear. I could just see by the dim light that his left foot lacked a second toe. That clinched it. I needed that confirmation.

I lay on my back and pulled my dress up over my hips. I slid my pantyhose and panties down around my ankles. Beck tore off his underpants and moved to lie down on top of me.

"Let me help you," I said, and moved my hand down as if to assist him. Instead, I grabbed a handful of pubic hair in a tight grip and pulled with all my strength. There was a tearing sound and a terrible scream. He rose up, his face contorted in pain and rage. I slid out from under him, propped up on my elbows, and double-kicked him hard in the testicles. Too bad he hadn't asked *me* to remove *my* shoes.

Beck gasped and emitted a dreadful moan. He doubled over in agony, both hands in his crotch. I hurriedly dressed, wiped the pubic hairs from my hand into my bag, and moved ass.

The Circumcision Room is thick-walled, and no one was near. Beck's cries had gone unnoticed. I climbed out of the garden and through the passageway to the Third Court. My bartender friend noticed me and smiled. I mouthed in Turkish *Allahu Akbar*—"God is great"—and lit out across the court toward the Gate of Felicity, biting my lip to keep a normal pace. It would not be fitting to run.

I thought it was an illusion induced by panic when I saw a square-jawed man with a crew cut amidst the celebrants as I sliced through the crowd. He reminded me of a man I'd seen in Orlando, and I thought I saw a glint of recognition in his eyes. Most everyone else's attention was focused on the belly dancers, who had just begun their act. I passed unhindered into the Second Court.

The impulse to run was still there but I resisted. A running woman would alert the guards. Once I passed through the Gate of Greeting to the park outside, I could book.

I sped back to the Basilica. In my room I did breathing exercises to regain a semblance of tranquility. I wanted nothing more than to change clothes, go outside, and run, run, run until all the fear, misgivings and tension dissolved in streams of sweat.

Discretion demanded that I stay put. I couldn't be sure how Beck would react. He might do nothing. He might go looking for me with vengeance in mind. He knew my hotel was near enough to Topkapi for me to walk there.

He might go to the cops and claim he was assaulted and robbed. They wouldn't find Violet Williams but it wouldn't take them long to locate a tall, slim, blonde-haired American woman. They'd make an extra effort since Beck was an influential figure in the politics of Istanbul. On the other hand, he might not want to bring in the authorities. Violet's accusation that he was trading sex for adoption would be unwelcome, especially because he was already known to be operating outside the strict letter of the law, leastwise, Islamic law.

The best thing for me to do was leave Turkey as soon as possible. It was too late for me to call the airlines in Istanbul. They don't operate on a 24/7 basis like airlines in the U.S. But I could place an international call to Delta in the States. I did so, and the earliest they could get me on a flight to the U.S. was Sunday. Saturday's flight was fully booked in all classes.

I considered flying somewhere just to be out of Istanbul and Beck's reach. Maybe Cairo or Rome. But wasn't I being irrational? Unless he had brass balls—and I didn't hear them clang—Mr. Sad Sack would have trouble walking to the toilet, let alone hunting me down. I did a few more breathing exercises, then called Delta back and booked myself onto Sunday's flight.

Under the strong light in the bathroom, I removed Beck's pubic hairs from my bag with my eyebrow tweezers and placed them in a pill bottle. I couldn't say getting them was an easy way to earn a couple of Gs. Of course, I hadn't earned the money yet. Ashley had to be convinced that Beck was one of her rapists, but his proclivity for the crime, and the intense pleasure it gave him, informed against him. How many victims of his carnal perversions were walking in the world?

It was well into the wee hours before I fell into a fitful sleep. I dreamed of sexual violence. The worst of these dreams was a faceless rape in which the sexual organs undulated in and out of focus like a cheaply made porno flick. At the end, the man ejaculated a fountain of blood, which washed over the sheets and became a river, and both man and victim were swept away. Finally I saw the faces. Afloat in the sea of blood were Thompson Beck and Ashley Bloodworth.

I awoke full of self-reproach. Though I had harmed Beck in patent self-defense, the entire scenario left me feeling soulless. Groggily, over breakfast, I tried to make sense of my dreams. The violence against Beck was bloodless but I may have had Ernest's blood-soaked demise in my subconscious, where logic doesn't always reign.

"I am not guilty," I repeated to myself, emphasizing each word. "Self-preservation is not wrong." By repeating these admonitions, lubricated with several cups of Nescafé instant coffee, I raised my spirits to the point where I could think about how to pass the day. In fact, I raised my spirits to so incautious a level that I contemplated leaving the hotel, rationalizing that Beck would be unlikely to launch a search and destroy mission in broad daylight.

I wanted to shop at the Grand Bazaar. It's the largest covered market in the world, comprising more than four thousand shops on several miles of streets. It also contains mosques, banks, police stations, restaurants and workshops. The nearest entrance is a ten-minute walk from the hotel. I could pass a pleasant day meandering in and out of the stores, eating lunch when I got hungry, and watching people from around the world test their bargaining skills against those of the merchants.

The market was very touristy. Touts badgered tour groups as they climbed down from their buses. The entrances to the bazaar teemed with T-shirt hawkers and rug merchants. The day was unseasonably warm and humid, but the change in weather hadn't penetrated the roof and walls of the enormous structure. Inside it was cool and dry. Away from the entrances in the central portion of the bazaar, the crowds were less thick.

When a person visits the bazaar for the first time it gives every impression of a maze. To the uninitiated eye, every souvenir shop or cell phone store looks like every other one. After a few turns you'd swear you were back where you started, and you might or might not be.

In fact, the bazaar is sensibly laid out. The tiny streets and alleys run parallel or perpendicular to one another. There are no dead ends and at the center is the clearly demarcated Old Bazaar.

I walked to the Old Bazaar, which was old when Istanbul was Constantinople. From there, I wound outwards, taking time to examine wares ranging from gems to leather goods to the latest European fashions.

Many shopkeepers invited me in for the ever-present tulip-glass of tea, and when I got tired I'd take one up on the offer. One time I sat in a shop of souvenirs with the proprietor, a friendly young man who wanted to practice his English. We had a bizarre conversation in which he'd speak English and I'd speak Turkish, each helping the other with grammar and pronunciation.

As I sat sipping tea and improving my language skills, I noticed that every few minutes the same two men would walk by. If you stand in one place in the Grand Bazaar, you'll often see the same people several times. That's because they're lost. By the third time, their faces will have the perplexed look that rats in mazes would have, if rats had facial expressions. But these guys didn't look perplexed; they looked menacing.

Besides, they were Turks. Turks do not get lost in their Grand Bazaar any more than rabbits get lost in their own warrens. One man, the dominant member of the duo, for he walked ever so slightly in front of the other, was tall for a Turk, nearly six feet. He had an ugly scar on one cheek. The other was of average height, thin with a face that tapered into a pointy nose. They appeared to be in their thirties. I didn't think they were out shopping.

I asked my companion in English if he had ever seen them as they passed by a fourth time trying to look casual. He hadn't.

"If they do frighten you, I will call the police," he offered.

I didn't want to deal with the police because I didn't know what had happened to Beck after our encounter. He might, for all I knew, have been found off limits by the palace guards and been obliged to make a police report. He may have filed a complaint against me. In that case, the police, if they found me, would prevent me from leaving the country until the matter was settled.

It was also possible, even likely, that the two men might want nothing more than a chance to pick me up. Blonde women have the reputation—greatly embellished in the fantasies of Turkish males—of being attracted to dark-skinned men. Whatever the case, reason dictated that I should leave the bazaar at once.

When I judged they were halfway through the cycle that would bring them back to the souvenir shop, I thanked the young man for his hospitality and left. I walked as speedily as the density of shoppers permitted, taking first one street, then another, always bearing toward the exit closest to my hotel.

I was a rabbit in a warren with weasels on the loose. As I rounded a corner, the two men came up on either side of me. The tall man took my right arm at the same time that the other one stuck the silver barrel of a .22 caliber revolver in my ribs.

"Come with us or be shot," said Scarface. Ferret face punctuated the command with a jab of the gun barrel.

The .22 is a quiet pistol. I could have been shot in a vital organ and the report gone unnoticed while the men escaped. Many scoff at the low caliber. They forget that Sirhan Sirhan used a .22 to assassinate Robert F. Kennedy with one shot to the head. For the moment, I'd have to go along. If the gun bearer relaxed his concentration for an instant, I'd make my move. Once out of the crowds, my future was dim.

They ushered me toward the east gate that led out in front of the Light of Osman Mosque. If I could help myself in no other way, I'd sprint for the mosque. I might get shot, but it's a rare Muslim, gangster or no, that will commit violence under the eye of Allah.

The men held steady. As the exit came into sight I heard my name called. In front of me were the four Scots I'd helped home the other night. They came toward us in open-armed greeting. When they were near, I said in rapid English, "HelpmeI'mbeingkidnapped." I rotated my body as I spoke, exposing the revolver.

The weasel hesitated, not knowing what to do for a second, but he recovered quickly. He brandished the gun, sweeping the barrel back and forth from one man to the other, and finally pointed it directly at the rugby player.

"Out of way!" he threatened.

The big man's eyebrows rose and his hands came up palms out and arms spread. The hoods had disregarded the woman, to their regret. Presto, her foot exploded into the hand holding the gun. The little pistol looped through the air and landed six feet away. Its owner scrambled after it just as the great Scot launched a straight right fist into the nose of his partner. There was a crunching sound and a cry of pain. The man staggered backward, looking for his friend. The weasel was bending over to retrieve his firearm when the foot flashed again, catching him on the forehead and jerking him upright. The other two Scotsmen closed in on him and he fled. His partner, hand over face, followed close behind. I snatched up the pistol and tucked it into the waistband behind my back under my shirt.

"Truly brilliant, lass," said one of the guys.

"You nailed him straight," said another.

"A Rocky Balboa to the rescue," I added, with a nod to the puncher, who was massaging the knuckles of his right hand.

"Ooh, I like to do a wee bit of boxing of a morning," said the Scot modestly. "But come, Dagny, give us the straight skinny."

The fracas happened so fast that few people noticed. The ones who did were standing agape, not knowing what to do or say. To my tremendous relief, no cops showed up.

"Let's get away from here," I said.

We went into the Bazaar a short way and found a café where we could sit. "Drinks are on me, mates. You're my saviors."

We ordered beer and the Scots waited politely for "the skinny" that I could not give them. I was sure my kidnappers were henchmen of Beck's. True, women are on rare occasions abducted in public and assaulted, especially fair-haired ones. It's true, too, that there is a tiny amount of Kurdish-inspired terrorism that might take the form of a kidnapping. But these incidents are isolated enough to be discounted.

I couldn't figure why a man who ran an orphanage, even a slime-bag like Beck, would employ thugs. On the other hand, he knew the city. The children he rescued—I couldn't resolve the dissonance of rape and rescue—came from the roughest suburbs where such men were for hire. Apparently he hired them, and they tracked me. It was the only explanation that made sense.

I told my rescuers that as far as I knew, it was abduction with a sexual agenda. What else could it be? They didn't buy it, I could tell, but they didn't press the issue. To them I'd always be the mysterious American woman they saved from harm. Their friendship with one another would be cemented by having shared in the experience.

In the café, I learned that the girl was a former Olympic gymnast. To stay limber and fit, she practiced several of the martial arts, including Thai kickboxing. And the mighty Scot, as I came to think of him, was, in fact, a rugby player.

The beer and conversation restored my nerve. I didn't think I'd be accosted again. I repeated my thanks and made to leave. They wouldn't hear of it.

"Don't argue with the mighty Scot," said the mighty Scot, for I had shared my nickname with him. I believe that all four would have slept in my room if I'd asked, but once back at the Basilica I knew I'd feel safe. Uncle Husnu always had one or two sturdy bellmen around. I kissed and hugged each Scot, standing on my tiptoes to reach the mighty Scot, and bending to hug the little kickboxer. We exchanged e-mail addresses and promised to write each other.

"One day," said the mighty Scot, "I'd like to know the rest of the story, if ever you feel like telling it."

I gave him an extra hug and ran my hand through his hair.

"You're a hunk, big boy. Maybe we'll meet again. Thanks. Thanks to you all." I got a little choked up, turned and went inside and gave them one last wave.

"I see you've made some nice friends, my little poppy," said Uncle, who had sidled up to me as I was waving goodbye to the Scots. "I'm so glad you're enjoying yourself. I wish you could stay longer."

"I'm thankful for the time I spent with you, Uncle. I'll try to come back, I promise. And you know, you could come to America. The hotel will survive without you. Come during the off-season. You're welcome any time. John would love to see you again."

I told Uncle that I had work to do in my room and that I'd have supper sent up. I didn't intend to hazard the streets anymore. I asked the concierge to order a cab for early next morning. My flight to the U.S. left at ten. I'd stirred up far more trouble than I could possibly have imagined and I was ill at ease.

My room was at the far end of a long corridor. I was halfway to it when I heard a rustling behind me. It was the two ruffians from the Grand Bazaar. Even at a distance I could see the swollen, discolored face on the larger of the two men. I screamed even as I remembered that Uncle had put me in an unoccupied corridor, and that I might as well save my breath. We all began to run at once, I for the safety of my room, they for the repossession of my person.

CHAPTER 20

I dug out my room key on the dead run, but they'd be upon me while I coped with the lock. At the end of the corridor was a door that I knew led to the ancient underground reservoir—the Cistern Basilica. It was my only chance of escape. I dashed up to it, tore it open and slipped inside, slamming it shut behind me.

The moment the door closed I was in pitch dark. I knew there was a stairway leading down to the water but I couldn't see a thing. The stone stairs were uneven and treacherously slick from the underground dampness. Fearful of falling, I felt for them with my toe, expecting the door behind me to burst open any second.

The men thought they had the pig in the poke. They ran up to the door but they weren't in any kind of a hurry to get in. Teasing me seemed like more fun. One said to the other in Turkish, "The infidel sow is hiding in the linen closet. We've got her now." They both laughed. Then he spoke loudly in English, "You may come quickly now out or we go in and whack you blue-and-black." There was more laughter.

That was the last I heard of linen closets and beatings. My eyes had adjusted to the dim light from below enough for me to negotiate the stairs. At the bottom was a raised walkway that led to the main entrance of the reservoir, the only way out other than the way I'd come in. But I'd noticed on a previous night that the main entrance was gated shut. If I ran to it now and couldn't get through the barrier, I'd be trapped like a rat in a cage. Escape could only be via the back stairs I'd just come down.

I was looking about for a corner in which to hide when I spotted the two dories that were used to show the reservoir to hotel residents. They were moored in the shallow water a few yards from the foot of the stairs.

I unloosed one boat and shoved it into the darkness. I got in the other boat and pushed off in the opposite direction. As my boat glided into the gloom, I strained my ears for signs of the two men.

The sound of cursing came soon enough, followed by the squeaking of rubber soles on wet stone. They didn't bother to keep their voices low as they were speaking in Turkish and would hardly expect me to understand.

They knew they were in the Cistern Basilica. The ancient reservoir, though primarily a tourist attraction, is well known to Istanbulers. One man asked the other why it was deserted. His friend replied that perhaps business was poor. It was apparent that they had assumed I'd escaped via the main entrance—a fact I was counting on—and both began to run on the walkway that led to it.

I had let my boat drift a fair distance from the stairs, though they were my only path to safety. As soon as the men took off running for the main entrance, I began to row frantically back to the mooring. But the flat-bottomed dory, which was happy to glide in a straight line under the impetus of a shove, moved haltingly when I manned the oars. Before I could get back, the men discovered that the main entrance was barred and knew that I must still be in the cavern.

They were rushing back to the stairway. They cast gray silhouettes in the meager light—short Weasel a step ahead of tall Scarface. My race with them would end in a tie, I judged, and in this league a tie was a loss. I retreated to a dark corner, and lest reflections off my hair, jewelry or clothes give me away, lay down in the dory.

In this position I planned to cogitate my next move, but as I slid flat something dug into the small of my back. It was the .22 pistol. I'd completely forgotten about it. This would alter the rules of the game.

I was in a far corner of the cistern behind two plinths carved with Medusa heads, one notably upside down. It's a popular photo subject with tourists. Now, the blocks of carved stone gave me a temporary hiding place, and very temporary it was. My adversaries, aware that the only way out was the way we'd all come in, were stalking me. Each took a different walkway, staring into the murky gloom for clues to my whereabouts. The supporting columns cast obfuscating shadows, and the men had to search painstakingly to make sure that they kept between the exit and me.

The water in the cistern is about two feet deep. That's enough to give tourists the impression of what it must have been like when it was a functional reservoir some fifteen centuries ago, but not so deep as to be hazardous. I slid silently out of the boat into the water, holding the pistol in my hand to keep it dry. I needed to know if it was loaded and it was too dark to tell without opening the cylinder. I did so slowly, carefully, without a sound. I could feel the backs of the cartridges. It had a full load. I closed it with equal care, but the click as it reseated, magnified by the stone and water, gave away my location.

The Medusa head pillars hid me from the view of the approaching man, now alerted to my presence. He came slowly, scanning the water and peering around each column. I sidled round the Medusa heads the way a squirrel sidles round a tree to keep it between him and a predator. As the man turned the corner, I gave the dory a shove in the direction he now was walking. He grunted and sped up to pursue the boat.

I climbed out of the water onto the walkway. I had a clear path to the exit. But it was impossible to run quietly as my sneakers were full of water and made squishy sounds with every step. I tiptoed warily towards the stairway, taking every opportunity to shroud myself in the shadows cast by the supporting columns.

I was halfway to safety when he caught up with the boat. Seeing it was empty, he saw my trick. He shouted to his partner and started to run back. I sprinted forward. I had a good lead on both men but not, I feared, good enough. I shouted in Turkish that I had a gun, hoping to make them hesitate. To make the point, I fired it toward the second man who was running to cut me off, and then turned to fire over my shoulder at my immediate pursuer.

I had as little chance of hitting a man as those deputies in old westerns have of hitting the bad guys they're chasing while seated on the backs of galloping horses. It was a wonder to me that they didn't shoot their own horse in the head half the time. But my shots had the desired effect. Both men stopped in their tracks. Unfortunately, as I twisted back round, I slipped on the wet stones and went sprawling. I lost my grip on the pistol and it slid into the water with a kerplunk.

I didn't even have time to say, "Shit!" The man behind me, quick as a ferret, tackled me as I rose to my feet. I threw an elbow at his head and stunned him but he kept his grip long enough for his partner to arrive and overpower me.

"You come with us, please," said one of them in Turkish, "or else we cut you up and drown you in the dark." He brandished a combat knife with a nasty-looking serrated blade.

They frog marched me to the foot of the stairs but before we started up we heard footsteps descending. Both men cursed under their breath but it was too late to retreat. I felt them tense for a fight.

They let go of me just as Uncle Husnu accompanied by two burly men in hotel uniforms came out of the darkness of the stairway. My kidnappers were about to spring when I stepped up to Uncle.

"What's going on here?" he demanded.

"I can explain, Uncle," I said. "I just wanted to show my two friends the cistern, but it's closed to the public. I took the liberty of using the hotel's private entrance. I'm terribly sorry if I did the wrong thing."

Uncle looked skeptical and said, "One of the bellmen noticed that the door to the cistern was open and asked me about it. Did I hear gunshots?"

"Certainly not, Uncle. You know the echoes down here can magnify sound. It might've been one of the boats bumping."

Uncle looked around. "Where *are* the boats?" he asked.

"Oh, I'll explain that in a minute. The boys here need to get back to their, uh, jobs."

I addressed the two hoodlums. "Thanks for coming to visit me, guys. It was great seeing you. You won't mind if I don't walk you to the lobby? I need to change my clothes." I gave each man a friendly squeeze on the arm and a gentle push up the stairs. They edged by the two bellmen, more than happy to leave.

With an ever-growing look of disbelief on his face, Uncle asked, "Why are you soaking wet, my little porpoise? And why did that man's face look as though it had been run over by a dolmus?" Then, in a more avuncular manner, "You must change your clothes and come to the office and have a raki, my dear. You will explain it all to your simpleton uncle."

Uncle sent his two men to retrieve the dories and the two of us climbed up to the hallway in front of my room. I promised to join him downstairs for a drink as soon as I'd cleaned up.

The raki warmed me both physically and mentally. I had to be evasive with Uncle, and Uncle knew it. All I could do was to explain that I could not afford to get mixed up with the police. Inevitably, it would postpone my return to the States. I pleaded for his understanding and silence in the matter.

He insisted only on one thing, "...and to this I will not take the answer no. My two men will accompany you if you leave the hotel, and they will drive you to the airport tomorrow, and they will stay with you until you board your plane. Do not argue with me, my little donkey."

He sighed, sipped his tea, and went on. "I'm sorry those men could walk into the hotel unchallenged. If anything happened to you because of my negligence, Dagny, I could never enjoy another moment of happiness in this life. I thank Allah for your safety. God is great!"

Uncle had dinner for the two of us brought to my room that night. His chef prepared one of my favorite Turkish dishes called adana kebap, which means spicy-hot roast meatballs. When the meal was over, Uncle rang for a bellman, and over my protests posted him outside my door. There was no arguing with Uncle, who could be as mulish as he thought I was.

Alone in my room, under the protection of the sturdy bellman, I brought the Ashley files up to date. There was plenty to say about "Tom." I entered the physical description of the assailants who had twice tried to kidnap me, and wrote a synopsis of those events. I speculated that the two hoods had been hired by Beck for the purpose of revenge. I shuddered to think of what form that might have taken.

I reviewed the wisdom of letting them go rather than pressing charges and having them arrested. While I hated to leave the two criminals at large, I also didn't want Uncle or his men injured in the fight that would surely have ensued had we tried to restrain them.

More selfishly, I had to admit, I didn't want the police involved. Apart from detaining me as a material witness, they'd almost surely discover my connection to Beck. That might lead to questions about my own conduct. For all I knew, Beck had enough influence to get his guys off, and me charged with a crime. Why shouldn't he tell the authorities that I had tried to seduce him as a bribe to help me cheat the adoption process, and assaulted him when he refused to go along? Everything considered, letting them go free still seemed like the best thing I could have done. Ironically, the worst effect of my decision would soon befall the two men whom it appeared to benefit.

True to his word, Uncle had me escorted to the airport the next morning. His men stuck to me like paparazzi, relinquishing custody only when I entered the passenger secure area. I was paranoid enough to scan my fellow travelers for anyone resembling Beck's hit men. Beck would have to be nearly prescient to guess I was on this flight, and thirsty for revenge indeed to send someone to America to get even with me.

The flight to New York was uneventful, if long, and there was no pleasure in getting back on a plane to complete the trip to Raleigh. I nearly missed my connection because JFK was so mobbed, what with it being Sunday and people flying everywhere to start the workweek. Even in my relatively short lifetime, globalization had turned the once rare and exotic occasion of a transoceanic flight into a mundane practice.

I called Janet from my car on the way home from the airport to ask her to drop off Hank and Midas. I missed them and I didn't want to spend the night alone. When I got home, Janet was just leaving. She took one look at me and said, "Boy, do you need a good night's sleep!" Then, as an afterthought, "and a hug." She administered the latter while telling me how good the greys had been, except Hank had lacerated an ankle and had had to be bandaged.

When Janet left, I cuddled with them, giving Hank some extra rubs because, like me, he had a wounded limb. Greyhounds are thin-skinned, which makes them susceptible to all sorts of superficial injuries. I lectured them both on the need to take better care of themselves, but received only quizzical looks.

I called Ashley. She had exciting news. DNA testing had confirmed that Harry was the father of Jeanne-Renée.

"But not of Benton?" I asked with surprise.

"No," said Ashley. "I might've been unclear on that point. The children are fraternal twins. It's not all that uncommon—about one in a hundred births, so I've been told. Two distinct eggs are each fertilized by individual sperm. In my case, the sperm came from different men."

When I asked her what, if anything, she intended to do about Harry, she was evasive. It wasn't my office to pry into her affairs, though the opposite was not true. She was keen to hear about every detail of my activities in Turkey. I promised her a written report, but under prodding gave a sketch of my actions. She was particularly pleased with how I finally obtained the DNA sample, and said several times how she wished she could have done it, and how much he had it coming.

Ashley asked if I'd drive to Kinston to deliver the vial of hairs. "It's not that I mind dispatching a courier," she explained, "but we ought to have an in-person talk before you embark on your final quest. 'Third man pays for all,'" she quipped cheerfully as she rang off.

BOOK THREE

DICK

CHAPTER 21

In the morning I slogged through my s-mail and e-mail, trashing the junk and triaging the rest into do-now, do-later, and do-much-later. I slashed and burned my way through the do-now list. The last message was from Ashley and had directions to Hatfield Hall. I printed it and stuffed it in my handbag.

Kinston, a city of 25,000, is a marketing and shipping point for agriculture some 80 miles southeast of Raleigh. Ashley told me her ancestors settled there before the American Revolution, trading first in tobacco, cotton, corn and livestock, and later in chemicals, textiles and china. Her ancestor, Fremont Bloodworth, was so ardent a patriot that in 1776 he insisted that the chartered name of the city, Kingston with a "g," be changed to Kinston to sever any associations with the British king.

According to Ashley, the Bloodworths had fallen on hard times recently. You wouldn't have guessed it from seeing Hatfield Hall, the family estate. It was so grand that a major Hollywood studio had paid them a large fee to use its façade for external shots of Tara in a remake of *Gone with the Wind* that was never completed.

Hatfield Hall stood at the end of a quarter-mile-long, oak-lined private drive. Halfway to the house a spur led off through the trees to a helicopter pad. Beyond that was a great expanse of land containing orchards, a corral, and dozens of acres under cultivation.

Ashley was awaiting me on the steps of the grand front entrance. She wore jeans, a white turtleneck of luminous material, a loose fitting black cardigan, and cowboy boots—perfect attire for the brisk autumn day. When she saw my car, she came down to the driveway and showed me where to park.

We entered the house through a side porch full of hanging plants, and passed through a large sliding-glass door to an inner room whose décor was that of a CEO's office. The walls were mahogany-paneled and generously covered with richly framed artworks. Bookcases and credenzas of polished wood lined two of the walls. A graceful ivory-colored sculpture of praying hands stood on a majestic pedestal of carved ebony in one corner. In another corner was a cluster of upholstered, leather armchairs. A grand executive desk and chair faced out from one wall to command the entire room.

Ashley invited me to take one of the leather chairs while she settled into another, crossed her legs, and drew a lime-green cigarette out of the gold cigarette case. A Grateful Dead song played softly in the background through invisible speakers. Sunbeams glinted off the leaves of the hanging plants as they swung gently in the autumn breezes.

Though I had told Ashley a good part of my story on the telephone, she nonetheless had me retell it again in its entirety, seeming to draw pleasure from the words as she drew down her cigarette. I concluded by handing her a written report, the final page of which was a schedule of my fee plus expenses.

She read the report carefully while I watched, and when she had finished she stepped over to her desk and wrote a check for the full amount. She included the $4,000 bonus for the two DNA samples. "We should be square now, except you still have the original advance."

"That's right," I acknowledged.

I'd earned some good bucks for a few weeks' work, but Ashley left me little time to celebrate.

"Does that bring us up to date, then?" she asked, immediately upon my putting the check in my wallet.

"As far as I'm concerned," I answered.

"Tell me," she said, standing in front of me so I had to look up, "Do you have any leads on tracking down number three? I guess we can call him Dick, wouldn't you say?"

"I really haven't had a chance to work on it. I've had some luck up to now. If it keeps up, yes, I'll have some leads."

"And you've not told anyone that you're working for me, I assume, per our agreement?"

"Of course not."

"Especially not this Harry Angelica or J. T. Beck?"

"Absolutely not," I said, annoyed.

Ashley was undisturbed by my pique. She played the boss's role well, right down to her body language. She took some steps backward and half sat on the edge of her desk and folded her arms.

"So, what do you think Beck thinks about what you did to him?"

"I can't imagine he thinks anything other than that he met a woman who would fight rather than be raped."

"But you let him get so far. I wonder whether he asks himself why you didn't just kick him in the balls earlier, since he knows you're capable of it. Maybe he wonders why you jerked out half his pubic hair."

"Look, he can wonder away. I tell you that he wasn't aware of my purpose, nor that I had any knowledge or connection to some girl he assaulted ten years ago. You'll just have to trust me to do my job. As to hair pulling, isn't that how women fight? He probably thinks I'm the vixen from Hell."

She slid up to sit fully on the edge of the desk and lit another cigarette with the harp-shaped lighter. She inhaled deeply, a look of skepticism on her face, and exhaled a long stream of bluish smoke.

"Then why send those men after you?"

"Revenge," I said.

She raised her eyebrows, not satisfied with my one-word answer.

I repeated, "Revenge, pure and simple, and certainly nothing that has anything to do with you."

I gave her my "any more annoying questions?" look.

She had one. "What do you think Harry thinks about his missing shaver?"

"Oh Christ, Ashley, I don't know, but unless you tell him, he can't possibly associate it with you."

"I don't want him to know about Jeanne-Renée, or that I know who he is, that's all."

"He had a lot of people in and out of his place. Anyone could've borrowed or stolen the damn thing. I didn't leave tracks."

"What if Angelica and Beck compare notes?" she said, punctuating the air with her cigarette.

To this question I did not have a pat answer. The two men knew each other. They were friends and cousins. Yet they had little in common. The one was a filmmaker and the other ran an orphanage. They lived in different countries. How far apart can you get? And even supposing they corresponded, say by e-mail, would Harry be likely to tell his cousin that he ordered his bodyguard to eliminate some female and it backfired? Would J.T. Beck be likely to tell his cousin that he tried to rape some babe and ended up getting kicked in the balls? And even if all that communication occurred, would one of them describe me so accurately that the other would say, "Hey, that's the cunt who got my bodyguard killed," or "Hey, that's the she-devil who bashed me."

I shared these thoughts with Ashley, and she was about to pursue it further when someone knocked at the door, opening it at the same time. A distinguished-looking man with graying temples and wearing a blue, pinstriped shirt open at the collar appeared in the doorway.

"Oh, excuse me, honey, I didn't know you had a guest. How'd you get by me unnoticed?"

"We came in through the verandah, Daddy," said Ashley. "This is Dagny Jamison. She's doing some private investigation for me."

Her father came into the office. His steely blue eyes, ramrod-straight back and deep baritone voice as mellow as aged Kentucky bourbon fit the image of the family patrician.

"I'm Taylor Bloodworth," he said, "Please don't get up."

I stood up anyway to shake hands. "I'm pleased to meet you, sir," I said.

"I'm pleased to meet you as well," he said. "Tell me, what do you investigate, Miss Jamison?"

Ashley slid off the desk and walked over to us. "Dagny is doing some background checks for some of my investments, Daddy. We're just finishing up."

"Oh, I see. Well, you're welcome to Hatfield Hall, Ms. Jamison. If I can do anything to help you in any way, please don't hesitate to ask." With that, Mr. Bloodworth left us standing alone in the office.

"If you're not comfortable with my investigation..." I began, picking up where we'd left off, but Ashley waved me aside.

"It's fine," she said. "You're doing just fine. Keep me apprised of your progress with the third man."

I took that to mean the meeting was over. I asked to use the washroom and indeed, consistent with the CEO aspects of Ashley's office, there was one artfully concealed in the paneled wall behind her desk.

A lavatory isn't generally a place that bowls you over with décor, but Ashley's proved the exception. The fixtures were farmhouse-style brass polished to a bright sheen. The porcelain was faintly pink without being garish. Matching throw rugs safeguarded the user from slipping on the marble-tiled floor. The tiny room was arranged so that one's attention was unerringly drawn to an original oil painting on the wall opposite the washbasin and crystal mirror. An engraved plate named the artist as Titorelli the Painter, and the place and year, Prague, 1925. The subject was the head of St. John the Baptist on a silver platter. It wasn't until well into my drive home an hour later that the full significance of that particular piece of art in that particular location dawned on me, and I had to hand it to Ashley for having a wacky, nautical sense of humor.

When I emerged, Ashley was on the side porch, waving her arm slowly. A private-school bus was making a U-turn about halfway down the long driveway. It had let off two children who were walking slowly toward the main entrance of the house carrying full book bags. Ashley walked out to meet them, with me trailing uncertainly behind.

Jeanne-Renée and Benton were like no fraternal twins I'd ever seen. The girl was light skinned, with blonde hair and a lovely, wide-eyed Nordic face. She already showed the promise of both her parents' good looks, for Harry, for all his evildoing, was handsome.

Benton was shorter than his sister, dark in color, narrow-eyed, small-mouthed. Where Jeanne-Renée emanated light, Benton seemed to absorb it, making him appear smaller than his actual size. Taken alone, he wouldn't be considered unattractive. His features were delicate and his body was well proportioned, if somewhat diminutive. He suffered by comparison with the budding beauty of his sister. I took a mental snapshot of him that might help me recognize Dick, if it ever came to that. I was certain that J. Thompson Beck was not the father of the dark, wiry child.

After greeting them coolly, Ashley hustled the children on their way. She turned and was surprised to see that I'd followed her. She escorted me to my car where we exchanged the usual "keep in touch if anything new happens." It seemed odd to me at the time that Ashley didn't introduce her children. But I doubted it was an accident. Little that Ashley did or did not do was by chance.

My stitches were itching like mad. When I got back to Raleigh I drove directly to Southeast Plastic Surgery PLLC and begged them to remove the damn things. It was the end of the day and I didn't have an appointment, but one of the nurses was kind enough to stay after hours. The lacerations had healed nicely. I could already see that the scars would be the thinnest of white lines, not one of them straight, but rather meandering around my wrist and thumb like brooks in a hilly terrain.

It was dinnertime when I finally got home. I was far too jetlagged to do anything other than eat, love the dogs, play the piano for five minutes, and crash. In the morning I updated my case file and by the time I'd finished, the banks had opened. I walked to my bank and deposited Ashley's check, keeping back just the right amount to replenish the original cash advance.

I turned my attention to the third man and was able to take advantage of some earlier work. I'd already highlighted the Dicks and related names and initials in Harry's purloined address book. There were five of them. Now I had only to crosscheck those names with the 31 Dick records from Marquis University. Lady Luck was on my side. I found a single match: Richard Sangfroid.

Sangfroid was in the same graduating class as Harry Angelica and J. Thompson Beck. After his graduation he attended the Marquis Medical School, where he earned his M.D. The last entry in his school record indicated that he had accepted a residency in surgery and transplantation biology at the teaching hospital of Los Angeles University.

Both Harry's and the university's record gave an address in Los Angeles. It appeared as though a trip to the "city of the angels" was in the offing. That suited me. I had attended UCLA and knew the city well. But best of all was that I would be able to see Charles, for he lived in Santa Barbara, only about a two-hour drive from L.A. I was psyched.

Throughout this case so far, the evidence leading to Ashley's rapists had been circumstantial. Now, with Harry known to be the father of Jeanne-Renée, and Beck known to be Harry's cousin and to have a missing toe, there was no doubt of those two. Dick Sangfroid was linked to them through the university and the entry in Harry's address book. Furthermore, the "Tom, Dick, and Harry" remark that Little had made to deepen Ashley's misery took on heightened significance now that two of the names were accounted for.

Two other minor points that had found their way into my case records now looked significant. One was the use of the nickname *Frenchy*. The name *Sangfroid* is French, and Ashley's meager description of Little fit the Gallic stereotype—shorter in height than average, dark in color, a smoker. Fatboy's remark about Little having ice water in his veins for the impassive manner in which he tortured Ashley fit the name, for in French "Sangfroid" means "cold blood."

I called the hospital where Dr. Sangfroid had done his residency but all I could learn was that he was no longer employed there. They were not permitted to give out additional information. At worst, the trail was now a mere three or four years old, a big improvement over the ten years I'd started out with. I was certain I could track him down, especially with Charles's help. Being a medical examiner, Charles was in the milieu of physicians and surgeons.

I decided to fly to California, find Dr. Richard Sangfroid, and try to determine whether he was the third man. It was morning on the west coast and Charles would just be arriving at his office. I called him and told him of my intention. He was exuberant at the prospect of seeing me.

I booked everything I needed on the Internet. Twenty-four hours later, I found myself in an airline seat on final approach into LAX, peering through the brownish haze that sat, as usual, atop the L.A. basin.

Charles was to meet me in the Regal Biltmore Hotel in downtown Los Angeles. It's centrally located and less than ten minutes from the hospital where Sangfroid once worked. As I neared the hotel in my rental car, my excitement mounted. It had little to do with tracking down Dick Sangfroid, and everything to do with seeing Charles. I'd suppressed my feelings for him during the past month to focus on my work. Now that we were about to see each other, my love welled up and drowned all my thoughts except those about him.

He was awaiting me in the lobby. I rushed into his arms and he took me in a clasp that would do credit to an Alaskan grizzly bear. He released me when he saw that I was turning purple, then held me again more gently and whispered some very sweet somethings in my ear.

The lobby of the Biltmore captured the flavor of ante-bellum Los Angeles, the "bellum" being World War II. The expansive lobby with its sturdy, lush furniture and rich adornments was a reminder of the opulence of the period. Autographed photos of presidents who had stayed at the Biltmore were on prominent display. Franklin Delano Roosevelt had taken a suite there when he came to Los Angeles, as had presidents Truman, Kennedy, Johnson, Ford, and Carter.

Our room was on the fifth floor of the middle tower. We gave our luggage over to the bell captain, who met us a long five minutes later in the room. He bustled around, puffing pillows here and removing invisible flecks of dust there. He explained in tedious detail the use of the room electronics and minibar, while I shifted my weight from one foot to the other, paying no attention whatever to his babbling. I almost took back the fiver I gave him at the door when he winked at me as I deployed the do-not-disturb sign.

"About Richard Sangfroid," began Charles.

I put first my hand, then my mouth, over his mouth. Abstention makes the heart grow bolder.

"First things first," I whispered.

Later, much later, we staggered outside, famished. We crossed Grand Avenue to Pershing Square and looked back at the recently restored hotel. The three towers facing the square, with their red brick and cream-colored stone façades and terra cotta overhanging roofs, reflect a Spanish renaissance style that captures the Hispanic heritage of the city. The Biltmore, I learned from brochures, has been a location site for more than 250 TV shows and motion pictures, including *Chinatown, A Star is Born,* and *Beverly Hills Cop.* Staying there makes you feel like a minor player in the history of the city.

We hoofed over to Broadway and then turned northeast toward Little Tokyo, where superb Japanese food may be found. We drank warm sake and ate shabu-shabu at the Koharu, an intimate "bisutoro" on First Street. No shop was talked, and when we returned to our room, we put third things third.

CHAPTER 22

Only after breakfast was over did Charles tell me about Dr. Sangfroid. I learned that, even as we sat at our ease in the plush chairs of the Biltmore's porch restaurant, the ruined remains of two California Breakfasts pushed aside, Dick Sangfroid was less than two miles distant.

Two years ago he had accepted the post of Director of the Western Regional Organ Bank Clearinghouse. This organization matches donated organs to qualified recipients, and is expected to follow the guidelines set down by the United Network for Organ Sharing. In effect, the criteria for receiving donated body parts are to be strictly medical with no regard to cost. The post is particularly sensitive in that there are always rich and powerful people who want to use their position to "cut in line," so to speak. One job of the director was to protect the integrity of the system.

Sangfroid had had two crises in his tenure as director, one offsetting the other. The first came when a Los Angeles newspaper suggested that he lived so far beyond his means as to cast suspicion on his impartiality. It was hinted, archly, that he took bribes. Sangfroid lived in a multimillion-dollar house built by Frank Lloyd Wright, and belonged to an upscale members-only country club with dubious connections to the sex industry. Such a life style, the reporter wrote, must mean duplicity in the selection of transplant recipients.

Sangfroid had countered these charges by noting that he had family money and anyway, it wasn't anybody's business how he lived his personal life. The public reacted favorably to this curmudgeonly defense. In California, people are sick to death of gauzy allegations on one side and vaporous excuses on the other. They more or less approved of Sangfroid's "attitude."

What put the coup de grâce to the first crisis was the second, which occurred six months later. Sangfroid claimed he was menaced by two hoodlums, who had ordered him to approve a liver transplant for a member of an organized crime family. Failing that, they said, he, Sangfroid, would have his liver forcibly removed without benefit of anesthesia.

Sangfroid went directly to the authorities and reported the coercion. A rival newspaper broke the story. Their reporter lionized him as a man of unbending principle. Sangfroid used the threats as a reason to institute 24-hour protection, and now lives like an American diplomat in the Middle East, traveling nowhere without a bodyguard. As for his private life, it was effectively off bounds to the law whose duty was to protect him, not investigate him.

The offices of the Organ Bank Clearinghouse (OBC) were located in a building on Wilshire Boulevard overlooking MacArthur Park. It was, as Charles had noted, barely two miles from the Biltmore. It took just over five minutes to drive there. I parked in a pay lot and the two of us walked to the building.

The OBC was on the third floor and was accessible only by elevator. Security guards patrolled the lobby and let no one into the elevators without a badge or a badged escort. I tested the waters by pleading to one of the guards that we wanted to sign up for organ donor cards, and if he didn't mind, we'd nip up to the third floor and sign away our guts.

"No way," was the terse response, with a nod in the direction of the house phone. I could call upstairs if I wished, and if they wished, someone would escort us.

I was dying to have a look at the man. If he was six foot six, blond-haired and blue-eyed, my search was in vain. I used the phone to call them up. The person who answered told me that their offices didn't deal with the public. She gave me a number to call for information. Turning my back to the guard so as not to be overheard, I asked if the famous Dr. Sangfroid, whom I'd read about in the newspapers, still worked there. She politely, but firmly, informed me that that was none of my business.

There was nothing to do but leave the building. I took Charles's hand and we crossed the street to MacArthur Park. The park, named for the World War II general, surrounds a beautiful, manmade lake. One can rent electric boats that glide so gently over the water that a child may safely take the helm. Landlubbers of all ages lounge in the grass under trees, or sit on the brightly painted benches that line the gravel walkways at the waterside. Food vendors ply the hungry with tempting treats, often selling goodies to boaters who pull up alongside the shoreline.

As we walked hand in hand in silence, I had a thought.

"Didn't you say Sangfroid lives in a Frank Lloyd Wright house?"

"That's right," said Charles.

"Then we ought to be able to find it, shouldn't we? All Frank Lloyd Wright's houses must all be in a register somewhere. Everything he built is a national treasure and protected by a preservation society. I think they all have their own names even—I mean the houses."

"Now you mention it," said Charles, "I think the newspaper article said where he lived. And there was a photo of him, too."

We had the same thought: "The library."

Conveniently, the Los Angeles Public Library is a few blocks from the Biltmore on Fifth Street. We left the car with the hotel's parking valet, and headed out on foot. On the way, I asked Charles if he remembered when Sangfroid had gained his notoriety. He thought it was the first part of the year. He remembered thinking that here we were in the last year of the 20th century, and the gangsters were still pulling the same load of rubbish that they pulled in the last year of the previous century.

"Plus ça change, plus c'est la même chose," he noted philosophically.

"Yeah, some things don't change much," I said.

Once inside the library, and having taken a minute to admire the splendid entrance hall, we followed the signs to the periodicals section. The lady in charge showed us the storage bins of microfilm and gave us a brief lesson on using the readers. She apologized for the obsolete technology and assured us that in the future the newspapers would be on DVDs. Given that the woman was at least as old as the Central Library Building, whose archway keystone had 1926 chiseled on it, you had to admire her sprightliness and "get-with-it" attitude.

We found the microfilm we needed. Each spool contained one month's worth of past editions. The search was tedious because we had to look at each page of each section of national news and metro news. More than that, actually. Since a Frank Lloyd Wright house was part of the story, we needed to check out the various features sections as well.

We sat at adjacent machines. Charles took January, I took February, and we began our search. Those months yielded nothing. While scanning March, I was stopped not by a headline but by a photograph of a man whose resemblance to Benton Bloodworth was unmistakable. It was Dr. Richard Sangfroid. The text beneath the photo lauded his intent to uphold the integrity of the OBC, blathering on about his bravery under fire, etc. It said nothing about the house he lived in.

"But of course not," said Charles, slapping his forehead. "They wouldn't be so crass as to publish the man's address in the same article that reports his death threat. The house was in the other paper, the one that didn't like him. It must've been the previous summer or fall."

"It's okay," I said. "This photo of Sangfroid leaves no doubt that he's the man I'm looking for, so the time wasn't wasted."

We traded in the current batch of microfilm for a new batch covering the months in question. Once more we began searching, page by page, week by week.

It was Charles's turn, after an hour of spooling, to make the find. "That's a stroke of luck," he said. "I nearly spooled past it."

So there it was: a scathing article about Sangfroid. It began by stating that only a person of unquestioned probity should fill the position of director of the OBC. The journalist asked, rhetorically to be sure, how it was possible for Dr. Sangfroid to possess the financial resources to own a multi-million-dollar home. This led to the merest of suggestions—mere enough to avoid a libel suit—that perhaps the good doctor "cooked the books" in favor of wealthy clients. To emphasize the point about Sangfroid's home, an archived photo from the 1930s of the noteworthy Fillmore House was in a side panel.

Another hour in the library rewarded us with information about the house. It was named for its first occupant, President Millard Fillmore's great-grandson, for whom it was built in the 1920s. An old *Architectural Digest* filled in some details:

> The home manifests the superb naturalness that was Frank Lloyd Wright's trademark. It is set smartly into the side of a hill above Silver Lake. However, it is thought that the great architect's role in its design was minimal. Rather, two of his protégés—Messrs. William Jenkins Williams and Bartholomew Babbitt—were the architects of record. They had clearly followed the master's lead, with a result that bears the unmistakable imprint of a Wright-architected home.

"I wonder what the place looks like now," I said as we were strolling back to the hotel.

"There's still some daylight left," said Charles. "We could have a look."

"I'd rather see it tomorrow," I said. "By the time we get the car, fight traffic, and find the place, it'll be nearly dark in the hills. Anyway," I added, "I know of a very romantic restaurant, pardon me, bistro, on Melrose Avenue."

The next morning we drove to the Silver Lake district. It's a maze of winding streets and cul-de-sacs in the Hollywood Hills, about four miles northwest of City Hall. Overlooking the lake are some of the most interesting and costly homes in Southern California.

The Fillmore House had the concrete-block structure typical of Wright's work of the 1920s era, just as the *Digest* had described it. It was difficult to find a spot from which we might view the house *in toto*. The problem was that Sangfroid or a previous owner had turned the place into a compound. High, imposing fences surrounded most of it, and a steel-barred electric gate protected the main entrance. We had to drive to different vantage points around the property to fully appreciate how seamlessly integrated the house was with the hill into which it was built.

A security guard was posted at the gate, and as we drove by a third time his suspicions were aroused. He pulled out his cell phone and moments later an LAPD squad car fell in behind us, blue lights blazing. I pulled over to the curb and shut off the engine. The cruiser stopped behind me and two officers stepped out. One kept back while the other put me through the "license and registration" routine. When he asked me bluntly why I appeared to be "casing" the neighborhood, I told him that we were interested in Frank Lloyd Wright houses. He explained that there had been some security problems with the home and the owner was wary, but if we'd care to look at the house through the gate, he and his partner would accompany us.

Though any notion of meeting Dick Sangfroid by walking up to his front door and knocking seemed remote, I could see no reason to refuse the cop's offer. Perhaps something would occur to me. We drove back to the front gate of the mansion. The cops exchanged a few words with the security guard and drove off. The guard, a pleasant enough fellow, opened a door-within-a-gate and allowed us to walk a few paces onto the grounds for a better look.

Now that I was outside the car, the view was different, and it wasn't the Fillmore House that arrested my attention, though I tried not to show it. Appearing above us about a quarter-mile away, clearly visible over a row of eucalyptus trees, were the two top stories of an apartment building. Small balconies jutted out from the individual units. Residents would have a bird's-eye view of the entire Sangfroid compound. This must have bothered the security people, but they could do little about it.

After an appropriate amount of oohing and aahing at the house, not all of which was disingenuous, we got back in the car. I suggested we try to find the front of the building that we'd seen looming. This was not easy in the twisted, irrational roads of the Hollywood Hills. After ten minutes of U-turns, fruitless winding, and equally fruitless expletives, we hadn't found it. I felt as though I was in one of those alienation dreams where everything you try is thwarted.

Eventually, one of our random turns—for we'd abandoned all attempts at a logical search—put us on the street that fronted the building. A large sign identified it as "The Vista du Lac Service

Apartments." A smaller sign said "Rentals—monthly or more." Despite the foreign-sounding name, the building was pure California, from the stucco façade to the potted palms surrounding the swimming pool just visible off to the side.

There was a rental office on the site. A "service apartment," I found out, is for people who need to stay in the area for too long a time to stay in a hotel, and too short a time to lease a regular apartment. It's completely furnished, right on down to knick-knacks on the mantel, and it contains a fully functioning kitchen with dishes, flatware, pots, pans, and small appliances. Daily maid service relieves the resident of any domestic chores apart from cleaning up after meals.

I asked if there were any single units available on the top two floors with a view overlooking the city. There was one. It was currently rented but, as luck would have it, the occupant was due to move out the next day.

We took the elevator to the sixth and topmost floor where the agent admitted me to flat 6G. Within a moment, I knew it would do for my purposes. Across the smallish living room on the far wall was a sliding glass door leading to a small porch. It afforded the best view yet of the Fillmore House. From the balcony, I could keep the entire property under surveillance, including the entrance gate.

As we rode around the streets of the Silver Lake district, I'd been thinking about how to gain access to Dick Sangfroid. He was inaccessible at work, inaccessible at home, and most likely inaccessible at times in-between. I had no inkling of what his private life was like. Did he hang out in bars or clubs? Did he attend parties? Did he have people over?

I couldn't stake him out at work. A car parked in that neighborhood for more than a few hours over the course of one or two days would attract attention, even without a blonde occupant. I considered trying to meet him when he went out for lunch, if he did. But then what? Ask him for a blood sample? Pull some hair and run? How about invite him to a hotel room and initiate intimacy until I got a sample? No thanks. My experience with Fatboy Beck had put me off that stratagem, and besides, when I was with Charles such thoughts were repugnant to the point of being unthinkable even while brainstorming.

As in all professions, when the going gets tough, the tough return to the basics. For private investigation, that means observation and patience, and the observation is best carried out surreptitiously. What better place for that than the very place that I stood having these thoughts? From here I could watch Sangfroid's comings and goings, monitor his visitors, and spy on him when he went outside. If I could learn something about his habits, I might give myself a chance to devise a means of recovering a DNA sample.

"What is the rental fee?" I asked the agent, "and if I lease the unit, what is the soonest I can move in?"

"It's $4,000 for one month, $10,000 for three months, $18,000 for six months. Beyond that, the rent is negotiated."

Charles sucked air through his teeth.

"As to when you can take occupancy," said the agent, ignoring Charles, "I could let you move in a week from today. We've got to clean the place, change the lock, and check inventory after Mr. Nishida moves out."

"Hmm, if you don't mind, I'd like to move in Monday if that's humanly possible. I'll take it for one month and pay $4,300 in advance. The extra $300 should take care of the weekend cleaning and the locksmith."

The agent was about to open his mouth to object, for it would be extra work on his part.

"…and for being so helpful," I continued, "please accept this." I folded two C-notes into his hand.

He brightened visibly. "Yes, ma'am, I mean miss, uh…"

"Jamison. Dagny Taggart Jamison. Shall we go downstairs and sign a lease?"

Charles observed the transaction with a look of adorable incredulity. He wasn't as used to seeing Ashley's money being spent as I was.

When we returned to the car he slid over and nuzzled my neck, whispering, "Mmm, I want you to know I loved you even before I knew you were rich."

I laughed and ran my hand through his hair. "You'll be disappointed if you're after my money. Maybe I need to fix you up with Ashley."

"No way, José."

On the way back to the Biltmore, I explained my plan for spying on Sangfroid. Charles couldn't find any flaws in it. Then I explained my short-term plan. It was for us to drive to Ensenada, Mexico, for a weekend of R and R. He found nothing wrong with that, either.

CHAPTER 23

Ensenada is a small resort about 175 miles south of Los Angeles in Baja California, Mexico. Visitors may enjoy both the tourist side of Ensenada and its Mexican village side. The several excellent hotels on the oceanfront are convenient for sunning, surfing and sailing. More English is spoken there than in many parts of Los Angeles.

A winery founded in the seventeenth century dominates the interior of the town. Free tours are available and educational. They're best taken early in the afternoon, for the winery offers generous samples of its wares, and their effects may be pleasantly napped away on the beach as the day begins to cool.

Charles and I spent a lovely, relaxed weekend with long walks on the sandy shore and strolls through the village. For thrills, we went parasailing, first time for each of us. Evenings, we sat arm in arm in the sand and watched the hazy sun sinking in the sea. Afterwards, we struck out for the cantinas for food, margaritas, and mariachi bands. It felt extra special to be with Charles, after having spent all those nights alone in the bars of the Disney World hotels in search of Harry. I cherished having someone care deeply for me, someone who let me care back in kind. The distress that had lingered inside me from the fearful events of the previous weeks receded in my memory.

The weekend ended all too soon. We drove back to L.A. early Monday morning. Reluctantly, we parted, I to take possession of my service flat, Charles to return to Santa Barbara and work. The challenge of finding a means of connecting with Sangfroid masked for the moment the deep loneliness I felt when Charles drove away.

I stopped at a grocery store for basic provisions on my way up to the Vista du Lac. The security guard was expecting me. He gave me the key to 6G and summoned a young man to help me carry my meager belongings.

The end of the day was cool and unusually clear for Los Angeles. A strong Pacific breeze had pushed the polluted air of the city into the luckless counties to the east. Left behind was a translucent atmosphere that blended with the glimmer of shimmering ocean just visible across the city to the southwest.

I padded the two wrought iron chairs that were on the balcony with throw pillows from the sofa. I sat in one chair and, using the other as a footrest, kicked back to watch the shadows grow, a glass of Mexico-bought wine on the floor by my fingertips. I had a fine view of Sangfroid's house and grounds, though for surveillance I'd need to invest in some serious scopes. The eight-by-forty binoculars that I usually carried with me wouldn't be up to this particular task.

Daylight Saving Time had ended a week ago Saturday, so it was getting dark early. Just after six, a car with two occupants was admitted through the main gate. In the twilight, even with my binoculars I could only just make out the figure of a man getting out of the passenger side and entering the house through a side door. The car returned to the gate, where it paused for a few moments by the guard shack. It then proceeded slowly down the hill and out of sight. All I could tell about the passenger before he disappeared was that he was a male of small stature. That was my first view of Dr. Richard Sangfroid—the Dick of Ashley's Tom, Dick, and Harry—not exactly up close and personal, but a beginning.

I must have nodded off, for when I next looked down in the direction of Sangfroid's house the streetlights had come on. A car with a driver in it was parked outside the gate and I wondered if Sangfroid was going out for the evening. Instead, about half an hour later, a woman came out of the house, passed through the door for personnel built into the gate, and got in the waiting vehicle, which drove away. Nothing happened for another two hours until, finally, the lights in the house in all but one room went dark.

Sangfroid's car collected him at 8:00 a.m. In the morning light I could see his features more clearly. I ate a breakfast of fruit and cereal while perusing the morning Times, which apparently came free with the flat. I updated my files with additions that I'd gathered over the past week. When I'd finished that, I drove downtown for a shopping spree.

I supplemented my wardrobe to the point where I'd have clothes to wear while I washed dirty laundry in the stacked washer-dryer unit in the kitchen of the flat. But the real fun was had in a gigantic shop of optical devices.

I bought two video surveillance cameras, one with a wide-angle lens and the other with a telephoto lens. Each one was capable of digital photography and of displaying images on a TV screen. A high-powered telescope and medium-powered binoculars, along with tripods for all, topped off the sale. The young sales person, clearly a neo-geek of lens-bearing devices, was deliriously happy. He volunteered to interface the cameras to my TV set, warning me that adapters might be needed. I offered him fifty bucks if he'd do it over his lunch hour, to which he happily agreed. I gave him directions to the Vista du Lac.

By the afternoon my flat had been converted into a spy center. The wide-angle video camera took in the entire grounds of the Fillmore House, while the telephoto video camera focused on the main gate. The images showed on the large screen of the TV set and alternated every five seconds, so I could sit indoors in comfort and observe any goings-on.

I set the binoculars on a tripod aimed at the front of the house. They had a wide enough field to take in the area between the main gate and the front door, and were of a power halfway between that of the two cameras. The telescope afforded an extreme close-up look at objects and was capable of resolving the lettering on the cap of the security guard.

No sooner were all the lenses in place than I realized that they were, to understate the scene, conspicuous. They'd be readily visible from the front gate of the compound, as well I knew since it was from there that I'd first seen the apartment. I hastily pulled everything inside and closed the curtain. I went downstairs to the lobby and asked the duty supervisor if he'd object to a few plants on my porch. He probably thought "geraniums" when he consented with an indulgent smile. Later, when four six-foot tall Leyland cypress trees in 10-gallon redwood tubs rolled into the lobby, he may have had second thoughts, but apart from a "Lord, why me?" raising of his eyebrows he didn't protest.

I'd moved from a Mission Impossible scene to one from Gilligan's Island. My lenses were now well concealed among the greenery of the young cypresses. The trees also screened me from view, and I could peer through the binoculars or the telescope without fear of arousing suspicion. But mostly I sat and watched the TV screen.

The car returned Sangfroid from work at the same time as on the previous night. For a couple of hours afterward not much happened. A few residents passed by the property on an evening stroll, and occasionally a vehicle drove by. Around nine o'clock a car stopped by the gate and let out a woman. I nearly tripped in my rush to the telescope. In the dim light I managed to see that she had a trim figure in provocative clothing, and a pretty face somewhat hardened by her profession. There was little doubt that she was a girl on call.

Though I couldn't be sure, I thought the waiting car was the same as the one I'd seen the previous night. I wondered if the girl was the same. About an hour and ten minutes later she emerged from the house, her appearance unchanged from earlier, though I imagined that she'd been in and out of costume. As her car pulled into the street, I focused the telescope on the license plate and recorded the four letters and three numbers. I wasn't sure what I'd do with it, but such observational habits had been instilled in me by my brother John.

The next day began as the previous two, except I got my first close look at Sangfroid through the telescope. What I saw was consistent with Ashley's sketchy description of Little. In the evening, though, instead of a car, driver and hooker, an ambulance came quietly to the property and was waved through at once as if expected. It stopped to let out two persons dressed in white, who walked toward a side door of the house and were quickly let in. The ambulance continued around to the rear where I couldn't observe it. It reappeared nearly four hours later, well after midnight, and was let off the premises by the guards on the night shift.

The daytimes were tedious. Only the comings and goings of domestic workers varied the sameness. Little else happened in Sangfroid's neighborhood. To break the monotony, I thought I might drive into the city and watch his office building to see if he went for lunch. I didn't have a plan of any kind. I just needed to treat my cabin fever. Anyway, the closer I was to Sangfroid, the more chance I had of contact.

That day I saw neither hide nor hair of Dick Sangfroid. I did think that I had sighted the square-jawed man with a crew cut whom I'd seen in the hotel lobby in Orlando, and whom I thought I'd seen in Istanbul. When I tried to follow him, he turned a corner and vanished before I could get a closer look. I felt sure I'd projected the actual man seen in Orlando onto similar-looking men here and in Istanbul. I feared that the trauma I'd suffered in Ernest's car was having some kind of weird effect on me, making itself felt through recurring false resemblances. My subconscious was too rational to make the dead Ernest appear. It wouldn't even dredge up Harry, who was too concretely fixed in my mind. But a fleeting image of a man in a crew cut might be just the thing for my psyche to feed off.

That night a whore came again. The man had both a sexual appetite and a bank account. It's a wonder that his journalist detractor didn't find out he was hooked on ladies of the night. That would have made good copy. I suppose he didn't have my, or I should say Ashley's, resources.

I dressed in different clothes and wore a cap for my second lunchtime vigil, and eschewed makeup entirely. I looked a bit like a vagrant and it nearly worked in my favor on that Friday. A few minutes after one o'clock my patience was rewarded. Sangfroid came out of his building accompanied by a shifty-eyed man with a small asymmetry in his suit jacket that meant he was packing. Rather than going to lunch, the men stopped at a nearby barbershop. Sangfroid went in and must have been expected, as he was seated immediately, despite several waiting patrons. The bodyguard stationed himself outside the shop and began idly to pick his teeth.

I formed a desperate, if not ridiculous, plan, wherein I'd obtain my DNA sample in one fell swoop, a single stroke that would, mythologically speaking, cut the Gordian knot. Across the street, I found a convenient light pole to lean against that provided a place of semi-concealment. That let me observe the barbershop without drawing the attention of the bodyguard, whose focus had now shifted to his fingernails.

When the barber had finished and was shaking out the sheet that had covered Sangfroid, I quickly crossed the street and entered the shop.

"Hi," I said brightly. "I need to earn a few dollars for a meal and I'd gladly sweep out your shop, if you'd help me."

Before the surprised barber could accept or reject my offer, I grabbed a nearby broom and began sweeping up the hair around Sangfroid's chair.

"Say, that's not necessary," said the barber, who'd gotten back his voice. "Here, I'll give you a couple of bucks."

"I don't mind at all," I said, looking around for something to sweep the hair into. "It's only fair."

I found a dustbin, but as I knelt down to use it, and at the same time nab a few strands for myself, the barber took firm hold of my elbow and raised me up.

"It is *not* necessary," he said firmly. "We don't need any extra help. Here, here's a fiver. Now, would you please leave? You're making the customers nervous."

Both Sangfroid, who was waiting to pay, and the bodyguard, who had entered the shop attracted by the commotion, were marveling at me. My last hope was to reach down, grab some hair, and bolt, but my nerve failed me. In the end, it was too crazy a thing to do, and I didn't want a run-in with the bodyguard. I thanked the barber for the five bucks and left.

CHAPTER 24

Charles had driven down to spend the weekend, ignoring my warning that he might be bored out of his mind. "I'm never bored when I'm with you, Dagny," he had said, but this would be a test.

Sangfroid's hooker of the evening showed up at the usual time and left at the usual time. The good doctor was a man of habit, if nothing else.

Maybe it was all the illicit sex I was privy too, or maybe a desire to live up to Charles's expectations that I was never boring. An hour after Friday's whore had left, only one light shone in Sangfroid's house, and I didn't think there would be anything more to observe that night.

I brought the wide-angle video camera inside and pointed it at the sofa where we were sitting. At first it was weird to see ourselves on the screen, especially because the image is the reverse of a mirror and you're not used to seeing yourself that way.

I tried to do a comedy routine I'd seen on TV but my acting abilities suck, and I can't tell a joke without laughing before the punch line, if I even manage to remember it. Charles tried too, and he proved to be more adept than me. He did an imitation of a stuffy Englishman whose wife is henpecking him over his driving, and somehow it was terribly funny, and eventually it became terribly darling and I had to kiss the comedian.

Suddenly we were into stuff that one doesn't usually see on a TV screen, leastwise not on the networks, and not on prime time.

Charles is as much an Englishman as any of the Henrys and Edwards that once ruled Britannia, and is far more English than most of the Georges were. He was, in other words, a sensible lover, not given to sensation. He wasn't the type that needed to make love, if only once in his lifetime, in an airliner lavatory. That was not to say he wasn't good or creative. He was great in all ways. He knew his anatomy, of course, and was kind, gentle and considerate when he made love.

"Oh, really, darling, are we really going to watch ourselves on the telly?"

"Why not?" I brazenly slipped out of my jeans. "There's so much more to see."

There was no arguing with that, and while Charles is not the voyeur I am—maybe that's why I chose to be a P.I.—he was soon into it.

Later we brainstormed about Sangfroid and getting a DNA sample. Charles had the idea of somehow finding one of his hookers and, assuming Sangfroid used a condom, bribing her to keep it and give it to me. That was slightly creepy but the main deterrent was how to find the girl before she went there. We had no idea which "escort" agency Sangfroid used, and I doubted we'd find out by calling around.

Morning came and with it a fresh idea. I love the way the brain works at night. Unencumbered by the mundane processes of vision, digestion, balance and the like, it's free to focus its power in other directions. This doesn't mean that I awoke with miraculous mathematical abilities. There are limits. It was merely that I had an approach to the DNA problem that I didn't have when I shut my baby grays, cuddled in Charles's arms.

One of my dearest friends in the world is Hilda, no last names, please. Hilda is a charming, warm human being who considers friendship to be the supreme relationship. I have known her since my college days at UCLA.

Hilda owns and manages a "modeling studio" in West Los Angeles, located on a dead-end street behind the Veterans' Administration hospital. The "studio" is actually a twelve-unit apartment house with a recreation room that serves as a central meeting place. The "models" work and sometimes live in the units, coming down to the studio to re-enact several times a day the charade that they're models and not whores.

Hilda knew L.A. noir. Although crime syndicates control prostitution and do not suffer competition, they let Hilda keep her pleasure dome on the strict understanding that she did not try to expand her horizons. It was a tribute to her ability to win friends and influence people.

What came to me as I slept was that Hilda could help me find Sangfroid's escort service. It was clear that the man was a sex junkie. He was surely well known in the murky netherworld of sex-for-hire. At least he was paying for it and not raping helpless coeds.

I could hardly call Hilda on a Saturday morning. Friday was her busiest night because her married clients would tell their wives they had to wrap up at the office to free themselves for a weekend of wholesome family activity. Neither she nor her girls would be awake until the afternoon.

No car came for Sangfroid, nor did he appear outside, leastwise not in view of my cameras. In the afternoon two men drove up whom the guards clearly knew. They were waved on in without any hassle.

When the hour was "decent," I called Hilda. She was, as always, happy to hear from me, and when she heard I was in town, she was insistent.

"You must come visit and bring Charles. I'll make the girls wear their tops."

Charles knew of Hilda, though he'd never been to her place. He was keen to meet her, not out of prurience, but because she'd been my good friend for so many years.

Saturday afternoons were slow in Hilda's trade. Only two girls were on duty, and true to her word, Hilda had made them dress modestly, or leastwise less immodestly. Charles did a good job averting his gaze while Hilda and I exchanged news. She wept a little with joy when I told her I'd passed the five-year cancer test the previous month, and gave me a long, emotional hug.

With the small, but important, girl-talk out of the way, and the ever-present bottle of fine, chilled Chardonnay uncorked, I stated my purpose. I asked Hilda if she could find out who was providing girls to Sangfroid, and what the chances were of getting one of them to do me a small favor. I'd make it worth her while.

Naturally, Hilda wanted to know the rest of the story. She wasn't about to get involved in even the smallest violation of the law beyond her prostitution ring, which was well protected. (Her clientele numbered civic and business leaders from L.A., Santa Monica and Beverly Hills, not to mention a number of cops and an occasional assistant district attorney.) Nor would she risk angering any of her organized-crime "colleagues" in the slightest degree.

I told her, with some hemming and hawing, what I wanted. I was astonished at how nonchalant she was about what I took to be a fairly bizarre request.

"Oh, Dag, you'd be surprised how often we're asked to collect semen samples. You're working on a paternity case, right? That's what it usually is. I mean, what the hey, we even have it price-listed: $500 over and above."

Well, live and learn. Never think you've heard it all. I added this one to my collection of arcane facts gathered in the line of duty.

The paternity case was the perfect cover-up of my true reason. Lies invented by the person to be lied to are perfect because they express what the person is willing to believe. Mind you, I don't make a habit of lying to friends unless forced to by need, and convinced that no harm could ensue. And besides, it was ultimately a paternity issue, so I wasn't truly lying.

"To be on the safe side, Dag, we should use one of my girls. That way, they'll never meet again, and the little secret will stay kept. After a girl's been with a man a few times, she might let something slip, you know."

"Aren't we getting ahead of the game, here?" I asked. "We don't even know the agency."

"Oh, Dagny, Dagny, don't underestimate your friend Hilda. A man who's spending a G or two a week will be known to the bosses. They're my associates, kind of, and we help each other out. We have a network, you know. Huh, we're talking about computerizing, can you believe it?"

"I'd watch out for computers, Hilda. They have a nasty way of remembering everything. It's the first thing the cops go for when they raid a joint."

"Ah, we're ahead of you there. One of the big cheeses is getting a computer that automatically erases itself—is that the right way to say it?—if anyone but its owner touches it. It's the latest in security."

"Sounds good to me, as long as they're careful not to be always deleting their own files. Anyway, how should we proceed?"

"Tell me his name and where he lives. Then you two lovebirds work on this bottle while I make a couple of phone calls."

I gave her the information and was even able to throw in the license plate number of the car she came in. Hilda returned well before the bottle was empty.

"This'll be easy," she said. "He has a standing order for Monday, Tuesday, Thursday and Friday. Apparently, he has his favorites, but he likes new girls, too. And best of all, get this, he worries about disease—just like a doc, huh?—so he uses a condom."

Hilda's private quarters, where we were sitting, were just off the rec room. She kept the door open to be aware of any activity, and to be able to call for service. She made the girls wait on her, which they didn't seem to mind. She rang a little silver bell and two seconds later a girl poked her head in the door and asked "D'ja ring, Hilda?"

"Come in, Lisa. I want you to meet my friends."

Lisa was a stunning woman of about twenty with glossy brown hair, large, perfectly shaped breasts, a narrow waist and a small, firm butt. It was too late to blindfold Charles. She would arouse envy in women, and arouse men, period.

Hilda explained that on Monday she was to work "out of the Rampart office"—that was the escort agency that covered the Silver Lake district—and that she was to "obtain a specimen."

Hilda told me that Sangfroid was paying $500 bucks a pop for his girls. I wondered, indeed, where he was getting the money. That's $100,000 a year and not even tax-deductible. I paid Lisa $1,000 in advance and gave her another $500 to compensate the girl she'd have to replace. Confidentiality was an expected part of the deal.

I congratulated myself a bit early on the easy conclusion to which I thought I'd brought my case. No dramatic thefts or car wrecks. No assaults, either on me or by me. Through my telescope, I watched Lisa enter Sangfroid's house Monday night at nine. She left one hour later, and in the yellow glow of the streetlights I thought she wore the expression of that proverbial canary-swallowing cat.

BOOK FOUR

ASHLEY

CHAPTER 25

I was far too excited to sleep, so when the phone rang at midnight I answered on the first ring.

"Come get your prize," said Hilda without preface. "He liked Lisa so much he gave her a huge tip and asked for her back."

"Oh, thanks Hilda, but it's kind of good news, bad news. I mean, good news about the sample, but I'm worried about Lisa blabbing at some later time. She doesn't seem like your brightest jewel."

"For sure, Lisa is no scholar, but she's a good little whore, and she's my little whore. I know what I said about the girls talking, but I'll go over the point with Lisa. She'll keep her mouth shut. Trust me, Dagny."

I hadn't much choice. Even if Lisa did blab on another visit, I couldn't see how Sangfroid could draw the right conclusion. And even if he did, so what? What could he do about it? I booked an afternoon flight to Raleigh, stopping on my way to the airport to collect the semen-filled condom, which Hilda had thoughtfully packaged in a zip-up plastic bag and placed on ice.

I called Ashley the morning after I returned to Raleigh with the good news. As usual, she asked for the details, which I gave her.

"At least you didn't use yourself, as I thought you had when you told me what the sample was. He was a disgusting goat, Little was. After your episode with Fatboy, I wasn't sure where you'd draw the line. You're a good team player, Dagny. I'm glad I have you."

"Do you want me to bring the plastic bag to you?"

"No, actually not. I'll send a courier, like we did the first time."

"Were you satisfied with Beck's sample? Was there an analysis?"

"Yes, as a matter of fact. He turned up negative for Benton's father."

"I'm not surprised. It's got to be Sangfroid. I'll send you his picture and you'll see the resemblance."

"I'll test the sample in any case, but I'll give you the benefit of the doubt, as I did before. Would you send me a final report and a final reckoning on the finances including your bonus?"

"Will do. Anything else?"

"Oh, feel free to keep or sell the surveillance equipment. I'm well satisfied with what I got at the price. So I ask you, is there anything else?"

"No, I believe that's it."

"All right, I'll have the courier there by two tomorrow. Goodbye, Dagny."

I spent the rest of that day and half of the next on paperwork. By the time the courier came, I was able to give him not only the semen sample, but Ashley's credit card, the remains of the cash advance, an invoice, and the neatly printed final report.

That evening I brought Ashley's case up-to-date on my computer and saved everything to a diskette that I filed under "Cases closed." Two days later an Airborne Express package arrived that contained a check for full payment including the bonus. Written on the "memo" line of the check was a terse "It was him. –A."

I basked all weekend in the glorious summer of the triumphant closure of a tough case. I took pride in having earned a substantial fraction of my usual annual income in six weeks. And it all seemed sweeter still on top of the afterglow of the lovely and loving time I'd spent with Charles.

The phone woke me Monday morning, edging out the alarm clock by ten minutes. I had readied myself during the weekend to return to my regular routine. I was actually looking forward to a bit of the mundane. My substitute, Barry Hernandez, knew of my return and we were scheduled to meet that morning. I assumed Barry was calling to change the meeting time and it annoyed me that he would call so early. But the voice at the other end belonged to Taylor Bloodworth, and when the conversation ended, it would be I who'd call Barry to ask him to continue in my capacity.

With his old-whiskey voice, in his slow southern way, Mr. Bloodworth told me that Ashley had taken the two children and left Hatfield Hall without speaking to anyone. She'd been gone two nights and hadn't contacted the family. When I suggested that two nights away was hardly reason to engage a private investigator, he demurred.

"There are other factors that might best be discussed in person," he said, "if you were willing. I'll pay you whatever rate Ashley was paying you."

"You could hire a competent P.I. for much less."

"Nevertheless, Ms. Jamison, I wish to hire you. At least I've met you and received a positive impression. I hope very much that you'll consent. Please come today and consider it a day of work," he urged, "and meet me at Hatfield Hall at noon."

Thus I found myself once more on the private roadway of Hatfield Hall. Nobody was outside to greet me this time. I parked in my old spot.

Autumn was crisping up now and the trees were nearly bare, with only spotty patches of reds and oranges for color. Wafts of smoke from wood-burning fireplaces floated on the autumnal breezes. A solitary seagull screeched its lonely call overhead as I made my way through the chilly air to the house.

A maidservant admitted me into an elegant foyer decorated with two waist-high Chinese urns and several Japanese scrolls in black and white featuring horses and their masters. She asked me to wait a moment and disappeared into the house, only to reappear a few seconds later with a request to follow her.

She escorted me to Ashley's office, where Taylor Bloodworth greeted me. He was dressed in gray slacks, a blue-striped shirt of expensive cotton, and a tie with a pattern of blue diamonds and yellow lightning bolts. "Please sit down, Ms. Jamison. Would you care for something to eat or drink? I'm afraid I've forgotten my manners, not to invite you for lunch at the noon hour. I am, to be frank, quite upset."

I asked for iced tea. When the maid left, there was a short, awkward silence as I waited for him to begin.

"I'm not sure how much you know about my daughter. She said that she hired you to investigate matters regarding her financial interests. I'm afraid I don't believe that. You were employed to do something special for Ashley. What that was I'm not asking you to reveal," he said, waving a hand. "I understand and respect the client-privilege relation."

"I'm glad of that, sir," I said. "I mean, I really can't discuss her case with anyone. It wouldn't be fair to her." I fiddled nervously with the straps of my handbag as he waited expectantly for me to say more. "If I may be honest with you, sir, I'm not sure whether it's right for me to even consider working for a family member of a client on a matter that regards the client. It's all a bit unusual, if you don't mind me saying."

As I spoke those words, I suddenly wished I'd conferred with my brother John before rushing helter-skelter into what, I realized, was a maze of ethical dilemmas.

Bloodworth finally spoke. "For the past six weeks or so, dating back, I believe, to about the time she hired you, Ashley hasn't been herself. I'm not even sure I know what 'herself' is anymore. Once I did, but something terrible, unspeakable, happened to her ten years ago, and afterward she changed. To use her own words, she redefined herself."

The maid came in with two glasses of iced tea, each with a sprig of mint, a little sugar bowl, a small jug of cream and individual wedges of freshly sliced lemon. She served us each in silence and, receiving a nod from Bloodworth, promptly retired from the room.

He picked up where he'd left off. "Now this time she hasn't changed to so great a degree, but there's an edginess to her, an agitation about her, that I've never seen before. And to take the children, my grandchildren, whom she's never taken anywhere, and whom I'm not sure she truly loves—to take them away without explanations or goodbyes..."

He stopped there, his eyes filling with tears.

Of course I knew the whole history. God, did I know it. If it was a horror to me, an unrelated stranger, what must it have been to her father! I dug my fingernails into my palm as I struggled to appear impassive.

When he had gained control, I asked, "How do you think I can help you, sir?"

"Very simple. I want you to find her, and if she's alive, I mean if she's okay—because I'm worried about that—I want you to give her this." He held out a brown, sealed envelope. "She will understand the contents. She'll know what it means."

I suppose the devil in me was saying *ethical, shmethical*, for I didn't ponder very long in thought. "I'll do that much, Mr. Bloodworth. But first, I must tell you that if I find her, and that is a very big 'if,' I cannot tell you where she is unless she consents. If you hire a different P.I., he or she wouldn't be under such a constraint. It'd be a simple missing-persons case."

"I still wish to employ you, Ms. Jamison. I believe you to be a good investigator and a good person. I know I can count on the goodness within you to help Ashley and the children. Surely that supersedes all other considerations. And, Ms. Jamison, I believe Ashley's disappearance has much to do with whatever it is that you worked on for her."

I opened my mouth to protest but once again he held up his hand.

"I'm not saying that you're to blame or that there's any fault on your part. I'm merely observing that certain events are juxtaposed in time. First she's edgy. Then she hires you. And when your work is done, she vanishes. Causal relationships are plausible, wouldn't you say? It's logical, isn't it? You don't need a weatherman to know which way the wind blows."

He paused to add sugar and cream to his tea, stirred it thoughtfully for a moment and removed the sprig of mint. When he looked up his eyes were molten pools of blue. "So you'll work for me."

It was a statement, not a question. I had already agreed to it in so many words. Looking back, I believe I did so because I feared for

Ashley's safety. Though she had protested that she wanted no interaction with the men who had raped her, apart from knowing who they were, and who had fathered her children, I never fully believed it. I'd wager diamonds to dog biscuits that she had left to seek out one or more of Tom, Dick, and Harry. In that regard, Mr. Bloodworth was right about my role.

A further, nagging thought was that Ashley was unaware that Harry, for whatever reasons, was accompanied everywhere by an armed bodyguard, and that Tom employed two vicious hoodlums. At least she was aware that Dick was under guard 24/7. She knew these men were capable of cruelty and even murder, but she didn't know that each of them was abetted by hired thugs.

Like Ashley, her father refused a contract, preferring to pay a large sum in advance. We shook hands and he said, "Welcome aboard," as if I'd just stepped off the gangplank onto his private yacht. Little did I know into what turbulent waters I was about to sail.

CHAPTER 26

Now that I'm 'aboard,' sir," I said, "request permission to search this room for leads." I suppressed the reflex to salute. In less than one minute I'd waded into murky ethical waters, but I had by then convinced myself it was all in Ashley's best interest.

"Yes, of course you may. I'm afraid I don't have keys to anything in this office but I'm sure you have your ways." He turned to leave, and after a couple of steps turned back. "By the way, if you need anything, pull this cord"—he indicated a braided rope with a tasseled end—"and one of the servants will come, okay? Stay as long as you need to. I'll have lunch sent in."

Without further words he left the room. A few moments later a young black woman brought a plate of sandwiches and more iced tea. I seated myself in Ashley's executive chair, bit into a sandwich, and revved up the old gray matter.

I saw little point in rifling through Ashley's files. I needed clues to recent activities, unlikely to be filed yet. The desk drawers were unlocked and their contents unhelpful. A dark computer screen off to the side invited me to try my luck booting up. The computer was probably password protected, but nothing ventured…

As the hardware whirred through its wake-up stages, I cast a glance at the statuette of the praying hands and appealed to no one in particular for access to the machine. It was my chief hope. The musical tones of the Windows operating system as it came to life brought me to the moment of reckoning. I was in luck. No password needed.

Though I'm hardly an expert—I couldn't write a computer program for love nor money—my job as a P.I. requires me to have more computer skills than the average bear. I know how to manage files and snoop into them. I have a better than working acquaintance with the Internet and the various Internet browsers. The computer wizards who are my next-door neighbors have given me hacking lessons for beginners. These skills I put to work.

I searched various files, sorting them by date and snooping into the most recent. After two hours, I had nothing. Then I noticed that Ashley had minimized her Web browser, but had left it open. I maximized it and began to click on the "go back" arrow. In essence I could read the browser pages that Ashley had been using, and I was, as Charles might say, "bloody lucky."

Among Ashley's Web pages was one showing the purchase of an electronic airline ticket. The record showed one first-class passage departing the previous evening from Washington's Dulles Airport to Atatürk International Airport, Istanbul, Turkey. While I sat in her office, Ashley was in Istanbul. I didn't like the idea one bit.

I pulled the cord and heard bells jingle in the distance. Quaint in this electronic age. It worked, however, and the same girl who had brought me lunch appeared at once. I asked her to ask Mr. Bloodworth to please come to the office.

When he showed up two minutes later, I filled him in on what I'd found.

"Turkey," he exclaimed, "why Turkey?"

"I believe there is someone in Istanbul whom she thinks she knows," I answered cautiously.

"Do you think she's in trouble of some kind? Is she fleeing the country?"

"Well, I'm guessing, but I think she's going to, not running from, and yes, I think she could be in trouble. With your okay, I'm going to fly to Istanbul."

"Yes, of course you have it, and you'll ask her to take care, and show her the...I mean, hand her that envelope."

"I will if I can find her. She purchased a single one-way ticket. That may mean that the children are staying with someone in the U.S. You have any idea?"

His brow furrowed in thought, but before he could speak, my own thoughts had raced ahead. "Of course she might buy them tickets at the airport, but why not online? I'll bet they're still in the country. If you'd follow up on that, I think my job is to get to Istanbul as quickly as possible."

He agreed. I asked him for a couple of snapshots of Ashley. When he went off to find them, I phoned American Airlines and reserved a seat on the evening redeye to London's Gatwick Airport. From there, I'd have to take an afternoon flight to Istanbul. It arrived at night and Ashley would already have had two days to get into trouble, but without a time machine it was the best I could do.

I departed in haste for home in order to prepare once more for travel. I called Uncle Husnu to see if his hotel would accommodate me in about 24 hours. He was perfectly sweet, called me his little turnip, and even though we'd just seen each other a few weeks ago, acted as if I'd been gone for years. He insisted on having his man meet me at the airport, and brooked no further argument.

The time between leaving Hatfield Hall and landing at Atatürk airport is a blur of frantic activity mixed with near unendurable boredom. You'd think that flying over 500 miles per hour would satisfy, but the faster you go, the faster you want to go. I wished for the Concorde instead of my Boeing 767 slow boat. The few hours of sleep I managed were heaven-sent. The layover in Gatwick seemed endless. The final leg to Istanbul, though less than four hours, felt like fourteen.

The driver sent by Uncle Husnu was the same man who had transported (and guarded) me two weeks ago. He was a bull-necked, sturdy fellow who took his job seriously in spite of my assurances that there was no danger. It was comforting nonetheless to be escorted to the hotel, and to my room. It was too late to do anything but try to get some sleep. Morning would come soon enough, and with it the formidable challenge of finding Ashley.

Naturally, I couldn't sleep right away. Beside it being late afternoon according to my internal clock, I still didn't have what I felt was an effective plan for locating her. If I thought she was here on vacation, I'd walk the Istiklal shopping area looking for, and asking about, a dazzling blonde westerner. She'd sparkle like a jewel among the swarthy Turks. But I didn't believe this was a pleasure trip. I feared that, driven by her demons, Ashley was here to contact J. Thompson Beck, Doctor of Divinity, rapist. And that when she did, she'd place herself in grave peril.

The next morning I enlisted Uncle Husnu to help me find Ashley. I gave him one of her photos and asked him to call the upscale hotels in Istanbul to see if he could find out where she was staying. The best use of my time was to stake out Beck's home to see if Ashley would come prying. I also thought I might get information from the cops watching the place. They would remember Ashley long after they'd forgotten a visitation from Muhammad's ghost.

Now that Uncle Husnu knew the kind of people I hung out with— the two hoods from the underground cistern were a dead giveaway—he was adamant about providing me with a car and driver-cum-bodyguard. I didn't refuse. I needed all the help I could get.

"He doesn't know a word of English," warned Uncle, "but he'll protect you with his life."

The driver knew where Beck's orphanage was. He had grown up on the Asian side of Istanbul and had been in the police force prior to coming to work at the hotel. Speaking Turkish slowly so as not to be misunderstood, I told him I wanted to watch the place to see who comes and goes, but I was worried that the cops would shoo us away.

He said he knew most of the cops and they might be persuaded to help, especially if a few million liras were to change hands. I didn't object to the idea but it turned out to be unnecessary. Concern about the controversial orphanage must have cooled. It was no longer under police protection. We parked the car in an inconspicuous place with a good view of both the house and grounds. The tedium of waiting began.

Uncle had thoughtfully had the kitchen pack lunch for us. After some hours we were about to break into it when a woman, clearly a domestic servant, came out of the front door and walked toward a nearby bus stop.

Over my driver's protest, I slipped quietly out of the car and ducked behind the right fender. As soon as the woman was out of eyeshot of the house, I approached her. She was surprised when I spoke to her in Turkish, and more surprised when I offered her a sum of money equal to a week's wages if she'd answer one or two small questions.

I showed her a picture of Ashley and asked if by any chance a woman who resembled her had visited Dr. Beck in the past day or two.

"Oh yes, ma'am," she said, "the yellow-haired lady came this morning."

Half of the woman's teeth were missing and I had to ask her to repeat herself. My understanding of spoken Turkish seemed to rely heavily on the speaker's dentition.

"Is she still there?" I asked, my heart beating faster.

"No, ma'am. She left shortly after she came."

"Can you tell me what she did, or what they talked about?"

She didn't answer. Rather, she focused her eyes on my handbag. I got the point. She had answered "one or two small questions" and having sensed the depth of the well, wished to ladle up more. I handed over another week's wages.

"They went into the doctor's study. I was running the vacuum cleaner so I couldn't hear them."

"Please listen to me, as Allah is great," I said, holding up yet another week's wages just out of her grasp. "I want you to tell me everything you saw or heard, from the time the blonde lady arrived until the time she left."

"I told you everything, ma'am. They talked, she left. That's all I know."

"That's all you know?" I mimicked, making to put the money back in my handbag.

"Except maybe one thing," she said, her eyes glued to the paper bills. "The master, he looked upset, and the lady, she looked like she had the evil eye, and she said 'I'll be back,' just like in the movies."

"How do you know she said that? She doesn't speak Turkish."

My informant proffered a semi-toothed smile and said in highly accented English, "I understand small English," and reached for the money.

I walked back to the waiting car. I ate lunch in silence, my mind racing over what I'd just learned. What did Ashley tell Beck? Or, more pertinent, what did she ask him for? And Beck, no fool, somehow talked her into coming back later. Later, when he was more prepared. And no sooner had that thought occurred than a car pulled up in front of the orphanage and out piled the same two goons who had harried me in the Grand Bazaar and the Cistern Basilica three weeks ago. The tall one led the way up the walk and Beck himself admitted them through the front door.

That clinched it. I'd have to wait for Ashley and confront her before she got to the house. I hoped that the message I bore from her father, still in its sealed envelope, would dissuade her from whatever crazy plans she had. If not, I'd be forced to take drastic measures.

The afternoon crept snail-like, unwillingly, toward dusk. After an interminable time, it began to grow dark, and I began to despair of my errand. Suddenly, out of the dark blue of the twilight, two police squad cars squealed around the corner and came to an abrupt halt in front of the orphanage. Two cops got out of each car, and the four went to the front door and demanded entrance.

Five minutes later the cops escorted Beck and his two hoods off the grounds and into the police cars. They shoved Beck and the small hood into one, and the big guy into the other.

Now it was clear. Ashley had used her influence or wealth to have Beck detained and perhaps tried for some crime, or kicked out of the country. She had come by his place earlier to either blackmail or taunt him. When she said, "I'll be back," she didn't mean it literally.

That was a satisfactory close to the affair. I was sure either that Uncle Husnu would locate Ashley's hotel, or we could go to the police regarding Beck's case and they'd give us Ashley's local address. My job was to find her, keep her safe, and hand over the envelope from her father. I was relishing the glow from the light at the end of the tunnel when the train ran me down from behind.

"Miss Dagny, they're not real cops," volunteered my driver.

"What," I exclaimed, thinking I'd misunderstood his Asian-accented Turkish. "Would you say that again? You mean those really aren't cops?"

He nodded and spoke carefully, "They are not really cops, and those are not really police cars. The number plates are wrong. And the way they put those men in the cars. It was not how cops do it. They are always careful of the head. I know what cops look like and how they act."

My smugness vanished. "Can you follow them?" I asked.

"Your uncle wouldn't like it."

"It's very important. It may be a matter of life or death. Please. Before we lose them."

He shifted the car into gear, shaking his head in that "I know I'm going to regret this" kind of a way.

CHAPTER 27

They were several blocks away by the time we started after them, but my driver was sharp-eyed and able to follow undetected. They didn't try to be evasive, but rather took a main avenue at a sensible speed toward wherever they were going. Eventually they turned off onto a secondary street and we closed the gap a little. They drove by a stadium and slowed as if looking for a place to park. We slowed too, exposing ourselves somewhat, but our quarry was too preoccupied to notice. They turned onto the grounds of the stadium. As we drove casually past I noticed that they had stopped.

"What is this place?" I asked my driver.

"It's a soccer field," he explained. "They also play American football here. That's become popular lately."

"I want you to drive back and let me out. I need to see what they're doing."

"I will certainly not, as Satan is evil."

"Satan is evil, and Husnu Oktalmus is your boss. Did Uncle not tell you to do as I ask?"

"Miss Dagny, this is too risky. Those men are dangerous, I can tell. Please don't go. I can't protect you."

"Listen, it's okay. I'll take very good care," I said. "I haven't told anyone, not even my uncle, but I, too, must protect someone. It's a matter of honor for me to see if she's in danger. For me, it's like a promise to God. It's my duty."

He relented, but insisted on coming with me. I refused. I told him that stealth was needed, not strength, and he'd serve me best by waiting in the car in case I had to flee.

I found a place to enter about a quarter of the way around the stadium from where the two phony cop cars had parked. I walked up some stairs and through a tunnel. From there I had a view of the field. I crouched in the shadows to watch.

Six men in uniform, two of them carrying bright electric lanterns, escorted the now handcuffed prisoners onto the field. The captives were forced to their knees in front of the goal posts that were used for American football. There was no sign of Ashley.

I decided to circle around, check the vicinity of the two squad cars, and if I didn't find anything, hightail it the hell out of there. With Ashley absent, this was none of my business, and I didn't like the way in which the scenario was unfolding.

I'd started backing away into the tunnel to leave when I heard the crack of a pistol shot. I froze in terror. Then a second crack. I had to look. When I stepped forward, I saw what I had dreaded. Both of Beck's henchmen had been executed, gangland style. One had fallen straight forward, his hands cuffed behind, his forehead on the ground as if in mockery of a Muslim in prayer. The taller man lay dead beside him. Beck was trembling in an agony of terror.

One of the "cops" unlocked Beck's handcuffs and ordered him to remove his clothes. Beck was babbling something, of which I comprehended only the frightened, pleading tone. The order to strip was repeated with a gun barrel under his chin for emphasis.

Soon he stood naked, shaking in fear and from the cold November night. His only adornment was the large crucifix that hung almost to the bulge of his hairy belly. Two men held him while one affixed a gag over his mouth. They forced him to the ground on his back and two more men pulled his legs apart. A knife blade flashed in the lanterns' glow, then again, and again.

In my benumbed mind his muffled screams of agony shook the stadium as if ten thousand fans had arisen, screaming, to their feet. A wave of nausea swept over me and I retreated into the darkness of the tunnel and began to sob, attempting to muffle the sound in my two hands. Still the screams welled up. There was no escape from them. I pressed my hands to my ears and cowered in a paralysis of horror.

A pistol shot quelled the screams abruptly. Now the utter silence that followed spooked me. I couldn't afford to make a sound. My nose was running from crying but I was fearful even of snuffling. I'd have to hide in the stadium until the men left. There were too many of them to keep track of, and it would mean death if they found me.

I sneaked back to my viewing place, expecting to see the men leave. But to my utter surprise they appeared to be starting a construction project of some kind. They brought out ladders and lumber, and several of them extended the crossbar of the goal post to either side. They erected a third post that bisected the crossbar, and when everything was securely in place, they dragged the bodies over.

They had created three large crosses. To the ones on either end, they tied the two dead thugs in a position of crucifixion. They hung Beck from the middle crucifix, arms akimbo, legs crossed at the ankles. In a final repugnant act, they prized open Beck's mouth and stuffed it with his bloody genitals.

They prepared to leave, careful to collect all their possessions. The last man to go had a camera with a powerful flash attachment. He took about a dozen photographs of the victims, zooming his lens in and out for maximum effect.

I was like a deer in the headlights. I couldn't turn away. Each time the flash went off the scene etched itself in my brain. The shadow cast by the three crucified men towered menacingly on the stadium wall with each strobe. The blood oozing from Beck's open mouth dripped onto his crucifix and left rusty tracks on his swollen belly. The black gap between his legs made me turn away. When I looked back for the final time I saw a tableau of grotesque horror that not even an ocean's water could wash clean from my memory.

From the street side of my tunnel I watched the men drive away. Only there were now three vehicles. A limousine had joined the two squad cars. The limo had darkened windows, so I couldn't see the occupants, but one window was lowered a few inches and through it I caught a fleeting glimpse of golden hair.

Sweat beaded my brow despite the cold night air. When I returned to the car the driver was as happy as a puppy to see me. He sprang out of the driver's seat to open the rear door, and though he was a stodgy, taciturn fellow, he took my hands and practically danced as he held them tightly, all the while muttering thanks for the goodness of God.

The Turkish authorities would go wild over this. I wouldn't be able to leave the country any time soon if they knew I'd been an eyewitness. But their initial investigation would focus on the protestors against the orphanage, leaving me, and of course Ashley, time to get out of Dodge.

Despite my misgivings about Ashley, I still wanted to find her, deliver the envelope in fulfillment of my professional duty, and then disown the whole affair. Events were tumbling out of control and I had no desire to become part of a murderous, vengeful bloodbath.

While I was away, Uncle Husnu had ascertained that Ashley had stayed at the Sheraton in the commercial district, but had checked out that morning. If she had checked in elsewhere, he hadn't discovered it. There were many flights out of Istanbul at night, several to nearby European cities such as Athens. It wouldn't surprise me if she had already left the country. My best bet was to do the same in the morning.

When I told Uncle I was leaving the next day, he was amazed. Turkish people rarely move around in this fashion, and to come one-third of the way around the world to stay for two nights seemed crazy to him.

"Dagny, my little artichoke," he said, cupping my head in his hands, "you are like a wolf from the Steppes, untamed, and ever restless."

I assured him it was my job, not me, and promised him a leisurely visit, perhaps with my brother John, of whom Uncle was equally fond. This mollified him somewhat and he was further comforted when I asked if he'd have my stalwart driver take me to the airport.

I caught a painfully early flight to Munich from where I could catch a nonstop to Orlando, Florida. If you've never shared an airliner with 400 Bavarians on vacation to Disney World, you've missed a unique experience. Which isn't to say it's either good or bad: simply that there's nothing like it. The flight attendants could barely keep up with the demand for beer. Drinking songs filled the air from wheels up to wheels down. My seatmate translated some songs, every one of which extolled the virtues of beer, elixir of the gods, soother of the soul, mender of the mind, balm for the brain, and so on.

The lavatory lines grew steadily longer as bladders filled and the aircraft drew nearer its destination. Half the passengers, it seemed, were standing in the long lines. Kids were everywhere underfoot. The order to fasten seatbelts as we approached Orlando was met with good-natured cries of "schnell, schnell" by those still waiting to offload their cargo of digested beer.

I had deduced that Ashley would most likely have one of three destinations. She could simply return home, having taken revenge on the one rapist that hadn't fathered a child. Or she could continue her rampage by going after Dick or Harry. If she returned to Kinston, it didn't matter what I did. If she was determined to hunt down another rapist, it would most likely be Harry. I'd impressed upon her how well guarded Dick Sangfroid was, and had not even mentioned Harry's bodyguard. Also, Orlando was a great deal closer than Los Angeles. To Ashley, Harry would be the next easiest target. The hypothesis wasn't a certainty—there are few of those in life—but it guided my actions.

CHAPTER 28

Immediately upon seeing the balconies of the Raphael Hotel, I knew that Harry had departed. Swimsuits belonging to a generously apportioned woman and two small children hung over the railing of his former balcony. They weren't Harry's kind of people. Nonetheless, I dutifully asked at the desk whether a Harry Beck, or a Harry Angelica, was checked in. The answer was no and no. I booked a room anyway.

While walking to the elevators I saw a pair of familiar pretty faces. It was Jamie and Jamie, the young couple that hung out with Harry. The recognition was mutual, except they knew me as Susan Radford.

"Isn't that that Susan person?" said Jamie-girl to Jamie-boy.

He acknowledged that it was, and they both said at once, "Hey, Susan."

"Hey," I said back, the standard manner of greeting in the South.

"Hey, we heard some weird stories about you. Like you did something bad to Ernie."

"Me? Hurt him? Do I look like David?"

"David?" they questioned in unison.

"Yeah, you know, David and Goliath."

"Oh, whoever. We heard Ernie got killed in a car wreck," said Jamie-boy.

"Yeah, and that you had something to do with it," said Jamie-girl.

"That's a lie, believe me," I lied. "Stupidest thing I ever heard. What's happening here? Where's Harry? What are you guys up to?"

"We had a breakup with Harry," said Jamie-boy.

"Yeah, he screwed us royal," said Jamie-girl.

"Yeah, me too," I said, truthfully this time. "What'd he do to you?"

"Well, you know Harry's real business, right?" said the one.

"Like the advertising gig's just a front," said the other.

It struck me in a flash. "I kind of thought he might be making X-rated videos on the side."

"Huh, on the side, nothing."

"That's what he does for the real money."

"So you guys were, uh…"

"That's right. We were stars, leastwise for the adult stuff."

"And the cocksucker owes us some big bucks and welshed out."

"What do you mean, 'the adult stuff'?" I asked.

Jamie looked at Jamie. "We shouldn't talk about this, here. Let's go outside."

We found a table to sit at in a corner of the outdoor patio.

I said, "Guys, I'd really like to hear y'all's story. Maybe we could help each other. You know, he screwed me too. Why don't we rat him out?"

"Oh, no way, man. First, we'd never collect if he got busted, and second, he's got some stuff on us."

The other Jamie added, "And third, the gorilla he hired to replace Ernie is a mean fucker. I mean, like, we want to go on living."

"So why not a little blackmail?" I suggested. "I'm willing to try it, and if you guys help me, I'll see that you get what's coming to you."

They looked at each other, unsure.

"So he's doing kiddy porn," I ventured to guess. "Is that it?"

"You got it. He makes a fuckin' fortune. I mean, like a hundred times over legit porn."

"Thousand times."

"Wow, who buys it?" I asked, at once repulsed and spellbound.

"Rich fuckers, I can tell you that. Businessmen, movie dudes, you'd be surprised. Politicians."

"One old rich Japanese fuck, he paid half a fucking million for the only copy of a video of a twelve-year-old girl being, you know, getting it done to her the first time."

"We don't approve of that. I mean, you know, we do it in front of cameras, but we're adults, and anyway, we do it artistically."

"Children?" I was still shocked. "Where does he find them?"

"That's the thing we don't get. I mean he's got a steady stream of, you know, really young kids, like a new one every week or two. They're brought in by these women and there's like a bunch of different ones. And they look, you know, way strung-out, the kids, I mean."

"The women too, if you ask me," chimed in the other Jamie.

"And after a week of shooting, they're kind of used up, right, so they're sent to adoptive homes."

"Don't the kids ever tell their new parents?" I asked.

"I don't know, they always seemed all fucked up with drugs. Maybe they don't remember. Anyway, I think they're foreigners, like, they don't speak English. They don't understand things. You have to show them."

"They definitely look foreign," said the other Jamie, knowingly. "Real dark-like, not like blacks or anything, but, you know, more like Mexicans."

"Except sometimes he gets a white girl, I mean a blonde."

"And Harry, he saves those girls—there aren't that many—for himself."

"Are they all girls?" I asked, not sure I really wanted to know.

"Oh he does gay porn. There's more girls than boys, but he does boys. Man, he makes oodles off the boys. Same kind of deal. They're brought here from somewhere, made to do, you know…"

"Sexual things. Then at least he finds them homes so they can grow up in America."

"Decent of him," I said bitingly. "Was he doing all this in the hotel?"

"Nah, we did some shooting here, but not all. On weekends when he wasn't doing younger kids, me 'n' Jamie would recruit older kids, like teenagers, for him, from the hotels around here. Would their parents be surprised!"

"Yeah, we'd give them some grass or coke, and they'd get stoned and we'd start to do stuff with them, and Harry would roll the video. And other kids might join in and next thing we had an orgy. People pay big money for it because they like, you know, off-the-cuff sex. But the kiddy shit, he does that in his house."

"His house? He has a house around here?" I asked.

"Oh yeah. It's 40 or 50 miles from here. Ernie was going there when he got himself killed. Got drunk, missed a curve, whammed into a tree. Harry thought you had something to do with it."

"Well, whatever. Can you tell me where this house is?" I asked, steering the conversation away from the murky waters of Ernest's demise.

"Oh shit, he'd have us killed for sure. I don't think we should."

"Hey, no one will ever know who told me. I'm just going to suggest to Harry, real subtle-like, that he pays me what he owes me, and when he does we'll split it three ways. That'll be a grand for each of us, and he'll never know how I found out, I swear."

Again they considered. Finally Jamie-girl said, "Awright. If we can get the two grand, we can go to the West Coast. He couldn't find us there, and there's plenty of work, 'specially in Portland or Seattle."

"So, will you do it?" I asked.

They did. In a schoolchild's handwriting, Jamie-girl wrote out the directions and even drew a crude map to a house on the outskirts of Lakeland, southwest of Orlando. Formerly a horse ranch, it sat on an isolated 20 acres, with its own pond and stables. Its nearest neighbor, according to Jamie, was a nudist colony.

They gave me their room number—they were still staying at the Raphael—and made me swear I wouldn't welsh out on them. In the meantime they'd be making ends meet by picking up "odd jobs," just as they had been doing. We'd just shaken hands when the square-jawed man with a crew cut exited the lobby.

I hastened after, catching up with him on the empty shuffleboard court.

"You've been following me, haven't you?" I began without ceremony. "You've been on my tail for weeks. Why?"

"Go home, Ms. Jamison. These matters are bigger than you are. You did your job, and you were well compensated. Your hour on the stage is over. Don't overstay your limit."

"Who are you?"

He shook his head deliberately from side to side and started to walk away. I snagged his elbow but he wrenched it free and kept walking.

"Why are you dogging me? Who do you work for?" I said to his retreating back.

He turned to face me, backpedaling away slowly. "Goodbye, Ms. Jamison. Our next encounter, should there be one, may be less pleasant than this one."

With that, he spun round and walked rapidly away, leaving me both angry—I didn't like the veiled threat—and confused. I now was convinced that he was the man I'd seen during my first visit to Orlando, in Topkapi Palace in Istanbul, and on the streets of Los Angeles. And now here again in Orlando. This cast the entire case in a new, strange light. Somebody had been keeping tabs on me since the very beginning of my investigation.

I spent the evening making my old rounds, barhopping furiously, leaving a trail of untouched cocktails, looking for Ashley as I'd once sought Harry. Unless I spotted her near one of the hotels, I'd have to concede that I'd lost her trail.

By midnight I gave up, dog-tired. From my room I called Mr. Bloodworth to see whether he'd heard anything. He had indeed.

"Ashley left the children with my cousin's wife, Olivia, on Sunday. They're from Columbia, Maryland. I asked her why she didn't call us, but she thought everything was normal until this afternoon. Apparently Ashley showed up, totally exhausted-looking according to Olivia, and didn't even stay five minutes but she packed up Jeanne-Renée and left."

"And goes where, did she say?" I interrupted

"She didn't know. She just said that Ashley made her promise to keep Benton in her home no matter what."

"Can you go there? I mean, is Benton safe there?"

"Oh, I think he's safe. I'm more worried about my daughter. I don't know what Ashley is doing, or if she knows what she's doing. And I'm worried sick about my granddaughter."

I told him there was a good chance that Ashley would come to Orlando, and added that my unswerving mission was to find her.

"What does Orlando have to do with my daughter and granddaughter?" he asked.

"I can't tell you, sir. I can't even tell you not to worry. But I can tell you that I'll do everything in my power to find Ashley and her daughter, and when I do, I'll hand over the envelope you gave me."

He pleaded for more information but nothing I might tell him would reduce his anxiety. The truth would only make it worse. Hell, I was anxious and on edge myself. All I could do was to say that I had some ideas, that I was competent when it came to finding people, that I'd spare no effort, and so on and so forth; I sounded more sanguine than I felt, but finally succeeded in getting off the phone.

The next morning I drove to Lakeland to check out the surroundings of Harry's house. I bought a map of the area in the BP station by the narrow road where Ernest had died, and where I'd had years scared off my life. That road, according to the map, was a shortcut to another road, which led to both the nudist camp and Harry's ranch.

I took it, at once curious and loath to revisit the scene of my "accident." As I approached the site, dread welled up in me. I nearly became unnerved and I had to fight off the desire to turn back.

Most traces of the smash-up and ensuing conflagration had been removed, but a sizeable gash could be seen in the giant oak, and the ground was still charred where the gas tank had exploded. My first thought surprised me: I wished that the injury to the tree did not prove fatal to it. It was a magnificent oak, even now while just partially leaved. Then, purposefully, I reviewed the events of that night. When my pulse had subsided and my breathing had become normal, I knew that I'd taken a step that would improve my mental health regarding the death of Ernest.

I continued on to the road that led to Harry's house and hung a left turn. Several miles later the road leading to the nudist colony forked off to the right; half a mile further on I came to a private road that apparently went directly to the ranch, as I could just make out what seemed to be one of the outbuildings about half a mile away. I dared not go closer. In fact, I was engaging in risky behavior as it was, for Harry would surely recognize me if he happened by.

The ground on either side of the road was flat—no surprise, it being Florida. As far as I dared explore, it was not swampy—a pleasant surprise, it being Florida. Properly clothed and equipped with a flashlight, I'd be able to case the house at night with little fear of discovery.

I drove into Lakeland and bought a pair of black jeans, a black shirt and black sneakers. At a camping supplies store I purchased a flashlight with a shutter and fresh batteries.

It was dusk when I got back to the Raphael. I was hurrying to snag a parking space when I saw a sight that nearly caused me to flatten an overconfident pedestrian. Two women were standing beside a minivan parked under a light pole. One of them was counting a wad of bills. The other held a sleeping child in her arms. Even in the poor light I recognized the child as Ashley's daughter Jeanne-Renée.

CHAPTER 29

The woman carrying Jeanne-Renée laid her in the van and climbed in behind her. The other woman took the wheel and carefully backed the vehicle into the traffic lane. For a brief moment I thought, "Hey, I was hired to find Ashley, not her kid," but logic prevailed. If I followed Jeanne-Renée, I might find Ashley, and anyway, I saw it as my duty to protect the child. I positioned my car to follow them.

I had two ideas as to what was happening. Ashley may simply have hired these women to child-sit Jeanne-Renée while she pursued her interest in Harry. More sinister, the women had kidnapped Jeanne-Renée for ransom. The sheaf of bills that the one woman was counting was far too large for childcare unless she'd been paid in small denominations—hardly Ashley's style.

The van took an all too familiar route. By the time we were halfway to Lakeland, I began to think that I was wading in waters far deeper than I'd expected. They had to be going to Harry's house. The coincidence was too great otherwise.

I'd been tailing them long enough to draw their attention if they were wary, even though I'd stayed back as far as I dared. When the van sped past the BP station I took a gamble that they were indeed headed for Harry's. I turned off to take the shortcut I'd discovered a few hours earlier. That would put me ahead of them and at the same time allay any suspicions they may have harbored about being followed.

If I was wrong about their destination, I'd call the police immediately and inform them of the kidnapping. At least I knew what direction they were taking. With all this going through my head I sped along that road of doom. There wasn't room in my thoughts to appreciate that I wasn't handcuffed to the wheel and in mortal fear. I didn't even notice the gashed oak at the road's bend.

When I reached the road that led to Harry's, I was certain that I'd gotten ahead of the van, providing I was right about its destination. I pulled off the road and doused my lights to wait, fighting irresistible urges to smoke, bite my nails, or chew off my lower lip.

Two extraordinarily long minutes later, the van cruised past. I pulled back onto the pavement with headlights off to follow them from afar, and to assure myself that they had indeed turned onto the spur leading to Harry's ranch. I drove slowly up to the fork in the road and once again pulled off the pavement, this time to cogitate.

I should have called the cops immediately. I had my cell phone. Why didn't I? On the one hand, I was afraid that Ashley, and now her daughter, might have their lives put in jeopardy if they were in Harry's power when the cops showed up to make polite inquiries. On the other hand, I could imagine that Ashley and hirelings had Harry strung up by the balls, a fate with which I was not entirely unsympathetic, but which the cops might misinterpret if they stumbled in. My client hired me both to find and protect his daughter. Getting her killed, or getting her arrested, wasn't what he had in mind. I needed to check more closely into the situation before acting.

My skulking clothes were in the back seat in their original packaging. I cut off labels and price tags, slipped out of what I was wearing and donned my nighttime ninja warrior duds. Because I'd come to Florida directly from Turkey, I didn't have my much-missed automatic. Instead, I was armed with a flashlight and my wits. I'd take the gun any day.

I walked stealthily into the fields surrounding Harry's property, thankful that I had explored earlier and found the land dry. As I crept smugly along in my black ninja suit, it dawned on me that, duh, I'd done nothing about my blond hair—that is, my shiny, lustrous blond hair that reflected every photon of light within miles. I pulled my black shirt up over my head, exposing my midriff, and continued skulking, looking every bit like a ninja moron.

I moved cautiously toward the main house, bent low, slipping from shadow to shadow. Several vehicles were parked in the front, including the van that had transported Jeanne-Renée. I approached the house from its darkest side. There was activity within and I could hear voices, both male and female, but I couldn't discern individual words.

I was outside a room that was completely dark and most likely unoccupied for the moment. I cut away the screen and tried to open the window. It wasn't locked but it made a distinct creaking sound as I lifted it. A dog barked and something inside changed. I retreated to the woods and a moment later I heard a voice say what sounded like "sook, Adolf."

Adolf "sooked" all right and the next thing I knew the largest German shepherd I'd ever seen was cantering straight at me. I lowered myself into a crouch to receive his leap, but instead he ran up and grabbed my wrist, the same tortured wrist so recently sewed together. I had the brief bizarre thought that the plastic surgeon would chew me out for being careless with her handiwork, but I needn't have worried. Adolf locked his jaws around the wrist just firmly enough to keep me in place, but without breaking the skin.

"Helta, Adolf," cried the voice, or so it sounded to me. "Nice boy," I cooed, and reached with my other hand to scratch behind his ears. Dogs are usually suckers for that, but Adolf growled in a manner that said, "This is business, don't fuck with me." When I tried to release my wrist from his grasp he bore down just a smidgen and growled deep in his throat. I was as good as handcuffed again, and my current captor was undoubtedly brighter than my former one, the late Ernest.

Within seconds Adolf's boss came running up, brandishing a short-barreled revolver. "Frei!" he commanded, and the brute let go. "Setz!" said the man, and Adolf sat. "Gut, gut," he complimented the dog. With Adolf watching alertly, the man frisked me and ordered me to precede him toward the house. His Schwarzenegger accent confirmed that he was speaking some form of German to the shepherd. *Won't Harry be surprised to see me*, I thought bitterly and correctly.

"Well, well, if it isn't little Susan what's-her-name," said Harry. "This *is* a surprise. You may not've been drinking and driving, but you sure are gonna get hurt. In fact, I'm gonna make a lot of money off a snuff video showing you tortured to death, enough for me to retire. You can think on that while we wrap up current business. You watch her, Ernst, like a hawk. She's Miss Trickery-slippery."

Ernst, German for Ernest. Two bodyguards with English names of Ernest. Didn't someone write a play about two Ernests? With a play on the spelling of *Ernest* and *earnest*? I couldn't remember, and as the idea echoed through my mind it irked me that my brain, threatened with imminent extinction, could find nothing better to think about. This latest Ernest was larger and smarter than the one who had died in the passenger seat of his own car. Even if I eluded him and escaped from the house, I'd have to contend with Adolf.

I was in a room with eight or nine other people. Neither of the two women who had brought Jeanne-Renée, nor the child herself, was present. Video cameras were set up in every corner. Bright lights focused on a central stage consisting of a large round bed covered with red satin sheets and half a dozen pillows with floral designs.

"Quiet, shooting," someone cried. The two women from the van escorted a dazed, dark-skinned, barely clad boy to the bed. He was tranquilized to a point of stupefaction. They probably used Thorazine, or a drug of that family, to ensure compliance from their subjects. A man came onto the set who "seduced" the boy in a sequence of 20 or so, carefully choreographed, sexually explicit, scenes. Two handheld cameras moved to tape the action from different angles, while three stationary cameras rolled continuously. The final gay-kiddy-porn video would be assembled in the editing room.

From time to time during the shooting the boy muttered. It seemed like incoherent babbling at first, but after a while I realized he was saying, or chanting, or praying, something in Kurdish, a language that I'd heard spoken in Turkey when growing up there. I didn't understand Kurdish—it's quite different from Turkish—but I recognized it. While I pondered that mystery, I waited alertly for an opportunity to escape. I'd rather take my chances with Adolf than the sadistic Harry, but Ernst knew his job.

A technician reloaded the cameras. I was to get a reprieve while they shot another sequence. It appeared that Harry himself would be the star of the next movie, for he stripped to the buff, not in the least mindful of his audience. Indeed, he seemed to be anticipating his part with gusto, for his genitals weren't in the shrunken state of an embarrassed man.

The director called for quiet and the two women escorted the latest victim into the pitiless light of center stage. It shouldn't have surprised me in the least that it was a wholly somnambulant, mercifully semi-conscious Jeanne-Renée. I watched, horrified, as Harry began to exploit her in a series of scenes. He went slowly, exaggerating every movement, directing the hand-held cameras to assume specific angles and distances. Each scene became raunchier, with Harry becoming increasingly aroused.

I couldn't stand it. I had to intervene and scream that he was abusing his own daughter. Perhaps others in the room would be so outraged that they'd help me. But these were hardened pornographers, used to the grossest kinds of sexploitation. A paralysis of indecision overcame me. I felt that the next moment, then the next, and the next after that, would be more opportune. The sequence of scenarios led at last to a scene where Harry was placing the hapless child on his lap. I drew a deep breath and prepared to spring into action, heedless of the consequences, when the sirens sounded. A hugely amplified voice penetrated the room with orders to lay down arms and exit the compound. Outside, lights from a platoon of law enforcement vehicles illuminated the grounds. Powerful shoulders were battering down the front door.

Harry tossed Jeanne-Renée aside and ordered the crew to destroy the videotapes. Ernst shifted his attention from guarding me to saving his own skin, and darted into another room. I snatched up the video camera that the cameraman had abandoned in a rush to escape and released the tape. Harry spotted me as I pocketed the evidence and leapt toward me.

The square-jawed man with a crew cut intercepted him, doubled him over with a stomach kick, dropping him to his knees, and then stunned him with a double rabbit punch. He grabbed my elbow and hissed "this way." I let him lead me because it seemed the best of bad choices. Behind us, cops swarmed through the house.

My last glimpse of the set was of a policewoman throwing a coat over the cataleptic Jeanne-Renée, and of two officers subduing Harry while self-consciously trying not to touch his still half-erect penis.

We passed through a long corridor and exited the house via a side door, where the two women were waiting for him. To my surprise, they were speaking Turkish to each other, but so excitedly that I couldn't understand.

My rescuer said, "I warned you that our next encounter would not be pleasant." He had what I thought was a cell phone in his hand. He pointed it at me and pressed a button. Two antennae popped out, looking like the newly formed antlers of a young buck. The moment the probes touched me I collapsed, breathless and numb, shocked by a hundred thousand volts from the stun gun.

I didn't lose consciousness, but the Taser had sent powerful T-waves through my body, jamming the nervous system and causing incapacitation. My brain started to work in a few seconds, but the frantic signals it sent to my limbs were scrambled, and I lay helpless barely able to breathe.

He removed the videotape from my pocket and inserted it into his own. Then he lifted me to his shoulder as if I was a sack of potatoes and carried me across the yard to the stables. He opened one of the stalls and laid me down on some hay in a corner, propped up in a sitting position. I was a rag doll, legs straight out in front of me, feet tilted apart, arms at the side, shoulders slumped and head lolling.

He kneeled down so we were face-to-face and said, "I'm going to lock you in the stall. In an hour or two, you'll be strong enough to climb out." He indicated a high transom with a head movement. "When you do, I strongly suggest you follow my earlier advice. I do not bear you ill will, Ms. Jamison, but you do tend to get underfoot."

I was able to make some weak sounds, but I couldn't form words. Apart from wanting to say, "fuck you, asshole," I wanted to ask what had become of the child, and where Ashley was, for I was sure he knew the answer to both questions.

The two women had followed us to the stable. They had calmed to the point where I could understand their Turkish, except now they were whispering. They sounded as if they were talking about Harry, and I thought I heard the Turkish expression that I would translate "hoist with his own petard," or perhaps, "what goes around, comes around." Languages do not translate seamlessly. In the next moment the stable door swung shut. A hasp creaked over a staple, and a padlock rattled into place and latched. The sound of their footsteps faded away.

I heard the occasional start of an engine and the sound of tires on gravel as one by one the police vehicles departed. My whole body felt oddly anesthetized from the electric jolt. When I tried to move an arm, it felt "asleep," like it had been slept on half the night. I focused on my fingers, flexing first one, then another, then a whole fist. I practiced clenching and unclenching my hands. Now I tried to rotate my wrists, and I could. And I could move them up and down, too. Moving my arms became possible, but I was so weak that tears of frustration filled my eyes. At one point I stopped trying to move and let the tears flow freely, tracking down my cheeks and salting my lips.

I resumed the struggle with better success. I could move my right arm, then my left. I could feel my toes, twitch my ankles, and flex my knees. Finally, I toppled onto my side. I lay there panting, my cheek pressed into the hay that covered the stable floor. My nose filled with the smell of horses and their excreta, but I was beyond minding odors. I managed to rise to my hands and knees, my arms quivering. I paused, gasping for breath and thankful that I was physically fit. Finally, I was able to wobble to my feet and remain upright, fighting off the dizziness that would have me totter and fall.

It was at least an hour before the transom stopped looking like Mt. Everest, though it wasn't but twelve feet above me. There were plenty of hand- and footholds, but my arms and legs were too weak to raise the weight of my body. Finally, with frequent pauses to catch my breath, I was able to inch my way up and squirm through the opening. I hung by my fingertips along the outside wall of the barn, stretching downward to minimize the fall. I let go and dropped the remaining five feet, ending up on my butt because my legs were so unsteady.

I was sitting on the ground, resting, when I heard a snuffling sound. I looked up and sucked in my breath. Slinking toward me from out of the shadows was Adolf. The vitreous gleam of his eyes and his half-opened jaw made him look every bit the Hound of the Baskervilles. From my sitting perspective he appeared even larger than I remembered, and in that posture I was entirely defenseless.

He crept within a few feet and stopped. I stayed very still and avoided direct eye contact, but, viewing him asquint, I could see he was doing the same thing: avoiding eye contact and acting cautious. His ears were folded back and his head and tail were lowered. Without Ernst to command him, he was a lost and leaderless dog. When I stood up, he did nothing hostile, but continued to eye me obliquely.

I had to relax and try to remember the German words that Ernst used, and for which Adolf was trained. "Sit" was *setz*, I thought I remembered, so I said, "Adolf, setz!" (I knew from dog obedience class that you first call out the dog's name, and then give the command.) The beast sat. "Good dog," I said, but then remembered the German: "Gut, gut, Adolf," I tried again, and he seemed pleased. I reached over to scratch behind his ears. This time he welcomed the attention, leaning into my hand. Adolf had accepted me, at least for the moment, as his new pack leader.

It was a long and, in my condition, exhausting walk back to the car. I was just in sight of the highway where I'd parked when something red glinted under my feet. I bent to pick up the butt of a designer cigarette. I placed it in a shirt pocket.

My car was far enough away from the scene of the crime to have escaped unwanted attention from the cops. By the time we reached it, I could barely crawl. Adolf willingly jumped into the back seat, while I lay down in the front. We both slept until the coming of dawn awoke us.

On the drive back to Orlando we stopped for breakfast. Adolf was still docile, accepting me as "Alpha," but to secure my rank I needed to feed him. All that the convenience store had in the way of dog food was puppy chow. Adolf didn't mind. He was a bit of an oversized puppy that happened to be trained as a police dog, not unlike some of the kids I knew in Raleigh, who happened to be trained as cops.

I didn't want to leave Adolf alone in the car while I checked out of the hotel. A 130-pound German shepherd who feels abandoned might be unkind to the upholstery. Using my belt as a makeshift leash, I brought him into the lobby and asked if he could accompany me to my room while I packed to check out. The clerk pulled a face.

"Well, then, perhaps someone could hold him for a few moments," I suggested as an alternative, eyeing first one, then another, of the clerks behind the counter. Although Adolf had but an hour ago worked his way through the better part of a five-pound bag of kibbles, he unquestionably had a lean and hungry look. They decided I could take him with me.

Adolf must have been trained to heel, for he walked naturally with his nose just a few inches next to my left knee. He was therefore not immediately visible to the square-jawed man with a crew cut, who greeted me with the pointy end of a .38 Smith & Wesson as I entered my room. I had little time to upbraid him for his lack of manners. I'm sure his mother taught him not to break into girls' rooms and point guns at them.

Apparently one of Adolf's triggers was the sight of a pointed gun, because before you could say "blitz," Adolf had him down with his gun hand clamped in his huge jaws. With his other hand, the man brought out the Taser. I had followed Adolf into the fray, and if Adolf was a red-dogging linebacker, then I was the free-safety backup. I kicked the Taser away and commanded that Adolf "helta."

Adolf held the man as he had held me earlier.

"Let go the gun," I commanded. He did, and I picked it up.

"Call the dog off. I came here to talk."

He was on his back looking up at me. When he attempted to rise, Adolf growled warningly at him.

"Do you always begin conversations with a gun in your hand? I don't suppose you lose many arguments that way, do you?"

"If I wanted to kill you, Ms. Jamison, you'd be dead. I truly am here to talk."

"Okay, so talk." I cocked the hammer of the .38 and pointed it at him.

"Jesus, be careful. That thing's got a hair trigger."

"Mmhhh, too bad, and me still a bit shaky from my recent electroshock therapy."

I continued pointing, my index finger resting lightly on the right side of the trigger guard.

"At least let me up, for Chrissake. It's a bit hard to form sentences with this devil slavering in my face."

"Listen, mister. You've been somewhat less than chivalrous to me. Tell me why Adolf here shouldn't shred your jugular."

"I apologize to you, Ms. Jamison. If you'd let me explain who I am, you will, if nothing else, have your curiosity satisfied."

He had a point there.

I said, "Adolf, frei!" as I remembered hearing Ernst say. The big shepherd let go and backed up, eyeing his former quarry warily. The man got to his feet rubbing his wrist, then walked over to the table and sat down. I stood a distance from him across the room with Adolf at my side and the .38 aimed at the center of his torso. I nodded for him to begin.

CHAPTER 30

Y̲ou once asked me who I am. My name is Owsley Bloodworth. I'm Ashley's first cousin, once removed if you care about such details. I'm a retired marine lieutenant colonel. I spent 20 years guarding American embassies and spying on foreign ones. Since my retirement, I've been employed by Ashley to perform, ummm, special services."

I interrupted. "And that included tailing me, I take it. Didn't I see you in Orlando six weeks ago when I first came here? And later in Istanbul? You were in Topkapi Palace that night, weren't you? And L.A. too, huh?"

"No secrets. Your job was to find Ashley's assailants. I commend you on your success. My job was first as a backup. If you failed for any reason to find the men, or if you found them and were unable to report back, which, I understand, nearly occurred, I was to take over. Secondly, once you found them, it was my mission to discover the details of each man's life, so that Ashley could fit their punishment accordingly."

"God, Ashley swore to me she wasn't out for revenge, that she wanted only to know who the fathers of her children were. I suppose I've been duped," I said dejectedly.

"You're not the only person in the world to have been taken in by my illustrious cousin. Her experiences, of which you and I have exclusive knowledge, have both scarred and shaped her life."

"So you admit that you and she were responsible for the atrocities in the football stadium."

"Ah, I wondered if you knew about that. I'd lost track of you that day when you staked out the orphanage. I had other matters to attend to. So you followed them. You're both brave and foolhardy, Ms. Jamison. Had they caught you, they'd've cut off your tits and left you disemboweled at Beck's feet."

"You, how can you justify an act of such utter barbarity? It's vile and inhuman. Civilized people don't behave that way. They live according to the rules of decency, if not of law."

"Well, well, aren't we little Miss Self-righteousness? If you'd been tortured, raped, and left for dead, you'd feel differently. Do you think the law would've touched the pious Dr. Beck? All he did was have sex with a student hippie stoned out of her mind on cocaine. He was wealthy when we caught up to him and could've afforded a better team of lawyers than O.J. Simpson had. What jury would convict him, Ms. Jamison? What court would sentence him?"

"That's not the point," I responded weakly, knowing that in a way it was the point.

"But I concede that castration while alive, making death welcome, would seem harsh to you. You don't know how truly evil a man Beck was."

"Tell me."

"You'll figure it out, Ms. Jamison, if you haven't already. I'm not going to tell you."

"And you discovered that Angelica was producing kiddy porn, after I finally tracked him down?"

"That's right. I'm surprised you didn't. It wasn't very well covered up. Harry was a lucky fool in many ways, a weak link in the chain."

"Why not simply collect evidence and turn him in? What maleficent mind would devise using Jeanne-Renée as a decoy? And allow her to be ravished! That was truly sick. What does Ashley have to say about that 'special service'?"

He was silent.

Suddenly light dawned on me. "Oh, I see, I really do see. Here's the piece that completes the puzzle."

I withdrew the red cigarette butt from my shirt pocket and flaunted it. "She was there at Harry's, wasn't she? Or are you smoking designer butts?"

He said nothing while I glared at him.

"And she was there in Turkey, right? I saw her in the limo, after the slaughter."

He remained impassive, shaking his head from side to side, a gesture I found ever more irritating.

"She concocted all this, this horror. You're just a goon."

I was shaking with anger and it was making him nervous. He put both his hands out in front of him to ward off an errant shot.

"Take it easy, please. Point that thing away from me. I've no reason to pull any tricks. You're blaming the messenger. Ashley wanted to be an instrument in Angelica's downfall. She wanted it related to his crime against her. The cops were slow last night, and things went a bit further than we'd planned."

"Allowing your own child to be sexually exploited in a porno flick is 'going a bit further than planned'? Is that all you can say? It's monstrous! A sane person wouldn't think this up. Sane people don't act this way." The pitch of my voice had risen an octave.

"Maybe so. But let me tell you this. The D.A. cut me some damn good slack for taking the cops to a bust where plentiful evidence would lead to multiple convictions. The cops were told to give me a free hand. I was able to set it up so that after the bust, Ashley told Angelica to his face who she was. She assured him that he'd spend life in prison for abusing his own child. And, she showed him photographs of Beck's martyrdom, being sure to point out what his mouth held. In so doing, she stepped back from the brink of insanity on which she had teetered for so many years."

"Does she know she's an accessory to the crime? Do the cops know she gave her child over to him?"

"As far as anyone's concerned, Jeanne-Renée was kidnapped by two unidentified foreign women. They're unlikely to be found as they're departing the country as we speak. "

"I thought there were some things a person wouldn't do for money but I guess I'm wrong. How in hell do you live with yourself?"

"This is crap, Ms. Jamison. You're preaching."

"If I had your morality, I'd shoot you right now. It'd be prima facie justifiable homicide in self-defense. I can see the headlines: 'Intruder shot with own gun.' I wouldn't even need a lawyer."

I slid my finger off the trigger guard and let it curl around the trigger. At the same time I grasped my right hand with my left, and brought both arms up into the classic sharpshooter's stance. I trained the .38 on his heart. "Is there anything else you want to tell me?"

"You don't scare me, Ms. Jamison. I've faced far more dangerous people than you on a daily basis. You won't shoot me. Leastwise, not deliberately."

He smirked as he made his last remark and I had to curb an ugly desire to carry out my threat. I let my aim drift up to a point between his eyes, and then back again to his chest.

"There's one other thing," he said in a steady voice.

"Talk." I continued aiming, my finger still inside the trigger guard.

"It's the reason I paid you this visit in the first place. You never asked. I came to tell you that insofar as you're concerned, my mission is complete. You'll never see me again. And insofar as Ashley's concerned, your mission is complete. You'll never see her again. A call to Taylor will verify that you're no longer employed. He asked me to tell you to send in your expenses, including the cost of getting home from here."

"What?" I nearly shrieked. "I want to hear that from him. Call him." I gestured toward the telephone with the gun barrel.

He walked over to the desk and dialed. "Taylor, this is Owsley. Ms. Jamison wishes to speak with you."

I made him put down the receiver and turn on the speakerphone. I motioned him back with the gun barrel while keeping him in the sights.

"This is Dagny Jamison. Is this Mr. Bloodworth?"

The unmistakable voice at the other end, sonorant and genteel, began with an apology and ended by explaining that he had spoken with Ashley and he was satisfied that all was well. And true, he no longer required my services.

"I wonder if he has any idea what outrages you and Ashley have committed," I said, after disconnecting. "It nauseates me."

"It's all over, unless you begin shooting."

"No, you're lying. It's not over. There's the third man. I saw you in L.A. What deviltry do you have planned for Richard Sangfroid?"

"Nothing that need distract you from your appointed rounds. Sangfroid's punishment will be diabolical, yet the least draconian. Ashley's revenge is to show him a graphical account of the ruined lives of his one-time cohorts, Beck and Angelica. My job is to flaunt their fate in his face, not easily done since the man is guarded day and night, but I'll figure it out. He'll learn from me that his former victim is now a cunning, demented harpy of infinite resource, and that she's biding her time until she swoops down upon him. After I succeed in conveying that message, he will not enjoy peace in his lifetime, nor does he deserve any."

He paused, thoughtfully. I was speechless, a rare moment for me indeed. His description of Ashley was remarkably apt.

"You did good work, Dagny," he continued, "if I may call you this. I sincerely regret that I had to ill-treat you earlier. It was safer than a conk on the head, you know, and I needed you out of the way—out of harm's way. Let bygones be bygones."

He put out his right hand. A menacing growl came from Adolf, who had watched the entire scene with unflagging attention.

"Just go," I said. "Get out of my sight."

"All right," he said, turning the extended hand palm up. "Be so kind as to return my property."

I flipped open the cylinder of the .38 and ejected the six cartridges. I opened the door to the hallway, and as he left the room I handed him the weapon and quickly shut and bolted the door.

My shoulders sagged from the tension, and Adolf, too, relaxed. He sat with one of his hind legs tucked sideways under him, a canine form of slouching. He looked up at me, focused on an invisible spot on my forehead. His eyes were lustrous pools of black opal in a rich amber setting beneath shaggy brows. The dog made not a sound, but the eyes said "high five."

There was no way I was going to leave Adolf in the pound for "adoption." Families don't generally adopt pets large enough to devour triplets. He'd be euthanized after a few weeks.

I called the rental company and received permission to drop my car in Raleigh. It was a 10-hour drive with pit stops, but flying would be slower by the time I'd arranged for Adolf to accompany me in an air-kennel. Besides, there was little urgency, and the long drive would let me think through events of the past few days.

Being now unemployed in this matter, I could let it drop, technically. But I was heavily invested, intellectually and emotionally, and I'm far too obsessive to turn my mind off a case with more loose ends than a janitor's mop.

I strove mightily to draw conclusions based strictly on the facts, free of sentimentality. In this case the facts pointed to conclusions so sordid that my mind revolted. Beck was culling children from the orphanage and shunting them to Angelica via a perversion of the "Underground Railroad." The Kurdish boy on the set, the presence of the Turkish women, Beck's wealth, the relationship between the two cousins, their proclivity for sex crimes, and Owsley's condemnation of Beck as truly evil—all lent their weight to that supposition.

Pieces of the puzzle remained that didn't fit. Where did the children go when Angelica had finished with them? At first, I imagined that they continued on to their adoptive homes. Their brief, horrid detour through Angelica's studio wouldn't come out later in their lives because of the drug-induced memory loss, not to mention shame at any surviving memory fragments plus the language barrier. But after some thought I rejected that notion. Letting those children join a normal family as an adopted child was too risky for the perpetrators. Surely they knew that if even one child said something to ignite suspicion, their lucrative trafficking in child pornography would be imperiled. I didn't think those kids ended up adopted.

So were they sent back to Turkey, back to the orphanage? No, I couldn't make that compute either. While the probability was small that any one child would be able to tell what had happened, out of ten or twenty children, there was a much higher chance that at least one would talk, and that's all it would take. From that point, word would leak out even if the children were kept sequestered in Beck's orphanage. If the rumor that Beck converted children to Christianity produced near riots, imagine what the actual truth would lead to.

I briefly considered the possibility that Beck murdered the returned children and buried them on the premises of the orphanage. There was ample property for any number of unmarked graves. But I found that explanation forced. Too many people would have to know about it. The truth would out.

No, they weren't adopted, and they weren't sent back.

I was well into Georgia by the time my thinking had gotten that far. After a break for lunch, and a walk for Adolf, I resumed the trip with my mind bent on another ill-fitting piece of the puzzle, namely Richard Sangfroid, the one Ashley had dubbed "Little."

Inconsistencies swarmed about him. First, his apparent wealth. Where did he find the money to pay for his costly lifestyle? A hundred grand a year on call girls alone. A multimillion-dollar house. Physical protection whose cost I estimated to be several times that of the women.

Balancing that, he earned a high salary, and perhaps the weekly ambulance had to do with some kind of moonlighting. Maybe his employer took on some of the protection costs. He'd been investigated and cleared of accepting bribes, but maybe he escaped detection, or maybe—I was into irony here—he bribed his way out of it. Hell, maybe he was born wealthy. I didn't know.

The security provisions didn't ring true. They were supposed to protect him from an organized crime figure, but for that purpose they were deficient. If a mob boss wanted him killed or kidnapped, the security at his home, the squad car patrols, and the bodyguard, would be gnats on a bull's rump. What he did gain was a degree of privacy not afforded the ordinary citizen. He was shielded from unwanted visitors such as Owsley Bloodworth; and against snoopers such as myself; and even against the invasive probes of media reporters. Was that worth the cost? And if so, why?

There was also the matter of Ashley's revenge. She named him, Little, as the cruelest of her tormentors. According to Owsley, they were going to show him what had happened to Beck and Angelica, with implied threats that a similar fate awaited him. I had trouble buying that. Ashley had already drunk the blood of a grisly triple murder, and had sacrificed her own daughter to slake her thirst for vengeance. Merely scaring Sangfroid paled by comparison. She needed more. I didn't think Sangfroid's precautions could protect him from Ashley. She had already showed the capability and willingness to hire guns and muscle when needed.

Owsley Bloodworth was too eager to get me off the case. He and Ashley must have persuaded Taylor that my services were no longer needed, but why the rush to tell me? Why not have Taylor sack me when I reported in? Why the dramatic break-in of my hotel room? Why the drawn gun? Owsley didn't fear me physically. It was all intended to intimidate me on the pretext of informing me I was fired. It, too, didn't compute.

I remembered a paragraph from my brother John's book, *How to be a Private Eye*. He once said that this was the basis of all detection and even of all science:

The universe is an orderly, logical place. When we perceive inconsistencies, it's because our observations and reasoning are flawed. Inconsistency does not occur in nature. Nature abhors inconsistency. Often when one inconsistency is resolved, others vanish as a result.

Such was the case as I drove past South of the Border—a gaudy amusement park with a Mexican theme—and entered North Carolina on Interstate 95. My mind had been forced to accept a passel of horrors over the preceding week, and I didn't really think things could be much worse. But of course just when you think that, they worsen.

I had fixed my mind on Ashley, still aghast at the deeds she had given rise to. I tried to imagine myself in her place—in the place of a hurt woman, heedless of acting evilly, devoid of moral constraints, intent on what her warped mind thought was poetic justice. What would I do next?

My mind began to experience the I've-almost-gotcha feeling that in me often precedes an insight. It's similar to the feeling you have when you almost, but can't quite, think of a person's name. And then it comes to you, mysteriously, sometimes unbidden—moments after you've given up trying.

When the idea came I thought that if I could see my face, it would be lit up. I nearly craned my neck to peer at myself in the rearview mirror until I realized how silly that was. But I was psyched. The fog had lifted. I had a hypothesis that explained the silence of the children, the wealth of Sangfroid, and why Ashley wanted me off the case.

But if I had brightened at the thrill of deduction, what I had deduced must have turned me a pallid gray. For I realized that so deeply had I waded into the waters of three evil men and a woman that I could see to the farthest shore, and what I saw chilled the blood in my veins, and made me see that evil lurks without bounds.

CHAPTER 31

I spent the rest of the drive formulating plans of action, rejecting them, formulating new ones. One plan was to do nothing, the null plan. It was tempting. Anything I did beyond nothing was at my own expense and risk. Still, the Bloodworths had paid me well, and though Ashley wouldn't see it this way, entangled as she was in her web of madness, I was acting on her behalf and that of her family, toward whom I felt both loyalty and pity.

The next day I called Cynthia to see if she'd care for Adolf until I had time to find him a home. I was lucky to catch her inside on an unseasonably warm Sunday. I gave her a brief account of how Adolf had come into my life and she said she'd be proud to mind so gallant an animal. "And by the way," I added, "he only understands German, so the two years of it that you had to take will come in handy."

"German! I have to speak German to a dog. That's weird."

"Hey, it's just a few words. I'll fill you in. Dig out your old German tapes."

"Sure, I'll do that, *not*. Bring him over anyway and I'll teach him good Southern and feed him grits 'n' gravy. Then he'll be ready for a new home."

Next I called Charles. I needed to know what human organs were worth. Charles, being a medical examiner, often handled the commodities. He knew the answers.

"Paahts is paahts," said Charles, trying to imitate the old Wendy's commercial.

"We're serious here, darling," I said.

"Right. Human bodies have a lot of recyclable components. The most widely known ones are the liver and kidneys. But lungs, hearts and pancreases can be reused under favorable circumstances. So can heart valves, intestines, bone, skin, veins and corneas."

"What are they worth, all these 'components'?" I asked.

"Well, the cost of organs and other body parts is presumably free, though the recipients must pay for their removal, storage, transfer and implantation," said Charles. Then, thoughtfully, "But there've been black markets from time to time. There, prices are bid into the hundreds of thousands, if not millions. If you were wealthy and you needed a liver to survive, what's a million bucks? Or a billion if you're an oil sheik?"

"And that's against the law, isn't it?"

"Definitely. In fact organ distribution is supposed to be blind to the recipient's means or status. The criteria for doling out any donated body parts are strictly medical. It's absolutely illegal to buy or sell them."

I then explained with much difficulty—the matter was almost too complex for a phone call—my hypothesis, what I planned to do assuming I was correct in the essentials, and how I wanted him to help me. It took a full ten minutes to get through it all, but Charles was a knowledge sponge and he stayed with me.

"Bloody hell, Dagny, why don't you just go to the authorities? You're risking your life."

"Lots of reasons. The cops have already given Sangfroid a clean bill of health. They won't investigate him without probable cause, and there's no time, and no clear way, to convince a judge to issue a warrant. Even with a warrant, if they botch the timing, the ending will be terrible."

Of course he agreed. Charles is quite good at going along with my schemes, cockamamie though they may seem to him. I asked him to meet me in the service flat in L.A. There were still ten days left on my month's lease.

I caught up with my mail, both s- and e-, and placed a couple of necessary phone calls. My last task before flying to L.A. was to take Adolph to Cynthia's farm. His introduction to the two greyhounds the previous night went smoothly enough, though I was careful to feed them all separately. Like middle-school kids, dogs are easily drawn into to food fights.

Cynthia and Adolph hit it off immediately. After letting Adolph sniff her hands for a moment, she got down on her knees and gently wrapped her arms around his thick, shaggy neck and muttered some guttural sounds in his ear. Although Adolph and I had a healthy relationship during the short time I'd kept him, he had never wagged his tail for me. As Cynthia spoke to him in lowered tones, his tail began to wag and then his whole rear followed suit, undulating as if he were trying out for a hula contest.

"Well," I said when Cynthia finally stood up, "this looks like love at first sight if I've ever seen it."

"He's gorgeous, Dagny. Do you really think I could keep him?"

"Yeah, I think you really could, provided that I get unlimited visitation rights."

We shook hands on that and then exchanged hugs. I said goodbye to Adolph, who gave me his "high five" look, his dewy pupils shining black, but not a single twitch of his tail did I receive. I guess it was all business between us, but I could look forward to seeing him many more times, and that made me happy.

I caught the earliest flight I could to Los Angeles, putting me into LAX late in the afternoon on Monday. I drove directly to Hilda's "studio," where I received a crash course in sex for pay. She lent me clothes, accessories and fragrances suitable for calling on gentlemen's homes at night.

The security guard welcomed me back to Vista du Lac. I told him I was expecting Dr. Clarke and to please send him up when he arrived. I was eager to see Charles, both for the obvious reasons and to make sure that he had his ducks in a row. His role was critical.

I also wanted to revisit my entire analysis of the matter for one last reality check. Charles was to be the final arbiter on the soundness of both my reasoning and my plans. Once he signed off on them, I'd write it all up in my database so they'd be on record in case something happened to me.

I'd left the envelope from Ashley's father in my travel bag. I was impatiently awaiting Charles's arrival when I decided to open it. Ethically, I should have returned it still sealed to Taylor Bloodworth, but I was at the point where every shred of information might have significance.

The envelope didn't contain a written appeal to Ashley, couched in personal, emotional terms, as I'd expected. Inside was a photographic portrait of—I couldn't believe my eyes—Ashley. Only it couldn't have been Ashley. The photograph was very old. Its faded, muted colors testified that it was from the age of early color photography.

The woman was dressed in a long-sleeved, white-ruffled, high-collared shirt, white gloves, and a full-length skirt with a floral design against a dark blue background. Her plentiful light-brown hair was wrapped in a tight bun pinned by several bejeweled hair sticks that held it high on her head. She had posed standing, in the stiff formal style typical of early photographs. In the background were plowed fields and half-leaved trees. Writing on the reverse side of the photo gave the month and year—April, 1907—and the name, Ashley Renée Bloodworth née Stuart.

The photograph had been taken when the woman was about Ashley's current age. The year and the family resemblance between the two women suggested Ashley's great-grandmother. I searched the envelope that contained the photo again, feeling certain that I'd overlooked a written message or some other artifact, but there was nothing more. I replaced the photograph in its envelope and put it in my handbag.

Charles brought dinner. We needed to monitor continuously to ensure that the rhythmic flow of life at the Fillmore House hadn't changed. Sangfroid's chauffeured car returned him from work at the regular time. One or another of his domestic helpers came and went, and most vitally, a girl and driver showed up at precisely the usual hour in the evening. I studied the girl's apparel with more than a passing interest. I watched the way she walked, held her head, and flirted for a moment with the guard.

Tuesday was a typical Tuesday for Sangfroid insofar as I could tell, and much the same as Monday. Richard was a man of habit, which was both good and bad. Good for predictability; bad because the success of my plan depended on his seeming to stray from the habitual—which might arouse suspicion.

Charles visited the coroner's office to attend to the details for which he was responsible. With a colleague's help, he borrowed two two-way pagers from the LAPD as well as a matchbook-sized signal emitter and a locator attuned to it.

Wednesday afternoon crept in a nerve-racking petty pace. We'd been over our plans again, and had nothing else to do but watch the house for anything unusual. Finally, poor Charles said that he was "knackered" from all the waiting, and to re-energize himself, would I mind if he took a walk down to Silver Lake and back. I encouraged him to go and said I'd keep my eye on things.

Sangfroid returned home at the usual time. That was my cue to begin applying makeup in the style of a lady of the night. I dressed in the same manner and sashayed out of the bedroom to flaunt myself before Charles. He was not amused to see his girlfriend in the guise of a whore. The security guard called to inform me that my car had arrived. Hilda had arranged for the same car and driver that the hookers used when they visited Sangfroid.

The phone rang moments later. The security guard reported in a voice that barely concealed his amazement that an Emergency Medical Services van had come for Dr. Clarke. With that piece of news, all preparations were complete. I returned to the video monitor to await the triggering event.

A surge of adrenaline coursed through my body when the anxiously awaited ambulance drove up to the front gate of the Fillmore House and was waved in. I watched through the telescope as it rolled slowly to the side entrance. There, the driver and passenger, both fully attired in green scrubs and surgical masks, jumped out and walked around to the back of the vehicle. They were hidden for a moment by some tall shrubs, and when next I saw them, they were at either end of a stretcher upon which rested a small lump under a sheet. A servant ushered them into the house. Strands of blonde hair wisped from under one of the scrub caps as they passed from view.

I turned on the signal emitter and put it in my handbag. We tested it briefly one last time. We also tested the pagers—they worked—and I reloaded my little 9mm semiautomatic with a full magazine, topping it off with a bullet in the chamber to give me an extra shot.

We took the elevator down to the lobby and exited the building. The doormen at the Vista du Lac were agog. Charles patted my butt—"to get you in harlot mode, love," he said. He kissed me, opened the door to my car, and wished me Godspeed. As I was driven away, I saw him get into the passenger side of the EMS van to await my signal.

I had barely enough time to light a Virginia Slim before we rolled to a stop in the space where the hooker's car usually waited. The guard was surprised to see us, but not suspicious, as it was the same car and driver that usually brought the girls. I hopped out lightly and asked for admittance.

"I'm afraid you've got the wrong night, sweetheart. He's busy on Wednesdays. No girls 'til tomorrow."

"Sure he has a few moments for me," I said. "I'm here to surprise him. I'm a freebie. My boss sent me on account o' him bein' such a good customer. You know, customer relations, and all that."

"Don't know about that. I'll have to call in and ask his permission."

"Oh, please don't spoil the surprise," I said. "This is something unusual, you know; something a little kinky; something he's reeeaaly gonna like." I moved closer to the guard and pulled out the top of my chemise to give him a glimpse. "I'll do him so sweetly he'll want me back every night. And you know what?" I moved even closer so he could smell me. "If you be a good boy, there's something in me for you." I glanced down at his crotch for half a second, then rounded my lips and took a slow, deliberate drag on the cigarette, just like Lauren Bacall in those old Bogie flicks.

I moved even closer to him and brushed his lips with mine for thanks. I walked through the gate and toward the side door, hips moving in what I hoped was a decent imitation of Marilyn Monroe. It was my night to imitate sexy actresses.

I rapped on the side door. A woman in a shawl quickly answered and, after giving me the once over, said in a businesslike tone, "You got da wrong night, lady, he's busy. Come back tomorrow."

Two things were apparent. First, charm would not work on her. Second, to judge from her appearance and speech, she was Turkish. I pulled the pistol from my purse and aimed it straight at her mouth. I said in Turkish, "You will be in Allah's bosom if you cause me the slightest trouble."

Her eyes went wide as teacups. When she got her voice back, she begged me not to kill her.

"Where are they?" I demanded.

She pointed toward a staircase. "Below, down the stairs," she squeaked.

I pulled open the door to a large coat closet. "Get in," I hissed, still speaking Turkish, "and make not one sound if you wish to see the crescent moon again." I shut the door and wedged a chair under the knob. I judged that the shock of a blonde whore speaking Turkish and wielding a gun would keep her speechless and out of my way for a goodly while.

I removed my shoes. High heels are utterly unsuitable for stealth. I walked to the staircase and began to descend one step at a time. The solidly built stairs hardly creaked despite their age. From below, I heard the hum of small motors and the buzz of fluorescent lighting. That would mask any small sounds I might make.

I was descending into a basement room so brightly lit that vivid shadows danced beneath me at the foot of the stairs. About halfway down, I could hear voices. I stopped to listen.

"This'll be a short night. All we have are the kidneys. Shame to waste the rest."

There were grunts from the others, followed by the sounds of a body being arranged on a table, and the clinking of glass against metal and the rustling of rubber tubing. It didn't strain my powers of observation to realize that I was privy to a homegrown operating room.

"Which of you is assisting? You'll need to come around here and prepare his arm for the IV."

"I am," murmured a familiar female voice.

More shuffling about and then, "Oh, for Christ sake, where are the containers? What's with you guys?"

"Sorry, my fault, be right back with 'em," said a male voice that I recognized.

His rapid footsteps were headed straight for the staircase. I darted up and rounded a corner just as he began to climb the stairs two at a time. So much for my dramatic rescue. I had to wait for him to return or run the risk of losing control of the scene.

He returned moments later carrying the containers. After a minute, I tiptoed back down the stairs. When I heard the first man speak again, I knew it must be Sangfroid. It was strange finally to put a voice to the man I had dogged so determinedly.

I also heard a heart monitor beeping, regular bleeps about three every two seconds: it was a child's heartbeat. I pressed the send-button on my pager to alert Charles, and activated the signal emitter so they could find me quickly when they entered the house. I withdrew the semi, cocked the hammer and slid my finger inside the trigger guard. I was a split second from bursting into the room when the familiar male voice commanded: "Stop! Step away from the table."

I froze.

"What do you mean?" exclaimed an outraged Sangfroid. "How dare you pull a gun on me?"

"It means you and your detestable practice have come to an end," said Owsley Bloodworth. "And my colleague is going to provide the details of your demise."

I risked a peek. The third person present removed her mask and cap, allowing her blonde hair to cascade about her shoulders. She spoke: "Do you remember me? I'll tell you the last words you spoke to me. You said, 'You've been fucked by every Tom, Dick, and Harry.'"

There was a stunned silence and I tried to imagine what Sangfroid must be thinking.

"Holy fuck!" he gasped, finally.

"There was nothing holy about the way you fucked me. You're thinking of your pious friend Tom, the Doctor of Divinity. Show him the latest on Tom, Owsley."

I could hear my heart pounding in my ears as Sangfroid absorbed what he saw in the tableau of Beck's crucifixion.

"You're mad," he sputtered.

"Perhaps you're wondering why you haven't heard from Harry, Dick. He's in jail. On morals charges. Seems he was performing with his own daughter when his porn studio was raided."

"That's bullshit. He doesn't have a daughter."

"Ah, but he does," said Ashley, "and you have a son. You both fathered children when you gang-raped me. Twins, of course. And your son is lying right here. Look at him. If you're not convinced by the resemblance, here are the results of the DNA tests. One of your whores was kind enough to provide a sample of your semen. This is you; this is the child. I'm sure you're able to understand the report, Doctor."

"This proves nothing. How do I know whose DNA is being compared?"

"I think you recognize your son. His name is Benton. He can join all the other boys and girls you've murdered for their organs. Turn that stopcock! Now! It's your life or his. If he doesn't, shoot him, Owsley."

Sangfroid hesitated. He looked at the sleeping boy on the operating table, then at Ashley, then at the gun. Reluctantly, he raised his hand toward the valve that would release the deadly drug. Just as his fingers closed about it, Owsley shouted, "No. Don't do this, Ashley. This isn't part of the plan. We weren't going to risk Benton's life."

"Give me the gun, Owsley," commanded Ashley.

"Oh, my God," said Owsley. "You *are* crazy."

"The gun!" she commanded.

She put her hand out to take it. In the split second that the gun was in both their hands, Sangfroid lunged forward to seize it. In the struggle, the .38 discharged. Owsley's head jerked back as the slug entered his left eye, and exited over his left ear, trailing bloody strings of brain and bone in its wake. The recoil threw Sangfroid off balance, and Ashley was able to wrest the gun from him.

"Turn the stopcock or join my late cousin," said Ashley, nodding at Owsley's bloody corpse. "Of all the children you murdered, this, your son, will be the one you think of while you're sitting on death row."

"I don't need to," said Sangfroid. "The valve broke and the drug is leaking through. Listen." The heart monitor bleeps had slowed significantly and become uneven. "Give me the gun and I'll save him."

Ashley hesitated, but only for a moment. "No, I won't be cheated of my revenge. Your moments of pleasure when you tortured and raped me will be avenged through the son that you fathered. Think of that. If it wasn't for your own child, you might've lived out your life in freedom and luxury. Because of him, you'll rot in prison waiting to die."

Ashley's expression had taken on a demonic cast, as of one possessed. Her eyes burned with the blue heat of madness. The change struck me so that I was for a moment unable to move. But a child lay dying, as I had foreseen days ago, and I'd come to prevent this third abomination that had sprung from Ashley's twisted mind.

I showed myself. While Ashley gawked in surprise, Sangfroid slipped out the back door.

"Damn you," she said. "I wanted him here for the end." She pointed the gun at me. "Why are you working against me? Wasn't I good to you? Owsley said you were out of the picture."

"Ashley, listen. I understand. I saw you crucify Fatboy, and I saw how you used Jeanne-Renée to entrap Strong. I knew you'd use Benton to get at Little."

"That goddamn Owsley told you. How else would you know what that little bastard was doing?"

"Ashley, I give you my word. I figured it out on my own. The children were disappearing after Harry used them. Sangfroid was in a position to launder organs for huge amounts of money. It was logical."

"The ever fucking logical Dagny Taggart Jamison. Atlas will not be shrugging tonight. Let's see you deduce your way out of this: Dr. Sangfroid will be caught red-handed with a child's corpse on his operating table."

At that moment, someone came barreling down the stairs. Charles burst into the room. Ashley calmly trained the gun on him. "Don't come a step further. Put your little black bag down, doctor. You won't be needing it."

The heart monitor bleeps ceased. I had one last desperate card to play.

"Ashley, your father gave me something for you. It's in my bag. I swear this isn't a trick. You once said we were of an age. You once trusted me. For the sake of that, I beg you to look. It's in the envelope."

As I spoke, I approached her, hands outstretched in front of me holding open the bag.

Her eyes narrowed suspiciously. She kept the gun on me as she reached for the envelope. She waved me back, opened it with her free hand and withdrew the photograph. I held my breath. Charles's eyes were fixed on the nearly dead boy.

Ashley stared at her namesake, at her ancestor double, for what seemed an eternity. Finally, her expression softened. She lowered the gun and big tears formed in the corner of each eye. She sank to her knees, hugging herself, head lowered. Then she looked up, tears streaming.

"Save him. Oh God, please save him," she implored.

Charles leaped into action. He had preloaded syringes for just such an emergency, and inside of ten seconds had emptied the contents of one into Benton's jugular vein. He began to massage the boy's heart externally, counting under his breath as he pushed and released.

My eyes were on the flat line of the monitor's screen. The line broke into a tiny wavelet, then went flat again. Then several wavelets, but still no sound. After endless time, a jagged wave attended by a single bleep made its way across the screen. It was followed shortly by another, and finally an irregular, but steady, musical stream of them. Charles stopped pumping and pulled a stethoscope out of his black bag. He pressed the bell to Benton's chest and listened intently. Finally, he looked at me and gave me a thumbs-up. I nearly melted with relief.

"Loads better," said Charles. "The boy is severely sedated. That alone could've stopped his heart. We'll use the EMS van to take him to hospital. Where's Sangfroid?"

"I'm afraid he bolted out the door when I made my grand entrance."

There was a commotion above, then a voice called, "Dr. Clarke, are you down there?"

"That'll be Sergeant McClaugherty," said Charles. "Yes, we're here."

Two plainclothesmen leading Richard Sangfroid in handcuffs came down the stairs into the operating room. "We found this one in a Porsche inside the front gate, honking like a madman. Too bad for him, after we entered the house the security guard lammed and left the joint locked up.

"Nice work, Sergeant," said Charles.

"We also found the original crew of the ambulance, bound and gagged in the back. They complained they were hijacked by a couple of hoods and wanted us to let them go. But there was something shady about those guys, so we had a patrolman take them downtown for questioning."

"Excellent," said Charles. "Hang on to them. They're part of this diabolical organ-reaping scheme."

Ashley had regained her composure and, for the moment, her sanity. "He's been murdering children and selling their organs. I have the evidence. *He* gathered it." She looked at Owsley, from whose death-wound blood and gore still oozed. "And I believe that Ms. Jamison also has knowledge of Sangfroid's evil little business."

I went to Ashley and helped her to her feet. I said to her softly, "You need to get help."

"I know," she said. "I'm ready at last.

> 'Let's make us medicines of our great revenge,
> To cure this deadly grief.'"

EPILOGUE

Nine-year-old Benton Bloodworth survived his ordeal, and, mercifully, had little memory of it. His twin sister, Jeanne-Renée, remembered her painful experience as a nightmare, her memory befogged by the large doses of the phenothiazine with which she'd been drugged. What might linger in their subconscious minds is another story.

Ashley escaped all but self-inflicted punishment. The murders in Turkey could not be traced to her. Owsley was the front man and he was no longer answerable. Likewise, Owsley had arranged for Jeanne-Renée to be "kidnapped" in setting up Harry. Only a very imaginative prosecutor would have bothered Ashley with that crime.

Insofar as events surrounding the entrapment of Richard Sangfroid were concerned, the law had every reason to thank Ashley's vigilantism. Sangfroid had become untouchable since his public exoneration. Now, the District Attorney could try an odious criminal caught red-handed and would probably get a promotion out of it. There was little reason to question Ashley's motives or methods.

Sangfroid offered no defense at his trial. Instead, he agreed to cooperate fully with the authorities in exchange for a no-death-penalty sentence. He pleaded guilty to 52 counts of murder, including Owsley Bloodworth's, and received 52 life sentences to run consecutively. I'm sure the D.A. hated to give up the death penalty, but its popularity is waning in California anyway.

The organ-laundering scheme was under the aegis of the same organized crime syndicate that had threatened Sangfroid. The threats were bogus. They were designed to raise Sangfroid above suspicion, and give him cause for the heavy security one needs when one is murdering children and selling their body parts on the black market.

Sangfroid was the perfect man for the job. In his administrative capacity, he controlled the records to allow both organs and recipients to enter the system in balance. As a surgeon, he could remove the organs from "donors" invented in the electronic "paperwork." The implanting of the reaped parts was done legitimately, or so it appeared, after Sangfroid had doctored the records. The disposal of the plundered bodies was taken care of by the syndicate—it was one of their several areas of expertise. Had it not been for Ashley's obsessive desire for her version of justice, there was no telling how long the children's Underground Railroad to Hell might have lasted.

A week after I got home I received a handwritten letter from Taylor Bloodworth on Hatfield Hall stationery:

My Dear Miss Jamison,

I am very much beholden to you for going beyond the bounds of duty and saving my daughter and grandchildren. I also apologize for the way I treated you when you were in my employ. My judgment failed me then, but I hope to be forgiven notwithstanding.

That you had the presence of mind to show Ashley the photograph of her great-grandmother fills me with admiration. I had hoped, when I gave it to you to show her, that it would remind her of her roots, and of who she truly was, and bring her back to her family.

You may be interested to know that Dr. Ashley Stuart Bloodworth, the lady in the photograph—after whom my daughter was named—was a Professor of English Literature, and the author of books on Shakespeare, Milton, and the Brontës. She also managed to rear a family, including my father.

After Ashley's "mishap" in her first year at Marquis, she became attached to her great-grandmamma. She kept the photo by her bedside. More than once, I heard her talking to it. Somehow, it helped her. Though my grandmother died 20 years before Ashley was born, Ashley drew strength and inspiration from her. She read all her books and all the works of the authors that my grandmother wrote about. As I had prayed might happen, my grandmother became a beacon in the darkness that swept over my daughter.

I hope that you will not find it crass that I have enclosed a check for $5,000. I left the payee

*unspecified. You are welcome to the money, or you may
redirect it as it pleases you. Your service to my family
has been invaluable, and you have my undying gratitude.
    Very truly yours,*
        Taylor Bloodworth

*   P.S. Benton and Jeanne-Renée have gone to live
with Olivia while Ashley undergoes treatment. Perhaps
this will take her mind off the loss of Owsley.
        TB*

I did not accept this extra money from the Bloodworths for myself. I arranged with Uncle Husnu to have the $5,000 donated anonymously to the orphanage in Turkey once run by J. Thompson Beck. It was a minuscule token when weighed against the enormity of Beck's crimes, but better something than nothing.

Charles came to Raleigh to stay with me for the winter holidays, three weeks to the day after the drama in Sangfroid's operating room. I showed him Mr. Bloodworth's letter.

"Huh, very interesting," he said after reading it. "Maybe that explains those poetical words she spoke about vengeance being medicine. Probably Shakespeare or someone. It wasn't quite what you'd expect under the circumstances." He paused a moment in thought. "But you know, she may find her medicine to be poisonous in the end. What she did, it can't be all that great for a healthy psyche. Poor, poor woman."

I took the letter from his hands and put my arms around his neck. "You're a sweet man to find it in yourself to feel sorry for Ashley. I know in my mind she's pathetic, but in my heart she will always be evil."

He enclosed me in his arms and said, "Speaking of evil, think of what you've done—of the children you've saved." He pulled me close and kissed me. "And of the evil that you've helped to end…"

www.ingramcontent.com/pod-product-compliance
Lightning Source LLC
Chambersburg PA
CBHW050516260626
47157CB00004B/1354